William Hardy lives in Spartanburg, SC, with his wife, Nancy. Not only being the published author of *Hell's Island*, he also is a founding member and guitarist with the J Teal Band, and wrote three songs on their album, *Cooks,* which was officially released on Rockadrome Records and distributed and sold worldwide. He is presently working on his next book, *Gullah Gravestones II*.

This book is dedicated to the people of Beaufort, SC.

William Hardy

GULLAH GRAVESTONES

AUSTIN MACAULEY PUBLISHERS™

LONDON * CAMBRIDGE * NEW YORK * SHARJAH

Ordering Information
Quantity sales: Special discounts are available on quantity purchases by corporations, associations, and others. For details, contact the publisher at the address below.

Publisher's Cataloguing-in-Publication data
Hardy, William
Gullah Gravestones

ISBN 9781638291824 (Paperback)
ISBN 9781638291831 (ePub e-book)

Library of Congress Control Number: 2022916511

www.austinmacauley.com/us

First Published 2023
Austin Macauley Publishers LLC
40 Wall Street,33rd Floor, Suite 3302
New York, NY 10005
USA

mailto:mail-usa@austinmacauley.com
+1 (646) 5125767

Special thanks to:

My wife, Nancy and daughter, Anna for their support and always accepting me for being me.

New York Times Best Selling Author, Brad Thor – for complimenting me on my first novel, *Hell's Island*. A very personable and kind man who not only gave me some of his (valuable, sought after) time to freely offer great advice and share some of his own writing experiences, but encouraged me to write a second novel which he suggested a title: *Gullah Gravestones*.

Shannon Matthews, Rock Hill, SC. Without her support, witty suggestions and especially all the effort she put in the work, this book would not exist.

I would also like to thank:

Patricia Matthews and her staff at ABS, San Diego, CA, my cousin Dorothy Randall, Atlanta, GA, and E. Gordon Summey, II – The King of the D on P.

Author's Note

The Gullah-Geechee people originally came from western/central Africa and have lived in the low country of South Carolina and Georgia since the colonization of America. They are fascinating and personable; holding strong to their beliefs, heritage, traditions and language. They speak a sea island 'creole' which is a combination of African/English.

This novel has some conversations using the 'Gullah' and 'Geechee' languages, but it's not completely authentic. It was written in a manner to be more understandable to the reader.

The author respects the ways, customs and the language of the Gullah-Geechee people.

Prologue: February 2001

STEVE RILEY PARKED his white Lexus right up to the front of an old office building on Bay Street. A brass plaque on the office door read: Thomas L. Ratteree, Attorney-At-Law. "We're here." He smiled, turning his head toward his friend and client, Johnny Sherburtt.

"Yep. And right on time!"

Getting out of the car, they embraced an unusually cold, miserable morning in Beaufort, South Carolina. A thick fog was moving across the small seaport city, spreading its nasty mist, while cold, bitter gusts of wind seemed to be coming from 'nowhere.'

"Damn! Is there ice in the air?" Johnny grumbled, rubbing his palms together.

"Sure feels like it. Let's get inside before we freeze!"

They hurried inside – into a cheesy, outdated reception room; dull walls, worn carpet, corny 'Muzak' blaring out of cheap speakers and no receptionist to greet them. "Does the Adams family live here?" Johnny tried not to laugh. "Look at this room. Is this not depressing?!"

"Yeah, but at least it's warm," Steve said, walking over to a long wooden bench placed against the back wall, "I believe this is an old church pew."

"I believe it is," Johnny laughed again. "Who in the hell found this place?"

"Ms. Watson."

"It doesn't matter as long as long as their's no problems with the closing," he said, still standing and looking around the room at its tacky furnishings. "You don't think Ms. Watson backed out...do you?"

"Why would you think that?"

"Because she's not here!" He spouted, plopping down in a winged back chair.

"She's probably on her way," Steve said, feeling his anxiety building.

"I hope so."

A young legal assistant came inside the waiting room and politely spoke. "Gentlemen, ya'll can come on back. Ms. Watson arrived early, and she's already been seated at the table."

"Alright, it's show time!" Johnny quipped.

Steve took a deep breath, thinking about the $200,000 waiting for him.

Two attorneys sat on opposite ends of a polished oak table inside the small conference room. They had prepared the legal documents to finalize the closing on a seventy-acre tract of land at Lady's Island; a once desolate community of mostly blacks that farmed and fished for a living. The island had become a desirable resort area and with demand growing and supply shrinking, Steve convinced Johnny that real estate values were ready to explode – shooting to the stars!

He sat next to Johnny on one side of the table, while an old black woman with curly white hair sat across. Her name was Lula Watson, the owner of the seventy-acre site. and it appeared she was eyeing them very suspiciously – Why?

One of the lawyers spoke. "Ms. Watson, are you ready to sign this final form?"

"Awright den," she replied in a Gullah dialect. "No one betta mess wid de grabeya'dd on de land – dat be dainjus! – Dat be ebbuh lastin eart' fuh de sperrits!"

"Ms. Watson, the deed specifically states that the graveyard cannot be disturbed; it will be protected," her lawyer said, reassuringly.

"You sho'?"

"Yes mam. I'm sure."

"Awright, I gwine to sign dat papuh." She hesitated a moment; then quickly signed the deed.

Johnny patted Steve's knee with a hidden thumbs-up that they could only see under the table, and handed his lawyer a certified check for over two million dollars. The deal was consummated. Steve got two hundred thousand for a broker's commission – Johnny Sherburtt now owned a large tract of coastal property – and Lula Watson became a rich woman. It was 9:40 a.m.

Steve, Johnny and Ms. Watson left the office, walking to the cars, when she spoke up with a stern warning, "Leebe dem grabes alone! Eeduh you don't…you be in bad trubbul!"

"Yes, Mam," Steve said, helping her inside an old Ford station wagon with bald tires, dented hood and rusty doors. After saying bye, he watched her slowly drive off – leaving a trail of *blue* smoke blowing out the exhaust pipe.

"I hope she buys a new car with some of that money," Steve commented.

"She could use one," he shrugged, not caring. "Anyway, we did it! Seventy acres on Lady's Island! Man…I can see those condos going up now! I bet this time next year, there won't be seventy acres left to develop!"

"Probably not," Steve agreed. "I was damn lucky to find it! Property is now going fast on that island!"

"It wasn't all luck. You worked hard."

"Thanks."

"Yeah, you found me prime investment property…I'm happy."

"I can't help but wonder what Ms. Watson plans to do with all that money," Steve pondered, curiously.

"Who cares," he replied absently, glancing at his watch. "It's only ten o'clock; that didn't take too long. The closing went smooth – No arguments – No re-negotiations…"

"Yeah, it sure did – but aren't you a little curious about that old woman?"

"No; not really. I'm not thinking about her. I'm thinking about getting back to Greenville. Now crank this car and let's go."

On the way back, all Johnny could talk about was the sale. "I'm so damn excited – I can't sleep at night!"

"You came out on top of this!" Steve said, stroking his ego, "It has to be worth twice what you paid – Probably more!"

"Yeah, but I wonder about that 'Life Estate Deed.' If I die, it goes back to the black woman."

"Any land undeveloped goes back to her. You know that."

"I guess she figures some might be left over to pass down," he mused.

"Probably."

"I have to die of natural causes before it can revert back to her."

"Yeah, that's right."

"What if I'm murdered?"

"I thought you understood – It has to be from a natural cause…like an illness."

"I don't plan on gettin' sick or dyin' for a long, long time!" Johnny laughed. "Just changin' the subject – I gotta great idea!"

13

"What's that?" Steve asked.

"Why don't we celebrate tonight at the Hyatt and if we decide to stay over, I'll pay for the rooms."

"I can't. We're lookin at a condo on Palm Island at ten thirty in the morning. I told her I'd leave Greenville in time to be there. Shit, I gotta get up at four and drive back to Beaufort…then it's another twenty miles to Palm Island."

"Why didn't you tell me? I would have driven my car so you could stay here."

"I didn't want to stay here tonight. I wanted you to ride with me. It's giving us time to talk."

"Yeah, that makes sense. By the way, are you and Kelly serious about moving to Palm Island?"

"That's what she wants," Steve replied, feeling more comfortable about the move knowing he had a $200,000 check locked in his console. In a few more hours, it'll be in his bank!

"I want us to go to the Hyatt! Tell her we got tons of business to go over and you'll see her tomorrow around noon or so," Johnny insisted. "Ya'll can look at it later that day or in the evening."

"That's possible since we'll be stayin at the one next door. When we get to Greenville, I'll call her."

"Hey, did you notice how serious the old Gullah woman was over that graveyard?"

"Yeah, I did." Steve laughed. "She thinks we might upset the ghosts!"

"What's the big deal on that?" Johnny asked.

"The Gullahs believe in graveyard spirits," Steve stated and continued, "I saw it and it is a little creepy – but what I found interesting; some of those graves are over three hundred years old!"

"Maybe it's haunted," Johnny jested. "The Boogie Man might live there!"

"Maybe so."

Chapter 1

It was a pleasant April morning, 2001 on Lady's Island, South Carolina, while Eddie Braxton was there, operating his yellow earth-moving machine. He was on a big cat – a big metal Caterpillar, preparing land for a pricey condominium project. On the right side of his dozer, he painted in sloppy black letters: 'eddie's Heavy Metal cat.' Eddie wasn't dumb, maybe not the brightest pickle in the barrel, just a low-country southern boy who loved four things: Fishing, drinking, women and golf – in that order! – not grading or hauling dirt.

Warm weather had already arrived in March and the demand for coastal property was on the rise. Beaufort had grown over the years and Lady's Island, just across the river, had become a hot resort.

Eddie marveled over the surrounding marsh and the deep-water creeks joining the waterway and the St. Helena Sound, while dreaming he was on a nice, large boat, headed out for the wide Atlantic Ocean. Suddenly, his foot slipped off the clutch pedal, and the 'metal cat' jumped a little – the wrong way! He was operating his dozer in a protective area, and his mind wondered into fantasy thoughts. "Damn it, Eddie – you stupid shit!" He scolded himself, knowing he almost knocked down a nice 'Spanish Oak.' *Quit fuckin' around...*

Again, he footed the clutch, releasing it slowly, pushing the throttle forwards and smiled as his Caterpillar injected sweet diesel exhaust into the morning's air. Operating the hydraulic bucket, Eddie began pushing down pines and scraping underbrush; carefully maneuvering around the large palmetto trees as his thoughts started wondering again.

He thought about the Gullah-Geechee people that have been here, on the sea islands, for over three hundred years. Originally brought here from Africa, they still hung on to their heritage and customs – including their belief in 'voodoo' also referred to as 'black magic.' It can be used for good or evil by witch doctors, also called root doctors that are capable of conjuring up spirits, healing the sick or placing curses. Whether it is true or not, it was, and still is, believed by many.

Eddie Braxton was twenty-two and was imagining owning a beach house, a brand-new Land Rover and that nice boat after taking over the grading company, owned by his father, Ed Braxton, Sr. But today, he's just a dozer operator, paid to clear off some land on a seventy-acre site. Studying the flagged utilities, and the taped off boundaries for an old *graveyard* required careful maneuvering. He squinted his eyes to see if the dump trucks had come back; it looked like they had stopped near the front entrance. "Why are they stopped up there...so far away?" he muttered.

Using the front-end bucket, Eddie began gathering rough flat stones thinking they were too small to pile up and load. He just banged and banged scraping them back into the sandy soil – stopped and turned his machine off – to take a five-minute break. "I wonder what those condos will look like stuck up in the air? And how many? They might look good with oyster shell exterior..."

SUDDENLY – NO WARNING, the ground under his dozer began moving. A muffled rumbling sound was felt and heard, followed by a heavy-crashing noise becoming louder, and LOUDER...exploding dirt and sand upward like an erupting volcano. The ground – began – separating – and EDDIE desperately held to his seat! – Not long! – In one terrifying moment, SKELETONS SHOT out of the breaking ground! GLOWING – YELLOW. They came at him! – Thrashing their violent arms and legs with – intense madness! Filled with – FEAR – HE tried to knock them away – before they began tearing his face to pieces – with tooth and nail. Their chalk white teeth – glowing yellow faces – became covered in blood! They were screaming in mad pleasure – spitting out pieces of his bloody flesh! Some were growling! – And some were laughing. Another explosion came – shooting smoke, hot ash and rocks into the sky leaving a large, frightening hole – filling with – wet bubbling muck – Eddie and his machine were sucked down the abyss – no means of escape! – As his final scream bellowed out the crater's mouth – he felt a bony hand slap his left jaw.

Hearing the explosions and seeing smoke, the two truck drivers leaped from their cabs – startled!

"What the shit! Did you hear those fucking blasts?" one screamed.

"Hell, yeah!" the other shouted.

"What happened?"

"Don't know – it came from where Eddie's scraping. Call Mr. Braxton."

A county patrol car pulled up and a deputy yelled out his window, "You boys using dynamite!?"

"No, Sir. One of our men is grading where those blasts came, and we gotta go down and check on him. We're calling his father right now. He owns this company."

Grabbing his binoculars, the deputy stepped from his car. "Point where he's at."

Focusing his glasses, he began scanning the backside of the site. "Oh, shit!"

"What. What is it?" a driver blurted.

"Don't look good. Your man is trapped in a large hole. We need to rush down there right now!"

"I got a chain in the truck!"

Mr. Ed Braxton Sr., came bouncing up in his Ford 250. "Ya'll just called. What's the problem?" he asked in a gruff voice.

"Mr. Braxton, I'm Corporal Smith. Your son had an accident. There's a large hole over there and he and his machine might be trapped down in it."

"What?!" He glanced at the three men, wild-eyed. "Why in the hell are we standin here. Hop in my truck and let's go get my boy out!"

All four men stood near the edge of the large crater, confused.

"What caused this damn ugly! Ass! Mess?" Braxton barked. "I don't see Eddie or his dozer – Shit, he wouldn't drive into nothin like this! Nobody would."

"I felt something move under my feet. I think we better step back a little," Smith suggested.

Water in the hole began to bubble and screeching sounds were heard. Then without any more warning, the ground began to rumble and crack under their feet.

"The damn ground is breaking away!" one of the drivers shouted.

"Step back!" Smith ordered.

Again the ground shook violently – breaking and cracking – as the screeching noises became louder and LOUDER! and then – the ground abruptly EXPLODED – up heaving nasty dirt, ash and smoke. The men were thrown to their feet scampering to regain a foothold. The SKELETONS shot from the crater – moving fast and mean toward them. Without mercy, the glowing – yellow – CREATURES OF THE DEAD jumped the four men – tearing at their faces and throats. And the men screamed in pain and terror – until – DEAD! Now sated by their victims' blood, the skeletons slung them into the deep abyss – into a red – steamy – quagmire – of infernal hell! The men sank bumping against Eddie's melting Caterpillar – the skeleton CREATURES screeched victoriously – sliding back into the hole.

The hot muck settled and the surrounding land ceased cracking.

***

After being notified about the incident, Sheriff Bill Price rushed to the scene, parked behind Smith's car and began investigating. And it wasn't long before he felt the hair on his neck and hands began to rise. A subtle but frightening fear started growing, while his confidence began to wane – this wasn't going to be a normal day!

Wearing tinted glasses, the six-foot tall, sandy-haired sheriff checked out the two abandoned dump trucks and Corporal Smith's car. "Where's everybody?" he muttered. Looking toward the distance, he could barely see a turned over vehicle. He pulled out his binoculars, focused the lenses and scanned the property. Seeing the nasty crater near the truck, he muttered, "Something ain't right here."

He started walking across the scraped ground, coming closer and closer to the pit. "What caused this? Where did that hole come from?" It looked like maybe a meteor hit there or maybe it was just blown up. He didn't know.

Moving a little closer he froze; goose bumps popped out on his arms and shoulders. A cold shiver shot down his spine. He reached for his cell and dialed his secretary. "Betty, Bill here. I'm at that property on Lady's Island, and we definitely have a bad situation here."

"What is it?"

"I wish I knew. All vehicles are abandoned and there is a truck turned over. There's no one here except me. Now get this," he took a deep breath. "There's a gigantic hole in the ground that I can't begin to explain."

"That doesn't make any sense! Why's it there?" she asked, puzzled.

"I don't know."

"And you say you're alone?"

"As far as I know, but I don't like what I'm thinking," he said, scratching his head. "I think the men working here and Corporal Smith might be dead or seriously injured."

"No," she blurted. "How!?"

"That's a good question. I wish I had the answer. Have you ever felt like you were at the wrong place at the wrong time?"

"I guess…maybe you need to come back to the office. I feel something's wrong…"

"Wait! God you wouldn't believe this. That hole is starting to send out a dark black smoke – that stinks like crap!"

"I better call the fire station."

"If I didn't know better, I'd say I was looking at a volcano. I don't like this."

"Hold on, I'm getting another call, can you hold a few seconds?"

"Yeah," he said, as he watched smoke rise from the hole – in disbelief.

"Alright, I'm back. That call was from the grading company. Do you see a bulldozer?"

"Nope."

"The owner's son was grading there."

"He ain't now."

"Oh my!"

"Yeah, send some deputies out here so we can get this place taped off and secured. It's dangerous and I don't want anyone here unless they're properly authorized."

"I will."

"And find out who owns this land and what the hell they're doin to it! ASAP! Can you do that for me?"

"Of course."

"I'm leaving now. I'll see you when I get there," Price said, climbing in his Crown Victoria.

It was mid-afternoon when Price walked into the Beaufort County Sheriff's Department, headed toward his office.

"Bill," Betty met him in the hall, "Find out anything?"

"I wish," he replied, frustrated.

"You're worried, aren't you?"

"Definitely."

Price walked in his office muttering under his breath as Betty followed in behind him.

"I called Lady's Island Fire Department. I called Johnson Civil Engineering, and sent four cars over there," she stated.

Price sat down at his desk and looked at her. "Did you call the owner?"

"I did, but no answer. I got his voice mail and left a message for him to call."

Sitting at his desk, he chuckled.

"What's funny?"

"I just wonder what those civil engineers are going to make over that hole?"

"Is it just a hole in the ground?" she asked.

"It's more than just a hole! It's a hole alright, but nothing like I've ever seen. Too mucky to see how big it is. And it's flat! Like a flat volcano – hell, I don't know. I really didn't get all that close to it. The ground surrounding it was cracked."

"That Sherburtt Development Company bought it in February. They're planning to build an expensive condo development."

"We'll see about that."

"They bought it from an elderly black woman that lives near there. Her name is Lula Watson."

"What did she get for it?"

"Two million dollars."

"Sounds like they got it at a good price but it'll cost a fortune to complete their project…if it's physically possible. Betty, there's a crater there, and I want to find out what caused it."

"Didn't you say an old graveyard is behind it?" she asked.

"Yeah, why?"

"I've always heard it was haunted."

"Stop it; you're leading to a bunch of nonsense," he laughed.

"Never know."

"I know explosions were heard, and I saw a hole and black smoke; I have no idea what caused it."

"I bet the owners won't be happy."

"Give me their number. I'm going to call 'em now," he said as he got the number, and quickly dialed it.

"Mr. Sherburtt, this is Bill Price, Sheriff of Beaufort county. I'm calling about some land you own on Lady's Island."

"Yeah, it's seventy acres and supposedly most of the prep work will be finished today. Why, is there something wrong?"

"Well, there's a problem. Seems like there was some type of land disruption and serious accidents there. I think, in your best interest. you need to come here soon as possible."

"What kind of land problems are you talking about!?" Johnny rushed.

"Mr. Sherburtt, there is a large hole or should I say a crater in the rear portion. It's dangerous, and I have ordered a stop to grading or anything disturbing this property…"

"Hey, you can't do that!"

"I can't do what?"

"That's my property, and I have a schedule to get this project up and running."

"Well, I hate that. But all work on that site is now ceased until it's investigated and deemed safe and physically possible."

"Tell me this is a joke!"

"Sir! You need to see me; and your property, ASAP."

"I'm in Charleston, I'll try to be over in the morning!" he spouted.

"Damn, Bill," Betty sparked. "He didn't ask if anyone got hurt! Sounds like a real ass!"

"Well, he's shocked over the bad news. He'll be here in the morning or maybe sooner. Changing the subject, it wouldn't surprise me that this incident hasn't spread to the media. We might be surprised at what we see tomorrow. I just got a bad feeling about that land…I can't figure out…"

"I can only imagine."

"Is Wilson here?"

"Yeah, he's here."

"Tell him to come on back. I need to talk to him."

"Hey, you wanted to see me?" Chief Deputy Charles Wilson asked, walking into the office of his forty-five-year-old sheriff.

"Yeah, I do."

Price spent a good fifteen minutes talking about what he saw. Abandoned cars, missing men, and the huge ugly hole surrounded by destruction.

"Wilson, what do you think?"

"I don't know…what to think!" Wilson said, shocked and perplexed.

"I believe men might possibly be dead in that hole," Price said.

"Sounds unbelievable."

"Yeah!" He thrashed his shoulders – feeling his skin crawl.

***

It was midnight. The Gullah man was fast asleep as winds began stirring around his bedroom window. He awoke to the sounds and sat bolt upright! The window panes shattered against a strong blast, spraying broken glass across the room. He covered his face and rolled off his bed in a sweat drenching panic!

Jumping from the floor, he found himself face to face with a skeleton dressed in a dark blue robe. He gasped – looking at the creature's skinless white face.

"Don't be scaret! I be a sperrit dat come frum de grabeyaa'd."

"De grabeyaa'd de men don dug up?" the Gullah man asked.

"Dat right. Dey tore up some ob de grabes, and I come to tell you wuh yu been chosen to do."

"Yessuh, but I don 'know wu dat could be," he said, unnerved.

"Don't jabber…I do de talk. De ancestors ob de invisible world dat were buried dey, be mad 'bout de mess dat bull dozer don.' Yu bettuh listen to me cause oonah be de one to make it awright agin."

"How I do dat?"

"De powers of voodoo will be yours. Yu are to make a curse to put on dat mahn dat bought de land. He will have to gib it back or he die. If oonah hab to…den make him die ob a sickness. De land will no longer be his and it and de grabeyaa'd will go back to de way it was. He don't hab to die – weeze hopes. Yu hab to use de mahn dat tawked him in to buyin' it."

"Wuffu?"

"Bekase *he* be de one dat can tawk dat mahn to gib it back! Oonah hab squeschun?"

"No. I do whu you sed."

"Yu bettuh or eeduh you be haanted by de sperrits all yo' visible life. De sperrits will come to oonah in yo' sleep dis night and de spell begins sun shot. You will hab vision ob what to do."

"Yassuh," the Gullah man said.

"Dat's all den," the robed skeleton spirit spoke, then moved to the broken window and flew away into the darkness of the night.

Chapter 2

STEVE RILEY WOKE to the pulsating sounds of an alarm clock. YAWNING, he slowly crawled out of bed hoping not to wake his wife, Kelly. After wiping sleep from his eyes and rubbing his tangled red hair, he put on a robe, walked quietly to the kitchen and turned on the coffee pot.

Sitting at the breakfast table, he gazed out the large window at the beach and the wide Atlantic Ocean. The view stimulated his senses – making him feel alive! Now that he was fifty-two, the early morning sun was much more friendly to his age and Irish complexion than the hot attacking sun that comes later.

After finishing his coffee, he tiptoed back to the bedroom, threw on a T-shirt, a pair of ragged shorts, slipped into a pair of sandals, left his condo and walked along the private boardwalk leading to the beach.

He winced at the gravel piles that were put down, replacing natural sand dunes as artificial barriers. Greedy developers and contractors built homes too close to the surf, not thinking about the reality of nature. They were thinking about money!

He liked the feel of the wet sand ooze between his toes while walking the surf's edge, looking for shark's teeth.

"Steve!" A voice cut from behind.

He spun around surprised to see a new friend, Bob Johnson. "You're out early!"

"I woke up early feeling restless," he said as his ash brown hair blew in the breeze. Being a small man in his sixties, he beguiled his age. "You huntin shells?"

"Shark's teeth. It's funny but I ain't ever found one."

"They're hard to spot. I can't find 'em either but my wife has a shoe box full." He smiled and continued. "I'm glad I ran into you. I'm in a foursome over at the course and one of our players dropped out. I know you play golf and was wondering if you might want to take his place. We play Saturday mornings. You think you might be interested?"

"I don't see why not! I'd like to be in a group playing regular."

"Can you play at nine tomorrow morning."

He rubbed his chin for a moment then smiled. "Yeah, I can play but I'm still trying to get used to the course. It's not like the one back home. Man, this one eats my lunch!"

"I've been trying to get used to it for years and still can't." Bob laughed. "Hate to call this short; but I have to head back to the house for now."

"Yeah, I need to get on back myself."

"Hey, you wanna meet out there at ten and hit some balls…have a drink?" Bob asked, before he started his walk home.

"Yeah, that sounds like a good idea. I'll see you then."

It was 7:30 AM when he glanced at his watch on his way back to the condo. It was one of twenty units, all with views of the ocean, private access to the beach and a manicured courtyard. It was what Kelly wanted, not him. But after a few weeks – he fell in love with it.

He walked into the unlocked door of the breakfast room to find his wife standing next to the table, sipping coffee while brushing her long black hair. Kelly's sexy brown eyes twinkled as she smiled at him. "Morning, honey."

He looked at her. Without a shower or makeup, she could slip into an evening gown and look like a fashion model. They had been married twenty-two years with twenty-one-year-old twin daughters and he always thought she could pass as their older sister.

The smell of sizzling bacon filled the room as Steve sniffed the sweet hickory aroma. "You got up early and already have breakfast cooking," he said, smiling, giving her a pop kiss on her lips.

"Wow! Just what have you been smoking?" she quipped.

"You got up earlier than usual."

"I didn't sleep well. I got out of bed right after you left for the beach."

"Something bothering you?"

"Um – can I ask you something?"

"Of course. What is it?"

"How much money did you make selling that property on Lady's Island?" she asked curiously, atypically.

25

"Don't tell me you don't know," he spouted, surprised. "What brought that up?"

"I find it hard you could make $200,000 on one sale," she commented, with suspicion.

"Why not? A commission is based on a percentage of a sales price. Not the number of sales…and just what are you getting at?"

"I don't trust Johnny. You didn't do anything illegal…did you?"

"You know I didn't," he stated, offended. "I'm flabbergasted! How could you think that!"

"I don't and I regret what I said! I know you couldn't do anything wrong; you know I love you!" She gave him a sexy smile and a teasing wink.

"So you love me, huh," he grinned, devilishly, passionately pulling her toward him.

"Careful, Red!" She smirked, "Maybe later."

Only Kelly and his close friends were allowed to call him Red. Too many red hair jokes growing up. Sometimes he didn't like Johnny calling him Red – but he put up with it.

"I think so," he answered her, trying to suppress his sexual appetite – and thinking about, 'maybe later'!

"How was the beach. Did you find a shark's tooth." Kelly laughed, playfully slapping his chest.

"No, but I ran into Bob Johnson. He wants me to play in his foursome, tomorrow at nine, and I told him I would. He's a nice fellow."

"I haven't heard you mention him. Well, I met a lady that moved here from Charleston named Elizabeth Ashley. Said it was too crowded there and likes it here."

"You like her?"

"Yes, I do…she's extremely nice and fun to talk to."

"That's good. Oh, I'm going to range and hit balls at ten."

"That's good. Elizabeth wants me to go shopping with her in a little while and I'll be gone most of the day."

"Well, I hope you have fun but are you ready to eat this breakfast?"

"Of course." She smiled, her brown eyes brightened. "You really think I could be a model?" She spontaneously jested, as she started prancing around the living room, posing. Kelly knew she was attractive, tall and slim, long black hair, big brown eyes. "*Maybe later* might be coming sooner!"

He couldn't wipe away his smile as he drove to the Ocean Palms Golf course, commonly called "The Marsh." He loved the challenging, beautifully kept, tournament course with its long fairways guarded by palms, pines, creeks – and of course – marsh. The marsh was a magnet for hackers.

It was ten o'clock when he rolled his new Lexus into the parking lot, stopping close to the clubhouse. Only two years old, the building was designed after a low-country antebellum home, boasting a large wraparound porch with round, white columns. The pro shop and locker room were in the front and the restaurant and bar were at the rear, overlooking a beautiful lake surrounded by palmetto trees and live oaks.

Getting out of the car, Steve was greeted by a young golf attendant. He popped the trunk, and the teenager eagerly retrieved his clubs and fastened them securely to the back of a green and white golf cart.

"Have a good round, sir."

"Just came to hit a few balls," Steve said, handing him two dollars.

"Thanks. Just follow the path to the range."

"Alright."

He walked into the pro shop and smiled at the assistant pro behind the counter.

"Mornin', Mr. Riley. Playing today?"

"No, just gonna hit a few range balls. I'll be playing tomorrow mornin'."

"Who with?"

"Bob Johnson and his group."

"Who's your partner?"

"Bob," he answered, checking out the new clubs on display.

"You and Bob better give them some shots," he laughed.

"Really! Why's that?" he asked, not knowing the other players in Bob's group.

"I've seen you strike the ball, Mr. Riley. I bet you were on your college team."

"No, but I did play in high school. Wasn't good enough for college."

"A three handicap! Come on now!"

"I'm afraid it's going to start going up. I'm not getting' any younger and ain't playin' enough," he said, taking his cap off – rubbing his fingers through his hair.

"It won't be crowded. I hear some Gullah event is happening on Lady's Island."

"Oh yeah," he mumbled absently, reaching for some complimentary tees offered at the counter.

The driving range lay like a large green blanket as Steve softly hit a few wedge shots to warm up. He gradually worked up to his four iron and was hitting two-hundred-yard shots, straight and pure. Lighting a cigarette, he pulled out his driver, thought for a moment, put his Marlboro down on the grass and smacked the ball two hundred and eighty yards with just a slight right to left draw.

"Jesus!" a voice bellowed from behind. "That damn ball was nutted!"

"Oh, hey, Bob," he turned around to speak to the man that has a habit of sneaking up on you.

"You trying to hit Charleston?!"

"No," he laughed. "But this one might!" He swung and the ball went sailing almost three hundred yards, straight.

"To hell you say! I got me a strong horse tomorrow."

"Well, let's just hope the hooves don't come off," he laughed again.

"What you hittin' there?" Bob asked curiously, admiring the driver.

"Big Bertha II."

"Can I try it?" he asked.

"Sure."

Bob placed a ball on the tee and took a smooth swing, sending it about one seventy yards, fairly straight.

"Nice shot!"

"Didn't go nowhere?"

"You hit that ball fine."

"Yeah, but getting over creeks and the swampy lakes; my drives won't do it."

"Can I show you something?" Steve asked him.

"Sure you can."

Steve put a ball on a tee and said, "Take that club straight back until your left shoulder is under your nose."

Bob took a practice swing, trying to follow his advice. "Boy, that takes an effort!"

"Take that club back like I said – then swing out at one o'clock."

Bob approached the ball and swung. "Damn.! How did I do that? It went over two hundred, didn't it?"

"You loaded up, which gave you more power. You hit it about two hundred and twenty."

"I've taken lessons for years and was never taught that. This is great! Hell, I'm going in the bar and get a drink!"

"Hit some more."

"No! I want to remember that shot!" he said, then hesitated. "I'm glad I ran into you earlier."

"I'm glad you did," Steve said. "Now let's have that drink."

Steve drove the cart back to his car and the same young attendant rushed over. "Hittin' good?"

"Yeah. You brought me luck. Here's ten dollars."

"Thanks again," he said, neatly placing the clubs in the trunk. "I must have brought you a lot of luck."

"You did," he smiled, thinking about his 'maybe later'!

Steve walked past the pro shop and entered the lounge called the Marina Bar. Seeing Bob sitting at a table drinking a bloody Mary, he quickly joined him.

"Damn, if you can't hit a golf ball!" Bob shook his head, amazed with Steve's ability.

"You can too!" he said, motioning to a waitress. "Can you bring me a cold Budweiser?"

"Yeah, boy, I believe we're gonna have a good round in the morning."

"I'm looking forward to it." Steve smiled.

"Still got that shot you taught me, fresh in the mind."

"I believe it will help. Helped me!"

"I believe you told me you were in real estate. Right?"

"Yeah, that's right. I've been a broker since 1978 and worked in Greenville. I retired a few months ago."

"You look too young to retire."

"Fifty-two."

"What?"

"It's stressful work! After twenty-five years, I thought I needed to. I get anxiety from time to time and don't need the stress; but I might get back in it later if I get bored and my money runs out," he said. "I did sale a large tract on

Lady's Island a few months ago that will be developed for ocean condos. I think the prep work started yesterday. The developer is a friend and trying not to brag, I did made a real good commission. You know, I've thought about getting involved in this project, help market them. Yeah, seventy-five acres of prime land on Lady's Island! I'm proud of that sale!" He beamed.

"You say Lady's Island?" he questioned with caution, looking disturbed. "You didn't tell me that."

"Yeah. Why?" he asked, confused and curious – looking at a face with a secret that needs to unfold. "Richard said some event is going on there. Maybe somewhere close? Anyway, are you familiar with the land I sold."

"No." Bob shrugged his shoulders, "I don't know…"

"What is it, Bob? Something I should know…about that property?"

"No, but glad to hear it worked out for you." He then quickly changed the subject – to himself. "I'm the principal over at Beaufort High. Been there twenty years."

"You like it…I bet it's rewarding," Steve said, knowing he was hiding something from him.

"It is. But it can be very frustrating and disappointing," he replied, stopping to gather thoughts. "Most of the kids are black and were afforded much of nothing. Don't get me wrong; we have many bright students, but unfortunately, they come from very poor environments."

"Yeah, I know there's a lot of poverty in this whole area."

"Very bad."

"Bob, I majored in anthropology in college and remember studying about the Gullah Geechees here."

"Oh yeah?"

"How did they get those names?" Steve asked, acting interested but was trying to weave a conversation that Bob may stumble or open up – to what he's hiding.

"I was told that Gullahs came from Angola as slaves, centuries ago and were called 'Golas.'"

"Really!"

"Not sure about the Geechees."

"What about St. Helena Island?"

"In the 1500s, St. Helena Island was discovered by the Spanish and they named it 'Punta de Santa Elena' in honor of Saint Elena. Later, the English came and by the mid-1800s, the island was nothing but cotton plantations."

"Why is part of St. Helena called Frogmore? Are there more frogs there?"

"No," he laughed. "The English gentry named Frogmore moved there. I read that they brought over boars to hunt. Nothing to do with frogs." He began to sense that Steve was interrogating him. And he knew why.

"What about Lady's Island.?" he asked, anticipating what Bob will say.

"There are several legends, but the one that stands out in my mind is that it was once called 'Our Lady's' to honor the Virgin Mary."

"What about voodoo?" He fired the question.

Bob looked at him suspiciously, feeling wary of Steve, "Yes, it is…you're asking a lot of questions."

"But it's not real!" Steve lit a cigarette, rattled his beer, took a big gulp.

"It is to some."

"You believe it?" he asked flatly, thinking, *What does Bob know?*

"I don't fool with it. There's been many strange and astonishing happenings over the years claimed to be the result of voodoo practices. There are children in our school with notes written by either their mother or grandmother saying they can't speak for seven days due to a hex. And, Steve, they don't say a word during that whole time. Now that's just one example, out of many, claiming to be the work of voodoo."

"Wow! So you actually witness this?"

"I'm not going to tell you about some scary happenings."

"Why not?" Steve insisted. "Go for it!"

"Well, if you want me to – and people swear by this one," Bob said and continued. "There was a man who hated his wife that had a twin sister living with them. The man went to a 'root doctor' and had a curse put on his wife to drive her crazy but he had to get a clipping of her hair. Well, as the story goes, he sneaked in her room one night to get that clipping but he clipped the twin sister by mistake. They said she ran out of the house crowing like a chicken – running all the way to Beaufort – then wound up in the crazy house in Columbia."

Taking a large swallow of beer, he choked, coughed, face turned red and finally sputtered, "Joke…right."

"No joke. It's believed to be true," he said.

"You really believe that happened?" Tapping his cigarette ash in the tray, looking more skeptical than he was.

"Look, these people down here believe it; but they're also very superstitious. Why do you think houses on these islands are painted blue?"

"I don't know." Shrugging. "I have no idea."

"The color blue protects them from Hainnts – you know, evil spirits."

"Why blue?" Steve asked, intrigued, but still suspicious of Bob. *Blue!?*

"I think centuries ago when indigo was farmed to make a deep blue dye, the slaves would paint their shanties with the leftover paint their masters gave them. Over the years, they began believing it would protect their houses from curses, hexes, spells, or whatever." Bob stopped and shook Steve's hand. "This has been fun but gotta go."

"Yeah, me too," Steve said, finishing his beer.

It was one o'clock when he drove home and couldn't help but think about the look on Bob's face when mentioning the property on Lady's Island. The surprised and disturbed expression on his face was too transparent – becoming flustered – jumping from the table – leaving a fresh drink! It wasn't normal. Bob knew something that he wasn't telling. But what!?

Walking in from the deck, he could see Kelly sitting on the sofa in the living room – with a disturbed look on her face.

"Hi," she whimpered.

"Are you OK?" he asked, shutting the door behind him. "What's wrong?"

"Johnny called," she said.

"Did he say what he wanted?"

"He's mad and sounded like a monster! And has been trying to call you all morning…and you're not answering your phone."

"I left it in the car."

"You better call him. He's pretty mad," she firmly suggested.

"Alright, I'll call him."

"Steve, he's weirded out. Something went wrong on that Lady's Island property – and he's blaming you."

"What went wrong!?" he raised his voice, reaching for a cigarette.

"He didn't say. Go ahead…call him. And try to be calm!"

"You didn't tell him where I was?"

"Yes, I'm sorry."

"That's OK. It's none of his business where I go," he said, lit his cigarette and huffed out a large cloud of smoke. "Alright, I'll call him now."

"He's not himself. He's got to be drunk! Watch your temper!" she said firmly. "Remember what I said this morning, I don't trust him. He's trying to drag you in to something – I can feel – it's bad!"

Steve dialed his cell and he answered on the first ring.

"It's about goddamn time!" Johnny blared in his phone "You can't answer your fuckin' cell?!"

"The phone went dead this morning. And why are you yelling?"

"Seems to be working fine now!"

"What in the hell's the matter with you?"

"Listen, Red! We got big trouble at Lady's Island, Get your ass over here right now!"

"Why?" he asked, reluctantly.

"Because I want you to see this fucked-up piece of land you talked me into buying! The property formed a bad sinkhole or something! Now it ain't worth nothing!"

"That doesn't make sense," he said as his hands started trembling. "I don't understand."

"Are you coming!?"

"I don't know. What can I do?" he asked.

"I'll cut to the chase – This land is fucked up like a two-dollar watch! – and I'm pissed off. Get your ass here now!" he growled, loudly. "It's turning into a stinking hell hole! The sheriff's already got it taped off. They think some men died here – You better be on your way!"

"Alright, I'll leave now," he said. "But I'm leaving unwillingly!"

"Too bad! You'll see my car parked on the side…now hurry!"

"Well," Kelly said, "I told you he's mad."

"Yeah," he said, knowing he was soon to embrace a bad, bad situation he wanted no part of. The morning started out great – now it's getting bad!

The phone rang. It was Johnny again!

He answered. "Now what?"

"Are you on your fucking way?"

"Why did you call back?!" Steve blasted. "You're irritating the hell out of me!"

"Look, I lost over two million dollars because of you, I wouldn't have bought it if I knew it was gonna blow up and crack everywhere, now hurry up and get here!"

"Listen. You calm down and quit blaming me! – And I'll see if I can help."

Johnny burst out laughing.

"What's funny?"

"You are!" He kept laughing. "You think you got it made living in your little condo and spending my money! But, Red ole boy, that's about to end!"

Chapter 3

STEVE HURRIED out of Palm Island, heading west on Sea Island Parkway, a narrow, two-lane road connecting the sea islands east of Beaufort. It was only an eighteen-mile stretch of road, but could take a half hour of driving if the swing bridge over Harbor River was open for trawlers.

Gazing south over the marsh, he could see the water sparkle from the sun's rays; but didn't care. Looking north, he saw the St. Helena Sound open wide into the olive-gray waters of the Atlantic; but could care less! Steve usually appreciated these views of relaxing scenery, but not this day. His mind was filled with worries and concerns about Johnny and the property – tapping his fingers on the steering wheel – feeling his knees weakening. His ears still rang from Johnny's screaming voice.

Taking a deep breath, he began reflecting on his early career in real estate, remembering the good times and the bad – especially the high-interest rates of the late 1970s and early '80s. That was a hard five years.

The *real* money came in 1990. It seemed like yesterday, remembering a phone call from Johnny, inquiring about a seventy-five-acre farm he had listed eight miles east of Greenville. Johnny was a hard-nosed businessman; and money was his passion.

After the farm was bought, they rapidly converted the pasture into an upscale subdivision. That was the beginning of Steve Riley's road to success. By the year 2000, his net worth was over one million and had no problem with finances, including his twin daughters' tuition at Clemson University.

Johnny was a medium-sized man around forty, fairly handsome with dark features and looked like an Italian movie star at times, Steve sometimes thought. Originally from Charlotte, he moved to Greenville to take advantage of the increasing real estate demand. Johnny had the nerves, along with plenty of spunk, to make tons of money...and with the help of Steve's expertise and ability to put together lucrative deals...he did! He amassed a fortune.

His mind came to the present as he saw a stopped Toyota in front of him. "Damn it!" he shouted. "The goddamn swing bridge is open!"

A trawler was moving in from the sound, headed for the marina on St. Helena. He watched its slow procession as his mind drifted back to the site and Johnny. "How could a large, solid ground of oaks, palmettos, and pines turn to ruins?" he asked himself. There was nothing wrong with that land. He had walked it. It had public water and sewer. "What in the hell is going on!" It was killing him. He took a deep breath as he watched the blue-and-white fishing boat slowly pass along the pewter-gray water, until it finally moved under and through. The operator brought the bridge back for road crossing, and Steve entered St. Helena. Driving behind a slow truck, he thought of Bob Johnson when seeing some houses painted blue.

His nervousness was building as he felt his heart pulsating through his entire body. He didn't know what to expect and it was killing him!

He turned down Lady's Island Road and froze as his eyes peered at the once-beautiful seventy-acre tract. "Good God Almighty!" he cried. Looking over at a large crowd moving around on the land, he would have thought the circus had come to town or Hollywood was filming a movie. Why were they here? Something bad had happened! There were TV cameras, reporters, men and women in uniforms – he took a deep breath!

He parked at the closest spot available, got out, walked toward the yellow-taped-off area, moved through the throng of people and stopped to watch an attractive female reporter from Fox News talking into a microphone.

"And this has been 'literally' an earth-shattering experience!" she wittily quipped.

Steve moved a little closer inside the property.

"Red!" a familiar voice shouted ten yards away. He turned around and saw Johnny running up to him. "Goddamn it, Red! What took you so long?"

"Got here as fast as I could," he replied, mopping sweat from his forehead. "The swing bridge was closed, and the traffic was bad."

"Can you believe this shit!"

"What in the hell is goin' on here?"

"I told you over the phone." Johnny took a long drag off his cigarette, then flipped it to the ground. "I've been here over an hour, damn it. This fuckin' land I own is now worthless!"

"What happened?" He stared at the spectacle, bewildered.

"Nobody knows jack shit! Look, there's news people and officials here! Hell, a sheriff's deputy told me that a team of geologists and seismologists are on their way."

"Looks like a hurricane hit this place!"

"Come follow me," Johnny demanded, walking right up to the taped area. "Look!" He pointed to the distant large hole. "Can you see it? Is this not fucked up!"

"It's a long way off but I see something. Looks like a large crater."

"Red, they say five men lost their lives here yesterday."

"What?" Steve dropped his jaw. "That's bad."

"You damn right that's bad. And also, this land is bad!"

Steve looked silently at all the people, TV vans, deputy sheriffs, and reporters.

"I am completely lost for words!"

"I'm not happy, Red!"

"Well, I'm not happy either." His stomach churned.

A reporter spotted Johnny and rushed over to him. "I was told you're Mr. Sherburtt, the owner of this property."

"How would you know!" Johnny shouted. "I have nothing to say!"

"But, sir, I—"

"Hey! Are you deaf? I said I have nothing to say!"

The reporter nodded and hurried off.

"This is devastating," Steve muttered. "Unbelievable!"

"Let's get the hell out of here. I need a drink. Drive me into Beaufort!"

Steve's white Lexus rolled over the Beaufort River Bridge, and he caught glimpses of yachts, fishing boats, and even a small dinghy moving across the wide river…wishing he were hiding in one moored at the landing.

Taking a deep breath, Steve gazed at the pre-Civil War homes standing proudly facing the bay upon the high bluff shaded by huge live oaks. "You know," he spoke, pointing at the stately homes, "if you look way out to the point, you can see the large home where they filmed *The Big Chill*."

"What!?" Johnny screamed. "What's wrong with you?"

"You know the movie, *The Big Chill*? That's the home where it was filmed."

"Are you crazy?!"

"I'm just commenting on a house that's been used in a lot of movies – Just making small talk."

37

"Well, if you're going to talk, why don't you make some big talk. Important talk! From this moment on, any conversation we have is to be serious business."

"Alright. I just don't know what to say."

Johnny spit some Skoal Bandit tobacco juice out his window. Some of it might have missed the outside of his door.

When they crossed the bridge, Johnny suggested they park at the municipal lot on Bay Street. Just steps away from the car, they walked into a small restaurant bar that backed up to the river.

"Can I help you?" the bartender asked as Steve and Johnny plopped down at the bar.

"Give me a vodka tonic on the rocks with a twist of lime," Johnny said. Then raised his right hand, "And make that a double!"

"I'll take a Budweiser," Steve said.

"You guys need a menu?"

"No," Johnny said.

Normally, Steve would be hungry by one o'clock, but he wasn't.

Johnny looked at Steve with dark piercing eyes. "Have you had time enough to think of anything to say about all this?"

"I'm still in a state of shock." He gulped his beer.

Johnny rattled his glass and pointed to him. "I'm not in a state of shock. I'm beyond that. I'm pissed off! I just saw millions of dollars sinkin, in a fucked-up piece of land! I'm not happy!"

"What in the hell do you want me to say?"

"Hey! This is how it stands. I don't like that land, and I want my money back. The site is ruined, and there's no way I can develop it. I don't want it!"

Steve was silent; staring at his can of beer.

Johnny pulled out a cigarette, lit it, and let a stream of smoke circle upward. "You didn't hear me?"

"I heard you."

"Well, just in case you didn't, let me reiterate – I don't want that property! I want my money back!"

"Are you holding me responsible?" Steve asked him, bewildered and blindsided.

"Fuckin A!"

"Have you lost your mind?" he spoke, preparing for an altercation.

"No, just my money because of you!"

"Be reasonable. Don't piss me off."

"Red, you go find that old Gullah woman and tell her to give me back my money, and she can have that damned land! Or – you can give it to me!"

"What? Are you serious? – Are you tryin' to piss me off!?"

"Yeah, I'm serious. You put a lid on that temper stewing, and tell me you're gonna fix my problem."

Steve rubbed his chin, trying to stay calm as he gazed out the back window of the bar overlooking the landing and the river. "Alright. I'll try…"

"You do more than try! You go find that woman and tell her that if she don't give me my money back, I'm goin' to sue her ass off!"

He had never seen him like this. Johnny had lost his mind? "Hey, can you be reasonable, for a minute or so while I try talkin' to you?"

"I don't know. Can you get me my money back?"

Steve threw his arms and hands up in the air. "I said I'd talk to her and…and maybe she knows somethin' we don't."

"Red, I don't give a shit what she knows. You sold me that property. You have to do somethin' – and fast!"

His Irish temper was cooking – hotly. "Now, you listen to me and you listen good. For one thing, you have owned that land for almost two months or maybe more, and when it was under contract, you could have backed out of the deal. Since you closed on it without bringing up any problems. there's really no way you can hold her responsible. But she might take it back. Maybe…"

"She better."

"You did your due diligence. You are the responsible owner. It's an 'Act of God.'"

"Act of God my ass! Don't give me that crap!"

Steve thought about the graveyard and the warning she gave, but there was no way he would bring that up now. "There's only one possibility I can think of. Sue the grading company."

"What! Hell, they died there. They'll probably sue me!"

"Johnny, how did you find out about this and get here so fast?"

"What – What's that got to do with it? I was in Charleston and the fuckin' sheriff called me so I hauled ass here. I'm so damn pissed about this crap, Two million dollars down the drain…"

"I guess we will have to figure out something…"

He cut him off. "We! 'We' is a French word. I want you to take care of this now!"

"I said I'd talk with the old woman."

"When?"

"Today!" He spouted, exasperated, feeling his temper ready to blow.

"Resolve this matter, Red!" He glared him with nasty eyes. "You better get my money back!"

"Look, son of a bitch – this don't seem to be goin' anywhere! And I don't like the way you're talkin' to me!"

"You men hold it down!" the bartender shouted.

"You don't get my money or I'll sue your ass!" Johnny yelled, ignoring the bartender.

The big, burly, man running the bar yelled back. "I don't know what your problem is, buddy, but any more of this shit – you're out of here!"

"Fuck you!" Johnny shouted at him.

He hopped over the bar and twisted Johnny's arm like a pretzel, shoving him against the wall.

Steve wasn't a huge man but was larger than Johnny. He was strong, solidly built with a rugged, manly face – and was certainly not physically intimidated by crazy Johnny – except being wary of his present mental instability. Realizing this was turning into serious shit and not wanting to wind up in jail, Steve soberly spoke, "Just let him go, he's drunk. I'll take him home."

"Just get his ass outa here! You can come back, but I don't wanna see him ever again!"

"I'm going to sue your ass!" Johnny huffed.

"Well, good luck!" the bartender said.

"Now leave!"

"Johnny, you heard the man. I'm takin' you back to your car!"

"Yeah, and I'm going to sue your ass." Then he pointed at the bartender. "And I'm going to sue your fucking ass. I'll see both of you in court!"

Chapter 4

STEVE sat in his car on the roadside of the nightmare, watching Johnny drive away in a pissed-off haste. "Good riddance," he yelled through his opened window.

"Yeah! You wish!"

His anxiety and anger kept escalating…witnessing more and more people flocking to the scene. Two news vans pulled up and crossed over the taped-off 'No Access' area.

"Unbelievable!" Completely dazed, he sputtered, "Did a spaceship land here? A comet? An earthquake?" It was time to pay a visit to the old Gullah woman and hopefully she'll shed some light on all this.

Driving down Lady's Island Road, he turned onto a short sandy trail leading to Ms, Watson's small house. Parked his Lexus, walked to her blue door and rapped on it twice. She answered – her eyes were weary. "Wuh you want? I ain't gwine buy nuthing!"

"Ms. Watson?"

"Dat me…Wuh chu bidness?"

"Do you remember me? I'm Steve Riley, the real estate agent who handled your land sale." His nerves were jumping. His heart was racing!

"I know you men would come back to me adder you saw whu de land did. Now you come on een de house, and don't yu leebe de screen do' open, or dem flies will come een. I hate dem flies!"

"Yes, ma'am."

"Hab a seat on de couch. Wuh chu want frum Lula?"

"Ms. Watson—"

She cut him off. "Call me Lula! Eberbody dat come in me house call me Lula. Oonuh bettuh call me Lula."

"Okay, Lula, I'll do that."

"Now, wuh be yu bidness, e awready know. You and dat udder man wants me to keep dat grabeya'dd frum stirring up de dead bodies – but dat can't happen bekase yu done tore up dey grabes."

"What happened there, Lula?"

"Oh, I's gwine tell you – And yes, Mistah Steve, you be de one dat sold it to dat mahn."

"Lula!" He rushed to get words in. "You sold that land to Mr, Shurbertt, not me! You need to understand that I'm not the one that bought it."

"Awrighty den, I beleeb you. So you didn't buy it?"

"No, I absolutely did not!"

"Not in yo name?" Her eyes warming to a soft milky brown. "Me's gwine plop en de rocker chair, but fus I gwine get yu a bowl ob gumbo. You hungry?"

"No, thanks."

"Oonuh don' want Lula's food?"

"Oh – I'm sorry…Yeah, I like gumbo…a bowl of gumbo sounds good," he said.

"Den me gwine ober e git some fhu you."

"Lula, do you remember how your land was sold?"

"Yassuh. Back winter time yu come by here and me members yu said dat udder man was wantin to buy it. Yu jus found it fer him."

Lula brought him a hot bowl of gumbo with okra and tomatoes mixed with ham hock.

"You hab dis. Eeet – it good."

"Thank you." He laid it in his lap.

"Mistah Steve, dat land don' gone bad since dem men busted een de grabe ya'dd. Me tol' ya'll not to do dat. Now it be haainted. Dem sperrits be mad dat yu messed wid it."

"The man who bought it is the one who caused it," he stated, matter of factly.

"Dat grabeya'dd don put out bad hex," she ruffled.

"The man who owns it wants you to buy it back from him."

"Mistuh, I tol' you people at de lawyers table not to mess wid it. Dat be where our people…families, and ancestors rest. It been dat way 'fore de Gun Shoot!"

"The what?" Steve blurted, puzzled.

"Before de Civil Waah. Dat wuh granny called it."

42

"Um…I see."

"De sperrits wont dere grabes back. Dat's all."

"Won't your taking the land back fix it?"

"Yassuh."

"Can you give the man his money back?"

"Nossuh."

"Why?" His head spun as his jaw dropped. "He's real mad his land is disrupting like it is."

"Me ain't got dat money no more."

"Please don't tell me that you spent that money! There's no way," he blurted in disbelief as his eyes jumped from side to side, glancing at her humble surroundings.

"Nossuh. I gib it to de po' dat lib in dese parts." She paused, then giggled. "I did kept a little fu myself."

"You gave all that money away!" He slapped his face.

"I sho' did. Dat's why I sol it. Lula don't need all dat money. Udders need it."

"Please tell me you didn't." He sighed heavily.

"You say dat swunguh Mistuh Johnny own it all. I didn't like dat mahn, all dressed up like a demy crack. He be a Jim Dandy, don't he?"

"Yeah, Lula, he's a Jim Dandy alright," Steve said…despondent and depressed!

"He be in bad truble! De sperrits ob de grabes hab him!"

"I guess I better leave; and thanks for your gumbo."

She stood on her front porch, waving goodbye, as he walked shakily back to his car.

"You be a nice man, mistah. Oonuh come back and seez me mo.'"

"Yeah, I'll do that."

Drifting back to his conversation with Bob about Voodoo, he almost cried. What in the hell was he going to do!? Seventy acres evolving into ruins. Mad spirits of the dead. And psycho Johnny. Driving home, his cell rang. It was Kelly.

"Everything okay?" she asked.

"Yeah," he lied.

"I was worried. Is he still mad?"

"I'm on the way home and I'll tell you when I get there."

"Where are you?"

"Just crossed over to St. Helena. I should be home in twenty minutes or so."

"How about stopping and getting about four pounds of shrimp at the marina. The girls are coming soon."

He had forgotten about his twins coming. They were on spring break from Clemson. "Alright. Anything else?"

"You okay? You sound a little upset."

"No, I'm fine."

"You sure?"

"Everything's fine," he lied again.

He drove up to the marina, parked, walked inside the retail section and said to the man standing behind the counter. "Four pounds of fresh jumbos."

"Alrighty, and they're really fresh. Ain't been off the boat an hour."

"You got a Budweiser?"

"I do…anything else?"

"No."

He paced nervously around the floor as his shrimp were being weighed and packaged – swigging his beer, and looking at his watch.

"You in a hurry?" the man asked.

"No. I'm just nervous. Been a hell of a day."

"Yeah, well, we'll have those days," he said with empathy; then handed him a plastic bag with ice and shrimp. "How do they look?"

"Not bad. How much do I owe?"

"Thirty even."

Kelly met him at the door. She had been anxiously waiting.

"Hey," he said, despondently.

"You don't sound happy."

"I'm alright."

"Didn't go well with Johnny, did it?"

"We'll talk about all that later."

"Tell me now. I need to know," she pleaded.

"He was mad!"

"Okay, the twins will be here anytime now, and you're right; it's best to talk later. And don't bring it up around our girls. It'll just upset everyone."

"I wasn't goin' to," Steve muttered.

"Why don't you go over to the sofa and rest before they get here."

"Gotta get the shrimp goin'."

"I'm so excited to show the girls the condo. I can't wait!"

"Yeah."

"Show a little enthusiasm! Alright?"

"It's been a long, nerve-racking day," he groaned, putting the shrimp in the sink. "And all I can say is – I need a drink!"

"Oh, you picked out some good ones! Nice fresh jumbos!"

"Yeah, I thought they looked good," he said, not caring what they looked like, popping another beer.

"I'll get the pot boiling."

The doorbell rang. The twins had arrived.

"Hey, girls!" Kelly greeted them both with open arms. "Come in! How was the trip? I worry about you being on the road; especially on a weekend?"

"Mama, it wasn't bad," Jenny said. "Was it, Lisa?"

"No, we didn't have any problems. Traffic wasn't near as bad as we thought."

"You have to see this new condo. Come on and I'll take you through it."

The girls followed her. Looking in the closets, looking in the baths.

"Hey, girls." Steve walked up, and hugged them both? "How do you like our new place?"

"It's awesome! What do you think, Lisa?"

"It sure is!"

"How long did the trip take?" Steve asked, desperately trying hard to hide his despair.

"Four hours."

"Ya'll hungry?" Kelly asked. "We got some nice, jumbo shrimp. You want to eat outside on the deck?"

"Sure," Jennie said as Lisa nodded a yes.

"Well, girls. You'll be graduating soon. At least, I hope," he laughed.

"Daddy?" Jennie spoke.

"What is it, Jennie?"

"There was a traffic stop on Lady's Island. I think it was near 'your' property you sold to Mr. Sherburtt."

"Well, it wasn't my property to sell. I found it for him, and he bought it from a woman named Lula Watson," he said, biting his lip.

"Oh. Well, anyway, they've got it blocked off. Lots of people there."

"Oh really?"

"Daddy," Lisa spoke, "Jennie's right, there's really something big happening at that land."

"Did you see what it was?" He knew what it was.

"Not really," Lisa yawned. "I just got sleepy, for some reason."

"I think we're all tired. I know I am," he said, "I'll be ready for bed pretty soon."

Nodding in agreement, Kelly looked at him. "You've had a hard day!"

***

Ross London, an assistant to a professor of anthropology at Ohio State University, was racing through Kentucky on his way to Beaufort, South Carolina. He had been doing research on the Gullah-Geechee people for six months and was determined to gather his final information to complete his dissertation: 'The History, Customs and Beliefs of the Gullah Geechies.' After receiving his doctorate, he will be given an assistant professorship. All the research he had done was sure to suffice – but he wanted some more credible information on voodoo. He had arranged a meeting with a young Gullah lady living down there who would share a wealth of information that was not readily available to just anyone.

He decided not to rest in Knoxville but to go all the way to Ashville, North Carolina, bed down, and leave in the morning at dawn. It would only be a five-hour drive from Ashville, and he could get there by noon, but the road out of Knoxville was murder. Especially near Asheville. Coming through the Blue Ridge Mountains, people drove their cars like moonshine runners. It was so treacherous that trucks were made to drive in designated lanes. But they seldom did. They would run 100 mph down the mountain. And 10 mph going up. He was anxious to get this part of the trail behind him.

It was eleven p.m. when Ross pulled into the Holiday Inn Express on I-26. He checked in and noticed that the small lounge was open. He settled his bags and belongings in his room and walked, dazed and tired, to the lounge. He had grabbed something to eat at a nearby Hardee's, so he wasn't hungry. A nightcap was what he needed.

"What you have, bud?" the bartender asked.

"Uh, I got road lag. Let me think. Jack Daniel's on the rocks."

"You got it."

"Thanks. I'm tired. Been driving awhile."

"Where you from?"

"Originally from Richmond but I'm living now up in Columbus."

"Great city. Friendly people."

"Oh yeah?" He took a swallow of his drink. "Wow, I needed that."

"Where you headed?"

"Beaufort, South Carolina."

"Been there."

"Did you like it?"

"No. I was at Parris Island doin' boot camp. Ain't been there since."

"Oh."

"Yeah, that was a tough six weeks. But I got through it. Went to the Gulf War and got through that too."

The small lounge was empty except for him and the bartender.

Ross rose from his bar stool and said, "Been great talking with you, but I better get some sleep. I have to get back on the road at six in the morning."

"Buddy, you take care."

"Thanks, I will. You do the same."

Ross woke at five AM, had some breakfast, and hit I-26 at six. He could make it to Beaufort by one PM…maybe sooner.

They went to bed early and hit the beach early the following day. Jennie and Lisa ran to the surf's edge, stepped in the sudsy water and Lisa screeched.

"What's wrong?" Jennie asked her.

"I think something bit me."

"Where?"

"My toes," she whined.

"We didn't get far enough in for you to get bit!" Jennie spouted. "OK, if you say so. Anyway, I want to talk to Mama and not go in the ocean right now. The water's too cold."

"You're not in the water?" Kelly was surprised as she lay on her towel near the surf's edge reading a novel.

"Too cold!" Jennie folded her arms and shivered.

"Oh really?"

"Yeah, it's cold!" Lisa added.

47

"Girls, you're lucky your skin's darker than your father's." She smiled, looking at her beautiful twins with their heart-shaped faces, green eyes, and long chestnut hair. She couldn't help but marvel over them.

"I know!" Jennie exclaimed. "He can't stay ten minutes in the sun without burning to a crisp! But you're so dark, Mama…"

"I was told my great-grandmother was full-blooded Cherokee and your grandfather was Italian." She laughed, knowing they've heard that story before. Inside the condo, Steve unfortunately was on the phone with Johnny.

"What!? You say that old woman doesn't have any money. What in the hell did she do with it!?" Johnny barked.

"I'm gonna talk calmly, and you talk calmly. This yelling ain't gettin' us anywhere. Now listen to me."

"I'm listening."

"You had all the time and resources to inspect your property before closing. If you had found anything not suitable, you could have backed out of the contract and gotten your deposit refunded."

"Hey! Whose side are you on?"

"Listen, Johnny. I'm tired, and my daughters are here visiting. I can't reason with you now. Why is that? You never acted like this before."

"I'm out of two million dollars!"

"I'm sorry." Steve started pacing.

"Red! You listen and you listen good. You better figure out a way to get my money back – and I mean soon!"

"How!?" Steve's temper was starting to boil.

"That's your problem!"

"You're about to piss me off, and you really don't want to do that."

"Oh, I'm real scared!"

"I'm goin' to tell you one last time. This is not my problem!"

"I'm making it your problem!"

"Well, it's not – so what are you gonna do 'bout it?"

"Red! You have no earthly idea what I can do since you don't have the imagination to figure it out. But you better solve this, or you'll regret it!"

"Regret what!? I got a lot of imagination by the way!"

"Oh you do? Imagine this! You do what I say or else!" Johnny screamed.

"Are you threatening me?"

"Call it what you want!"

Later, Bob called him. "Hey, are you okay? You didn't show up at the course."

"Yeah, I know…" he said, almost snapping. "I had some serious problems come up. I should have called to let you – but – I got bombarded with shit you wouldn't believe. I'm really sorry I let ya'll down. I really am."

"Wanna tell me about it? You sound upset, but don't worry about our golf."

"Let me rest awhile. I think I would like to talk about this! I'll call you back – And hey – I'm real sorry about not showing up this morning."

"Forget it. Call me when you got some time."

He hung up, went to the fridge, pulled out a Budweiser, and plopped down on the sofa. Ten minutes later, Kelly came walking in from the beach and saw him just sitting as if he was in a trance, oblivious to anything and everything.

"You okay?" she asked cautiously as she sat down beside him. "You don't look too happy."

"I don't know," he answered, feeling defeated, sad, confused and mad.

"Didn't go well with Johnny, did it?"

"What do you think!?" he growled, reaching for a cigarette. "It just doesn't make any sense why he's acting this way. There's got to be more to it…"

"Well, did you ask him?"

"I'm afraid to ask him anything right now. He's not himself! This is all crazy and it's driving me over the edge!"

"Have you seen today's paper?"

"No, I didn't see the paper."

She went to the bedroom, grabbed the newspaper that she had hidden, went back to the living room and handed it to him.

"I picked this up while the girls and I had breakfast at the Cabana. Look at this! That's the property Johnny bought!"

He read the headline: VOLCANO OR EARTHQUAKE ON LADY'S ISLAND! then handed it back to her.

"Shit!" he shouted. "I don't need this!"

"I was afraid to show it to you. Big deal – right. And you don't know what caused it?"

He just looked at her and said, "I have no idea."

"I don't think Jennie or Lisa saw it."

"I hope not. God, I don't know what I'm going to do about Johnny. He's off the deep end."

"It's going to be alright."

"Why didn't you wake me this morning. Ya'll were gone when I got out of bed."

"Girls' morning out!" she said, forcing a smile. "Anyway, you were sleeping too good."

"I don't see how I slept at all!"

"You didn't until about five!"

"Let me see that paper again."

"Here."

His eyes widened with fear as he read the headline again and stared at the photo. It took up the whole front page. He was speechless.

She sat down beside him, placed her hands on his shoulders and asked softly, "Are you going to be OK?"

"This is un-fucking real!"

"Not so loud. The girls might hear you."

"They're on the beach!" he snapped, looked up at the ceiling and spouted, "Fuck!"

"Easy, Red! Quit saying the F word…the girls will pop in any second!"

"I'm sure it's nothing they haven't heard before!"

"Steve! But not from you."

"Damn it! I give up."

"Why didn't you tell me all this earlier? I knew somethin' was wrong when you came home yesterday. You hardly talked to me or the girls. They asked me on the beach if something was bothering you."

"I didn't want you upset. This all happened at once – like a bolt of lightning!"

"I don't know what to say?"

"Not much you can say."

"Have you told me everything? I mean everything!"

He lit a cigarette and exhaled a long flow of smoke. "Johnny blames me for this catastrophe and is demanding his money back."

"What?" she gasped. "He can't do that!"

"Tell him that! He's turned into a mutha fucker!"

"Steve!"

"I mean it. This man's gone crazy. I always knew he was driven by money, but I never thought he could be like this! Hell, he spent a fortune on that

50

property and had high hopes for a development…a development that can't happen. He's pissed and blaming me!"

"What about that woman he bought it from? Could she be responsible?"

"No."

"You're not responsible?" she asked, fearfully.

"No, I'm not!"

"Why is the property torn up??? Just what happened? Must be a reason."

"I have no fuckin' idea! I saw it. It's a mess."

"I can't believe he blames you for…"

"I told him I wasn't gonna assume any responsibility!" he spouted.

"What did he say?"

"He threatened me."

"He did what?" Her eyes were flaming.

"I said, he threatened me. I'm just hoping he'll cool down and realize what a son of a bitch he's being." Steve hesitated, crushing out his cigarette. "He's lost it!"

"I never liked him. I just pretended to for your sake. He's an egotistical bastard!" she stated. "Let's forget about it for now. The girls will be back soon. They don't need this."

"No, they don't," he agreed.

"Are you hungry?"

He shook his head no. "I'm just going to lay here for a while and try to nap."

"OK." She smiled. "Try not to think about what happened."

He laid on the couch and quickly drifted off to sleep. The sound of Johnny's voice began echoing in his head; and the vision of the site was torturing and tearing his mind apart. He pictured Lula Watson at the closing table months ago, demanding that the graveyard be left alone. It was creepy the way she said it…and she said it more than once. "But what if she's right and there are angry spirits out there. Haants!" he muttered. "You don't really believe that! You're just scared, that's all – and you're thinking too much! But *why* in the hell did some fool have to drive a Caterpillar into those graves? And why did she give that much money away?!" He could see her giving away a large amount – but TWO MILLION. That didn't make sense. And are spirits really at that graveyard…?

Kelly heard him fretting and moaning in distress; obviously having a bad dream! She went over to his side and began rubbing his neck and shoulders "Honey, are you OK? You've been talking in your sleep."

"What time is it?" he asked, sitting up, rubbing his eyes.

"It's only noon; but you didn't get much sleep last night; go on and lay back down and try not to think bad thoughts!"

Chapter 5

ROSS LONDON pulled into the parking lot of the Quality Inn on Bay Street, driving a white '99 Toyota 4 Runner. After parking, he walked into the hotel lobby carrying two overnight bags. It was 12:15 PM.

"Hey, Ross," the pretty desk clerk said, grinning. "You're back in town so soon?"

"Home away from home. I guess that's what I'll start calling this place."

"Doin' more anthropology work? Still working on your paper?"

"Yeah sure am."

"Gullah people, right?"

"'History Beliefs and Cultures of the Gullah-Geechee People.' And by the way, it's not just a paper. It's a dissertation I'm preparing for my doctorate," he said proudly, rubbing his hand over his blond hair. "I'm not getting any younger."

"How old?" she winked.

"Twenty-nine."

"You're still a young man! And smart! I bet you write a big book one day," she smiled, handing him a key. "Good thing you had a reservation. We're filled up."

"Really? College spring break?"

"Oh. No. Big land problem at Lady's Island. Some kind of large sinkhole happened all at once and can't be explained. People are coming from everywhere. And like crazy."

"Oh really?"

"Oh yeah. Bet you couldn't find a place in our lot to park; could you?"

"Had no problem finding a space."

"If you leave and come back late, you will!"

"Thanks for the warning," Ross said.

He settled in his room, placed his bags on the bed – opened one, retrieved a 35 mm 'Canon' camera, clipboard fastened with paper and pencil and a Panasonic tape recorder. He checked his camera and recorder then put them back in the bag. "All there." He nodded a confident yes as he looked at himself in the mirror. Young, blonde-headed, lithe Ross London was eager to start his investigation. He had timed this trip perfectly!

After a quick shower and a change of clothes, he was ready to go to the Coosaw, a small restaurant on Lady's Island, and couldn't wait to talk with the young Gullah girl he had never personally met. He just knew her name was Suzie and she could give him information about DR. HAWK, the most famous 'root doctor' who had ever lived – in the coastal Southeast. He was feared by many but also respected by many. He died in 1949 and supposedly was buried somewhere on St. Helena Island, but his grave was never found from what he had heard. Through Internet conversations, the young Gullah woman, Suzie, said she could lead him to the grave – at a price. He wanted to see that grave. And he wanted to know her price. Better not be a whole lot!

Passing over the Beaufort River onto Lady's Island, he saw the Coosaw restaurant and pulled in. Walking inside, he went right up to the owner, Preston Reynolds.

"Hey, Preston." Ross said.

"Ross, ole buddy." He ran over and gave him a hug. "Yu back again?"

"Yeah."

"Can't keep you Yankees away, can we?"

"I guess not," Ross laughed. "But I'm not a Yankee! Just livin' up there awhile."

"What yu drinkin'?"

"Miller Lite."

"Hungry?"

"Yeah. How 'bout a fried grouper sandwich?"

"You got it buddy!"

"I'm supposed to meet a young black woman who is going to help me finish my dissertation."

"That's right. You're gettin' your doctor degree," he said then faced the kitchen and bellowed, "One fried group...sandwich."

"Yeah, this girl I'm meeting is the granddaughter of a one-hundred-year-old woman living on St. Helena. She's a medicine woman."

"What!? Why? A medicine woman…!"

"Yeah, a medicine woman who sells special stuff to the root doctors down here!"

"To hell, you say!" Preston broke out in a laugh. "What's her name? This is funny."

"Willa Mae," he replied. "Heard of her?"

"No, I haven't. Who's this granddaughter you're meeting?" Preston asked still laughing.

"Suzie Smith."

"What are they helpin' yu with?"

"Are you goin' to keep laughing?"

"I don't know." He started coughing. "Tell me – can't wait to hear!"

"They're going to show me Dr. Hawk's grave."

"Get outta town. You must be crazy!"

"You've heard about him?"

"Oh yeah. He was a legend in these parts, some time ago. People been tryin' to find that grave for decades. Some say they know where it's at, but I think he's just buried somewhere in the woods."

Suzie walked in the door and asked, "I'm looking for Ross London. Is he here?"

"I'm Ross London," he said, rising from his stool. "Are you Suzie?"

"Yeah. You told me to meet you here."

"So we finally meet," he said, thinking she was fairly pretty, around twenty – probably been up and down those tracks a few times. "Let's go to a table, and we'll talk."

After fifteen minutes of conversation, Suzie said, "You won't tell nobody 'bout this and where my granny lives?"

"Not if you don't want me to. But you know I'm writing a long research paper, and I have to document my information."

"Yu can't use my grandmother's name if she shows you Dr. Hawk's grave. And yu can't use mine!" she firmly stated.

"Why?"

"We don't want no hexes put on us!"

"You serious?" he said, holding back a laugh.

"You can use fake names. Now, if you're ready, you can follow me to Granny's."

"I'm ready as soon as I finish this sandwich."

As they were walking out, Preston ventured to say, "Ross, there was an explosion close to here that caused a large and dangerous sinkhole on some vacant land. Also, there's an old graveyard there – they say it's haunted. You might want to check that out! There's all kinds of people there. Reporters, scientists, and – cops."

"Hell yeah! I'm going to! I could see all the cars there. I'm goin' to check it out, later."

He followed Suzie to St. Helena – the home of VOODOO – and turned onto a long dirt road, not much wider than a walking path heading to a small wooden house painted blue. They walked up to the door, and she gave it a loud rap.

"Me's coming!" a voice hollered.

The door flung open. "Suzie, me chile! You here to see po granny! Who dat man?"

"Dis is Ross. He wants to ask yu somethin."

He looked at the old woman. She had a ring on every finger. She also was wearing gold necklaces, bracelets and a scarf wrapped around her head. She looked like a gypsy fortune-teller.

"Mistah." She grinned with several gold teeth. "Whu yu want ob me?"

"Can you tell me where Dr. Hawk is buried?" he ventured timidly.

"Whu!" she shouted. "Why you wanna know dat? I ain't gwine tell!"

"Granny," Suzie spoke, "he gwine give you fifty dollars."

The old medicine woman's eyes lit up. "Yu can't come in de house, and you can't tell nobody I tol you. Let me see dat fity dollas and me tell yu."

He pulled out a crisp fifty and showed it to her.

"Yu gonna get some goofer dust frum his grabe? It don't hab no powers in daylight cept bring good luck."

"I might," Ross said, knowing it was used as a root, gathered at midnight, to cast voodoo spells. But so what. All he wants to do is identify a grave.

"Dut around his grabe. And yu betta leeb a case qwatuh. It be good charm the root doctor gib if'n yu leeb him a present."

"I know," he said.

"Bad luck if yu don'."

"Ross," Suzie said, "now yu give me that fifty dollars, and Granny will tell yu where to go."

Grumbling about the extra fifty dollars he gave, he got in his SUV and drove off.

He headed down to the back portion of St. Helena and spotted the dirt road leading to the little white church and parked in the sandy lot, got out and walked into a small graveyard – hunting Dr. Hawk. Seeing the large unmarked headstone, Ross eagerly ran toward and began taking photo after photo, talking into his recorder, and marveling over all the diggings at the OTHER graves. "Goofer dust. I got to scrape up some of that!" Lying next to the grave marker was a small empty jar, he grabbed it scraped up some dirt with his pocketknife and placed it in the jar. After leaving the church's lot – Ross had forgotten one thing – to leave a gift – and was now flirting with a powerful spirit and had taken goofer dust from the most feared root doctor known – risking his life and soul over a handful of dirt.

Driving back, Ross saw the Lady's Island Road lined with cars and people. Finding a place to park, he was amazed to see so many people, news vans, and police at this vacant tract of property – until spotting the hole.

He leaped from his SUV and could see the unbelievable hole, and then saw something that was even more unbelievable – suddenly red and yellow bubbles shot from the hole, then disappeared. Shocked, Ross fumbled the camera from his pocket, not realizing he was stepping over the yellow tape.

"Mister," a county deputy spoke. "I'll have to ask you to step back to the road. This is off-limits to the public."

"Did you see what came out of that hole!?"

"Sir, I'll ask you again to please step back."

Ross looked at him and pointed to the crater. "I want to get closer. I see people walking around."

"They're authorized."

"What's going on!?" Ross clamored, confused and excited.

"A serious land disturbance."

"I can't believe what I saw," he said, gasping.

"Young man, you look shaken up. It might be best if you leave here."

"I'm alright, I promise – been driving down from Ohio."

"You drove that far today!"

"No. I left Ashville NC early – by the way, how do you get authorized to go over there?" he asked, still astonished at what he witnessed.

"Go to the Beaufort County Administration building and apply for an authorization badge. You'll need one if you plan on stepping over this yellow tape."

"I'll do that," he said. "You didn't see those funny red bubbles?"

"No," the deputy said, looking at him questionably.

"I heard screeching sounds too." Ross stopped, realizing he was offering information deemed to be crazy.

"Oh I'm sure you did," he humored him. Another crackpot and Funny bubbles.

"I saw and heard anomalies too!" He regretted saying – talking too much.

"What in the hell are anomalies?"

"Never mind. I guess I just imagined ghosts in that hole."

"Young man, you stay behind the marked-off area. You understand?"

"Yes, sir."

The deputy walked away. Ross was going to get a badge in the morning and come back. He would get some recordings and photos!

As Ross walked over to his vehicle, a man wearing a T-shirt with binoculars hanging from his neck approached him.

"Excuse me, young man. I couldn't help but notice you talking with that officer and pointing to the hole."

"Yeah, why?" Ross spoke, looking at him apprehensively.

"My name is Jack Nolin. I'm a parapsychologist. Did you witness possibly the same things I saw and heard?"

"What did you see?" His curiosity began to stir.

"First, let me say that I'm a doctor in metaphysical science and also a certified paranormal investigator. You saw something?"

"A meta physician?"

"Yes, but don't think I'm crazy! I want to know what you saw."

"I'm an anthropologist and have taken a few courses in metaphysics. I'll tell you what I saw and heard. I saw bright red bubbles and screeching sounds come out of that hole!"

"I know!"

"By the way, I'm Ross London." He quickly introduced himself, shaking hands with Dr. Nolin. "I saw them but it happened too quick to get a picture. I asked people including scientists here if they've seen anything. None have...wonder why?"

"Ross, I believe only a few people can witness the supernatural. But most can't. There are definitely spirits in that hole – I believe came from the graveyard – directly behind it."

"Scary!"

"Don't you believe in spirits? You just saw some."

"I don't know."

"Sure you do." Nolin smiled. "You saw them!"

"Let's say – I saw something extremely unusual."

"You sure did." Nolin started to walk away.

"Jack. Wait. I want to ask you about something. You're from around here, right?"

"Yes, I am."

"Um, have you heard much about the old root doctor, Dr. Hawk?"

"I have!" His eyes opened, surprised and curious. "Why?"

"I just left his gravesite."

"Whoa. You were at Dr. Hawk's grave?"

"Yeah, I was. I'm doing research on Gullah customs and of course – VOODOO."

"Voodoo is a belief held by extremely superstitious people and Dr. Hawk was their man."

"Do you believe in it?"

He laughed. "I don't know…probably…but I stay away from it. But I believe it's here now!"

"Yeah, I saw his grave and dug up a little dirt around it."

Jack stared into his eyes "I hope you left him a present for taking that dirt."

"Wait, I didn't!"

"Hope Dr. Hawk doesn't put a curse on you!"

"Are you serious?"

Jack patted Ross on the shoulder and said, "You'll be alright."

"I hope so."

"Mere superstition," Jack reassured him. "Well, I have to go. The wife's expecting me."

"How come you don't have one of those VIP badges?" he asked.

"Ha. They don't give those out to quacky ghost busters! But – this place is haunted! There could be voodoo working here, I'm wondering."

Excitement raced through Ross's mind as he returned to the Coosaw restaurant. He needed a beer!

"Hey, you're back!" Preston said, surprised. "I thought you might still be down in Voodoo land."

Ross plopped down at the bar. "I got pictures of Dr. Hawk's grave."

"You sure it's his grave?"

"Yeah, I do. But it's unmarked and people wouldn't know whose grave it was. I dug up a little dirt around it."

"Goofer dust?" Preston laughed. "I hope you left a gift."

"No, I forgot."

"Hey, the old root doctor might put a curse on you!"

"Yeah, right. Anyway, I'm not going back there to leave a gift. That's just bullshit superstition!" he said, deceiving himself.

"Well, here's a Jack Daniel's on the house."

"Thanks," he said, reaching for it and feeling his hand tremble.

"Hey, buddy, you nervous?"

"Maybe, I feel a little edgy."

"Dr. Hawk?"

"I don't know."

"Aw, you were just down at a spooky grave."

Ross thought about the weird noises and the bubbles coming out of that hole. He thought about digging around the root doctor's grave. "Hey, Preston…"

"Yeah, what, buddy?"

"You got any garlic heads I can take back to my room?"

"Garlic heads!"

"Yeah."

"Hey, I know what you're thinking. You think they'll ward off evil spirits. Now come on! Hey, man. You don't really believe all that shit?"

"No. I guess I'm just tired. So, do you have any garlic heads?"

"Of course, I do!" He mocked. "You need some fresh rooster blood?"

"Yeah, give me some of that too!" He spouted.

"Ross, here's three garlics." He smiled and chuckled. "Come back soon. Missed you around here! And keep away from the 'hainnts'!"

"Thanks, I will. By the way, do you know where 'goofer' got its name?"

"Never thought about it. Tell me."

"It's an old African word meaning *corpse*." Ross went back to his hotel room and placed the garlic heads on top of the dresser and mumbled, "This has been one hell of a day!" Feeling fretful and restless, he strolled over to the hotel's lounge. Walking in, he was surprised to find it so crowded. Only one bar stool was empty, and he jumped to grab it.

"What you havin'?" the bartender asked him impatiently.

"Jack on the rocks. Sure crowded this afternoon."

"Yeah, hotel is maxed out with all the people rushing in to see that big sinkhole across the river."

After several drinks, Ross felt his nerves settle. He thought about that site and planned to return but not tomorrow. He had to go to the county administration building to get a VIP badge. No telling how long that would take! Also, he had some serious writing to do.

He overheard a man next to him talking with his friend about the site. Obviously, he was a local, wearing a ball cap and talking in a low-country drawl. He ventured to impose. "Um, excuse me, I don't mean to eavesdrop, but I heard you talking about that sinkhole over at Lady's Island."

"Yeah bo, somethin' bad happened there. I've lived here all my life, and I ain't seen nothin' like it."

"I guess that's why it's crowded here. Everyone wants to see it."

"I guess so."

"I wonder what caused it."

"Shit bo, they got all them college fuckers studying it, and they don't have a clue." He stopped, turned his beer upside down into his mouth, and resumed talking. "I know what caused it. There's a 'hainted' graveyard on that land. Been there forever. The Haints came out. You know what haints are, bo?"

"Ghosts."

"Evil ghosts!"

"You believe that?"

"Yeah, I sneaked over there last night, but by God I won't be going back. I ain't messin' with that place."

"How did you get in?"

"Hey!" He stared at him. "Yu want me to buy you a drink? What you drinking?"

"No thanks."

"Hey, bo." He slapped Ross on the shoulder, drunker than hell. "If we're gonna talk, then we're gonna drink!"

"Let me buy you one."

"Alrighty! Now, what was you asking?"

"You said you sneaked over there. That place is guarded. How did you do it?"

"You got somethin' up your ass, don't you? What you wantin' to see over there?"

"I don't know." He shrugged his shoulders.

"All you gotta do is go over to the Coosaw restaurant, and you'll see a path out through the marsh, and it'll take you right into the woods behind that graveyard."

"Really!"

"I ain't shittin' you! Hey where are you from?"

"Virginia."

"Where in Virginia?"

"Richmond," he answered absently, thinking about the graveyard.

"Umm, so are yu goin' over there?"

"I don't know."

"Damn, you ready for another drink?"

Ross thought for a moment with his head reeling in alcohol. "No thanks."

He paid his tab and stumbled back to his room. He too was drunk!

***

Rhonda Shields sat at a table in the lounge of the Ramada Inn, talking with her production manager.

"It's been a hell of a day, hasn't it, Rhonda," he said. "I bet you could use another drink?"

"One more," she agreed, reaching into her purse for lipstick. "This is the largest event I've covered."

"You know, you have reached the big time! The whole world is watching you!"

"Oh really?"

"Yes, Rhonda. I think you have hit it big. You've done excellent coverage. The whole team is proud of you."

"Well, I don't even know what's going on there."

"No one does! That's why it's news."

"I know, but it's sad people have died in some crazy unexplained crater."

"It is, but it's not our fault."

"You know, sometimes I feel guilty about drawing fame and money from tragedies."

"That's our job, honey." He held her hand.

It was 7:30 PM.

Chapter 6

JENNIE WATCHED the sun with its reddish glow dabbing its colors along the wet marsh while she and her sister were having sandwiches and beer at a sea food place on St. Helena Island. After visiting her 'parents,' she was anxious to get to Myrtle Beach tomorrow. "Now that'll be fun as long as Lisa doesn't complain all the time." Knowing she really wouldn't want go anywhere without her.

"Look out over the marsh," she said, taking a bite from her sandwich gazing out over miles of water and saw grass.

"It's great! I love it!"

"Yeah, when we leave here, we'll head into Beaufort. I heard about a great place called the 'Iron Mike.'"

"Oh really?" Lisa said with apprehension.

"We're going to have some fun. I got the scoop back at school. They're having a good band – oughta be great!"

"When we goin?"

"As soon as we're done here."

"I'm done. Sure hope it's not a rough place – It better not be! Like other dives you've dragged me in."

"No, it's fine…I promise! Now, if you're ready…let's go," she said, eagerly.

Jennie drove their '95 Mustang across the Beaufort River bridge, then parked in the municipal parking lot that was filling up fast. Bay Street had limited parking due to all the new businesses that had recently moved in; changing Beaufort from a little fishing town to a small bustling city. Jennie locked their car and they began walking up the street toward the bar. Jennie wore a white T-shirt tucked inside her designer jeans. With her high-heel boots, she stood almost two inches taller than Lisa who was wearing sneakers.

"I love twilight." Lisa smiled happily.

"I love action!"

They entered the bar, bracing the thunderous sounds from a band and the screaming and yelling of the crowd, Jennie shouted, "God – this is great!"

Lisa just looked around wondering what to expect.

Spotting two wooden stools open at the bar, the two chestnut-haired girls jumped on them.

"How 'bout it, ladies!" the bartender shouted over the music.

"Two Ultras."

"You got it."

At the other end of the bar, two young men spotted the twins, and they confidently walked over with a warm greeting. "Their drinks are on us," one said to the bartender.

Jennie turned to face them and with a coy wink said, "Thank you."

Both men smiled.

"Hey, don't be so friendly." Lisa nudged her.

"Why?"

"They could be ax murderers or something," she whispered in her ear.

"Stop it, Lisa. Why are you so paranoid?"

"I don't know."

"My name is Josh, and this is my friend, Todd. Do you mind if we join you," he asked as there were now two open bar stools next to the girls.

"Sure." Jenny smiled.

"Jennie, I'm going to the restroom. Come with me."

"We'll be right back."

"These guys seem creepy," Lisa said as they entered the ladies' room.

"What is your problem?"

"I don't feel comfortable."

"They seem alright to me and good-looking."

"Something's not right. And they're not all that good-lookin'."

"Come on Lisa. They're OK."

"Well." Lisa looked at her sister, still doubtful. "Alright."

They returned to their seats, and Jennie looked into the green eyes of one of them with her own wide green eyes and said, "Nice to meet you, Josh. I'm Jennie, and this is my sister, Lisa."

"Ya'll twins, right?"

"Yep. Wonder what gave it away?" Jennie smarted off.

65

"Where you from?" Josh asked admiring her sassy wit.

"Greenville."

Todd lit a cigarette with his sterling silver Zippo, hoping the flash of lighter fluid would give a sexually enticing aroma to Lisa's nostrils…it didn't. "So, Lisa, you don't live in Beaufort?"

"No, just came down to visit our parents," she answered, being a little 'short.'

"Stayin' long?"

"Goin' back tomorrow."

"We go to Clemson," Jennie interrupted. "Off on spring break."

"By the way," Lisa spoke. "You guys live here?"

"Yeah, we do," Josh replied. "We're car salesmen over at the Toyota place."

"It's time for me to go to the little boys' room." Todd smiled.

"Me too. We'll be right back, so don't go nowhere!"

The two men entered the restroom, and Todd spoke. "You trust that black dude?"

"Yeah, I think so. I hate we have to do this."

"How did he find us?" Todd asked, flipping his cigarette butt in a toilet.

"Don't worry 'bout it, Todd…Now listen, let's go back and act normal."

It was 10:30 PM several beers later, and they were still at the bar. Jenny spoke up and said, "Look guys, this has been fun, but we need to head home."

"Noooo." Josh threw his hands up. "It's still early!"

"It's time we head home," she reiterated.

"Hey. We'll all go over to the 'Anchor.' There's a big party crankin' up over there," Josh insisted. "You'll love it."

"I don't know," Jenny said, rubbing her hand through her hair. "I don't think so."

"We better not," Lisa spoke up.

"Aw, come on. We won't stay long. We'll drive and bring you straight back in less than an hour."

"Where?" Lisa asked.

"Just over Carterret Street."

"Well, Lisa." Jennie looked at her, not slurring.

"I guess," Lisa slurred a little.

Josh led Jennie out of the bar with his hand and forearm clutched tight around her waist as Todd led Lisa out behind them.

"A Lexus," Jennie commented, looking at the shiny red car glistening under the streetlights. "My daddy has a white one."

"You like it?" Josh grinned arrogantly, as he opened the door for her. "We're going to have fun. No problems, No worries."

"We can't be long," Jennie said.

"We won't," Josh lied. "Half hour at the most." He really lied!

Todd and Lisa climbed into the back seat. Todd was becoming a little creepy and quiet; obviously making Lisa uneasy. "Todd," she whispered nervously, "I'm not sure this is cool...is it?"

"Yeah," he answered, with that new, creepy-looking face.

"Jennie!" she hollered. "I don't want to go!"

"What's the matter, Lisa?" Josh looked over his shoulder.

"I said, I don't want to go."

"Aw, sit back and relax!"

"Hey, dude!" Jennie popped him on the shoulder. "She said she doesn't want to go so you back this car up right now!"

"Sorry!" he shouted with an ugly, wicked laugh. He was also creepy and becoming angry. A creepy – angry – face! And it turned into an ugly – wicked – face! But she became frightened as she quickly realized – it was a – dangerous – evil – face!

As the shiny red Lexus raced from the parking lot, Jennie and Lisa screamed, "Where are we goin'? You're fixin' to cross over the bridge. Take us back. Now!"

"Shut up!" Josh pulled out a gun and waved it in their scared – innocent – rich girl faces, as he sped over the Beaufort River Bridge and on to Lady's Island. "I'm driving! You're not!"

They turned down a long sandy road, and Josh drove slowly through the dense fog. The twins sat scared and silent. He parked in front of a small shack. "Come on, Todd. Help me get them out of the car before I shoot 'em!"

"Why are you doin' this?" Jennie yelled as they were jerked out of the car physically and at gun point.

"Walk to the door," Josh ordered.

"You're goin' to be in big trouble," Lisa cried.

A tall, masked man wearing thick black gloves and holding a shining flashlight came out of the door.

"Here they are," Josh said. "Where's our money?"

The man motioned them inside the small wooden shack. He closed the door and focused his flashlight on two stone footings with anchor bolts holding chains, motioning the men to lock the girls' wrists inside the shackles at each end.

"Todd! Lock these girls to these chains."

Todd complied.

"What are you doin'?" Jennie panicked as she tried to kick Todd.

"Shut up!" Todd backhanded her.

"Why are you doing this!?" Lisa desperately cried out. "Why?"

"Nothin' personal," Josh said without remorse.

"Nothin' personal!" Jennie shouted. "You assholes are goin' to be sorry!"

"Todd," he said, "get their cell phones. They won't be needing them."

"Where do you want me to put em?"

"Go in the woods behind the shack. Crush them, then bury them."

The two young men followed the masked man out. The door creaked shut. He handed them two thousand dollars each. Josh grinned while Todd just took his money with no expression.

As they counted their money, mentally gloating, a machete suddenly sliced across their throats. They never uttered a sound.

The masked man looked down at the two greedy fools wiggle on the ground in their own blood. He laughed, watching them squirm in agony. He laughed again, picking up the money he had given them. He just looked at 'em. Didn't say a thing. Just two pigs – a wallowin in a pool of blood. – Soon dead in their blood!

Once they were dead and his pleasure satisfied, he dragged them, one at a time, to their car. Opening the trunk, he heaved them in. No one was watching. The light of the bright full moon with dark shadows moving across its face made the masked man feel his powers.

He drove the red Lexus down Coosaw Road, then turned on a sandy, dark trail bordering a wet marsh. At the edge of a dark wet bog, he got out and looked around. He hadn't expected anyone to be around close. Of course not. The only sounds he heard were from crickets and bats. He took the car out of gear, pushed and heaved until it rolled into the marsh lake. It began sinking slowly and lazily. When the shiny red top disappeared below the ugly, nasty, deep, mucky water – he left.

Jennie lay on her back, staring up at dark rafters supporting a roof. The room was damp, and she could hear the wind blowing against the exterior walls of the shack; a steady creaking sound reaching her ears. In the room's darkness, she couldn't see much more than a silhouette of Lisa and pulled her blanket up to her chin, trying to stay warm as possible. She wasn't sleepy, but shut her eyes anyway. Shocked and confused – and determined to find some logical explanation to why they were chained up in some remote barn or whatever it was. "You doin' alright, Lisa?"

"No. We're in bad trouble. I told you not to trust those guys."

"I know. But we'll figure something out. There's got to be a way."

"How?" she whimpered in fear. "We're locked in chains!"

"Damn it, Lisa! I don't know; but I know this a weird deal. We're here for a reason and I'm goin' to find out what the hell it is! I don't understand why they just left us here and didn't rape or kill us. Someone knew we were at that bar and got Ross and Todd to bring us here. I wonder if that man with the mask is behind this – but why?"

"Yeah, that Masked Man. What's he goin' to do with us?"

"I don't know," Jennie muttered, looking down at her chained arm. "He must be holding us for ransom. I bet Daddy and Mama are being blackmailed."

"I bet those asshole dudes knew we were at the Iron Mike. But how could they know we'd be there? Why did they pick us?"

"Lisa," Jennie gasped. "Did you notice Daddy's reaction when I brought up the land he sold on Lady's Island? It shook him up a little."

"He didn't want to talk about it. Did he!?"

"It hit a nerve, but he was being distant all evening. Something was on his mind, and I think he's in some kind of trouble."

"You're saying he's involved in that property and might owe somebody a lot of money – And that's why we're here?"

"Maybe. Hey! I didn't say that."

"Daddy said he never owned it."

"I don't know what's with that property except what we saw in the paper this morning. They say it's cracking away due to an earthquake or a volcano. Whatever happened has something to do with us being here...you think...maybe?"

"I can't understand! He was just the realtor. That earthquake isn't his fault!"

"No, but he knows something he's not telling," Jennie said.

"I bet that masked man knows what he's not telling."

"He either knows everything or nothing, but I'm sure he'll be back and I'll find out!" Jenny spouted bravely. "I'm goin' to find out somethin'!"

"I don't think Daddy had anything to do with this. He loves us."

"You're right, Lisa. But for now, all we can do is lay here and hope for the best. Let's try and sleep, we'll talk more about it later. That Masked Man isn't goin' to hurt us, or he would have already."

"I won't be able to sleep," Lisa whined as she glanced at her watch. It was 2:00 AM, Sunday morning.

***

"Steve!" Kelly shouted at him as he lay on his back snoring. "Steve!" she said forcefully. "Wake up!"

"Wha—" he muttered groggily, then rolled onto his other side.

"I said wake up!"

He bolted upright. "What?" He rubbed his eyes.

"They're not here!"

"What time is it?"

"It's three o'clock in the morning, and they're not back!"

"What!?" he rose up, his blue eyes opening wide. "They are not here!"

"Shit," he growled, getting out of bed. "Why aren't they back?"

"I don't know, but I'm worried."

"Have you called them?"

"Yes! Five times and no answer." She shook her hair, upset and mad.

"I'm going to make some coffee."

"There's a pot already made."

"Well, when they get home, they better have a good reason. I don't care if they're twenty-one. They came to visit us and promised to be back before midnight!"

"What if something happened to them?" she shrieked.

"Now, don't go jumpin' to conclusions," he said, softening his tone and placing his hand on her shoulder. "I'm sure they're fine."

"How, at this time of night."

"They lost track of time. They'll be home soon."

"Why don't they answer their phones?"

70

"Yeah. I do have a problem with that." He frowned.

"What do we do?" she asked with tears running down her cheeks.

"I don't know. Let me think."

"We have to do something," she pleaded, almost in a panic.

"Wait a little while longer, and if they're still not back, I'll call the police."

It was 8:45 AM. Steve dialed 911.

"What's the emergency," a female voice answered.

"Sheriff's Department, please."

"I'll connect you."

Steve drummed his fingers on the kitchen counter top as the moments followed.

"Beaufort County Sheriff's Department."

"Yeah, I want to report two missing girls who were out last night."

"I'll connect you with the officer on duty. Your name, please?"

"Steve Riley." He lit a cigarette as Kelly stood next to him.

"What?" she asked.

"Kelly, I'm holding."

"Hello, I'm Officer Jones. How can I help you?"

"Officer, our twin daughters went out last night. They were supposed to be home by midnight, but they never showed up!"

"Where did they go?"

"They went somewhere downtown to watch a band. Like I said, they didn't come home!"

"How old are they?"

"Twenty-one."

"They're adults."

"I know, but I think something has happened to them."

"Hold on," he said, hesitating for a few moments.

"What?" Kelly pleaded.

"I don't know. I'm on hold."

"They're not here," the officer said.

"What do you mean?"

"I mean that we don't have them."

"You mean in jail!?" Steve huffed. "Damn it! I'm trying to find my daughters!"

"Alright, calm down. I'll have a detective call you shortly."

"When?"

"Sir, you sound upset."

"Damn right, I'm upset. I want to talk to the detective now!"

"Sir, he will call you in a few minutes. Give me your number."

He hung up the phone and looked at Kelly who was crying. "A detective will call back soon."

"What did they say?"

"Nothing yet." He kissed her on the cheek. "I hope those girls are somewhere safe and I wish they'd call."

"Steve! It's almost nine in the morning. They would have called earlier!"

"I don't know what to say!" She ran to the front door, holding her head with both hands.

"Please be out there," she cried as she flung the door open. But there was no one there.

The phone rang, and Steve jumped to answer it. "Hello."

"Mr. Riley?"

"Yes, this is Steve Riley."

"I'm Detective Rob Pinckney. I was told to contact you about your missing daughters. When did they leave the house, and how old are they?"

"They're twenty-one, and they left around six o'clock last night."

"Sir, they're adults."

"Detective, I promise these girls would have been home by midnight, or they would have called. Something happened to them!"

"Give me their names and description. Also their vehicle information, and we'll do some immediate checking. Can you come down to the station?"

"Now?"

"Right now, if you can."

"We can. You're on Duke Street, right?"

"That's right."

"It'll take us at least a half hour."

"That's fine."

Steve and Kelly arrived at the Sheriff's Department at 9:30 AM and were given a missing person report to fill out. Minutes later, the detective entered and gave both a warm handshake.

"I'm Detective Pinckney...please follow me back to my office."

They were seated in two chairs in front of his desk.

"Would either of you like a cup of coffee?" Pinckney offered.

"I would!" Kelly blurted.

"Before we discuss your daughters, let me ask you if they drove a white Mustang."

"Yes!" Kelly jumped.

"It was parked in the municipal lot on Bay Street, and it's been there all night."

"How did you know it was theirs?" Steve asked, curiously.

"You gave me the license number over the phone, and also it's the only car impounded. It needs to be fingerprinted in case there were others in the car and possible foul play."

Tears ran down Kelly's cheeks as she reached in her purse for a tissue. "I just can't believe this is happening."

He placed his hand on hers.

"Mrs. Riley," Pinckney said, "I think your girls are safe. I believe they ran into a group of people at a bar and maybe went to a party. These things happen on spring break. They're young. They'll call you, especially when they see their car gone."

"My girls would never go off to a party in a strange town with people they didn't know."

"I understand," he sighed audibly, refraining from rolling his eyes. "I'm exploring reasonable possibilities."

"What are you going to do, Detective?" she asked, her brown eyes pleading.

"I'm going to check all the night spots. Have you got pictures of your girls?"

"I do." She reached into her purse and handed him several photos.

"Beautiful girls." He hesitated and then resumed. "I hate to ask you this, but is there anyone you know who would willingly kidnap them?"

Steve sighed and went into a lengthy explanation about the land transaction and how his client reacted – including Johnny's threats.

"Uh-huh." He looked at Steve. "You sold that land over on Lady's Island to Mr. Shurbertt."

"I brokered it," Steve replied flatly.

"He threatened you? We'll put a stop to that! I might want to talk with him?"

"He's real mad, Detective," Kelly spoke up.

"He wants me to refund the money he paid for the property."

"He wants his money back? I'm not a real estate man, but how can he do that?"

"He can't, legally. He bought the land in February, had it inspected, and then closed on it. I told you what happened. He wants me to give back his money."

"Do you have that kind of money?"

"No, I don't!"

"Well, he must believe you have access to it. Like equity, savings."

"I doubt I could raise that much but I wouldn't plan on giving it to him even if I could. I expect him to set them free and unharmed. I want that mad man in jail."

"Where does he live?"

"Greenville."

"Uh huh. He needs to answer some questions for sure. If he's responsible, he'll spend a long time in a federal pen!"

"I'm sure he's responsible. You should have heard our conversations."

"Uh-yeah," Pinckney replied, and rose from his chair. "I want you two to go home and rest. I know that's goin' to be difficult, but for the next twenty-four hours, I would feel better if I knew you were in your house. Keep your doors locked. You know after a certain time period, the FBI takes over a kidnapping case."

"You think Johnny has our daughters?" Kelly asked him.

"I don't know, but I'll tell you what I think."

"What, Detective?" She asked.

"I think they might have had too much to drink and spent the night out somewhere. You know – crashed…" He hesitated seeing her eyes showing shock. "But that's OK. It's better than drivin' intoxicated. They probably feel nervous and ashamed. But they'll be in touch pretty soon."

"I just can't believe this." Kelly started crying again. "They would have called."

"Mrs. Riley? I'm going to check out every place they could have been. I'll find out where they are." He stopped and smiled. "Try not to worry."

"What about my client, Johnny?" Steve asked.

"That too. I'll call Greenville and have him checked out, but I still think your daughters will show up soon," he said and hesitated. "I'm going to have to come up with a reason why Mr. Sherburtt would stoop to kidnapping, knowing the legal consequences. Like I said, if he's caught and found guilty, he'll spend many years in prison."

"I don't think he's worried about that now. He's crazy!"

"If he drove back to Greenville Friday, how would he be able to steal them last night?"

"Hell, he drives everywhere. He could have been here Saturday," Steve said, rubbing his brows, frustrated.

"I'll know if he did, and by the way, did he know your girls were here and were out last night?"

"I don't know. That's a good question. He wouldn't have known from me or Kelly."

"Alright folks. I'm going to get started on this today and let you know what I find out."

"Thank you, Detective." Steve shook his hand. "Please just find them."

"We'll check out all the night spots today. I'll let you know something one way or another. And I'm not dismissing your client, Johnny Sherburtt." He stopped and smiled at them. "I have a good feelin' that they'll be callin' you anytime now. And your worries will be over."

**

The morning came with a hangover for Ross. But he was able to leave his room and grab some breakfast before heading to the Beaufort County Administration building. Due to the overwhelming problems happening on Lady's Island, the county offices were now open on weekends.

After gobbling down two eggs and some bacon at the nearby Waffle House, he went straight over to the county building, walked inside, and approached the information desk.

"Can I help you?" the receptionist asked.

"Where do I go to apply for a permit?"

"The permit office down the hall, third door on the left."

"Thank you."

Walking inside the office, he was told to take a seat. Ten minutes went by, and a short gray-haired man came out and said, "Ross London?"

"That's me." He rose, and followed the man to his desk.

"Have a seat, Mr. London," he said. "How can I help you?"

Ross explained to the county worker what he wanted while sharing information about his studies in Anthropology and the research he's doing.

"Mr. London," he said, looking at him and giving a sigh, "I'm afraid I can't help you."

"Why not?"

"Well, I've looked at the list of occupations that have been approved to have physical access to that property. Unfortunately, 'anthropologist' is not one of them."

Ross looked at the man, disappointment written all over his face. "Are you sure?"

"I'm sorry, Mr. London," he said, and continued. "Only those who have a certain expertise in physical land disturbances, along with county law officials."

"What about the media? You knew reporters and camera men have been on-site."

"I'm sorry."

"Well, alright. Thanks anyway."

"Mr. London," he spoke. "You might check with the Sheriff's Department."

"Thanks," he replied walking away with his back turned to the county worker.

He left the permit office heading straight for the Sheriff's Department, just a few doors down. *Worth a try,* he thought.

"Can I help you?" asked a man sitting behind bullet-proof glass.

"Yes, I would like to speak with someone who can offer me legal permission to enter the property on Lady's Island."

"Did you stop in the permit office? Right now, that property is off limits to the public."

"I know," he hesitated – agitated. "That's why I want to talk with someone who can help me. You see, I'm an anthropologist, and I'm doing research in this area."

"Alright," he stated flatly. "Have a seat, and I'll have someone come talk to you."

An older deputy came out into the reception area and said, "Hello young man. Tell me your business and why you need to go in a dangerous area."

Again, Ross gave his story and then watched the deputy shake his head no. "I'm sorry, young man," the deputy said with a slow southern voice. "That area has been deemed extremely dangerous. You can't have permission to access it, but you're free to do your research from the road. Just stay behind the taped-off area."

Jack Nolin, PhD, arrived at the site at noon. People were everywhere with cars and trucks lined up on both sides of the road. He drove his Chevy Trailblazer slowly, heading to the back section of the land where the old graveyard lay. No one except him ventured this far since all the action from the reporters at the site's front was drawing the crowd's attention.

Jack found a spot, isolated from the crowd, near the graveyard. He stopped his SUV along the roadside and could see the large hole in front of the graves. He got out and opened the back end of his vehicle and dropped the tailgate to lie flat. He placed an anvil case on it anxiously and propped it open. "Ah-ha!" he muttered excitedly, looking at his photo and recording equipment. "Oh-Yeah!"

A young deputy walked up, followed by a seismologist, curious and somewhat disturbed that this man was in the restricted area with cameras and recorders. He had no VIP badge. The deputy liked having a problem with that. Who does this old, crazy, jerk think he is? "Sir," the deputy spoke, "did you see the sign that said 'No access past this point'?"

"No, sir, I didn't," Jack replied. "I didn't see you walk up. I was checking my equipment."

The deputy peered down at the contents in the anvil case and asked, "What all you got there?"

The seismologist looked down at the case and commented, "Looks like some sophisticated equipment."

Jack looked at the scientist who was wearing a khaki shirt and blue jeans, then looked over at the young deputy and introduced himself. "Dr. Jack Nolin."

"Dr. Robert Stevens." The scientist shook his hand. "I'm a little curious as to what your function is?"

"Yeah, Dr. Nolin, why are you here?" the deputy asked matter of fact.

"I'm a parapsychologist," he answered matter of fact and with confidence.

"A what?" the young deputy sputtered. He never heard that credential before.

"I plan to investigate this phenomenon that cannot be explained by the natural laws of science. I hope to show evidence that there is a supernatural – And has so far not proven factual…And then the whole world will know!"

"Dr. Nolin, can you expound on what you just said?" the scientist asked, his eyes showing seriously doubt – but were actually hiding his growing fascination.

"Dr. Stevens, that hole over there is not the result of an earthquake," Dr. Nolin said.

"Oh really," Dr. Stevens said nodding his head up and down.

"Yes, oh really, but you must think it is or you wouldn't be here."

"To be truthful, Dr. Nolin, we don't have a significant magnitude reading, but South Carolina does experience what is known as 'intra plate earthquakes.' So far, our studies have not come to a factual conclusion – that there was an earthquake here. We're still monitoring."

"Excuse me for butting in," the deputy spoke up. "I want to know why you, Dr. Nolin, drove past the No Admittance signs. You couldn't have missed them. And what are all these fancy gizmos in your case?"

"Some do look fascinating," Dr. Stevens became intrigued, looking closer in the case.

"Dr. Stevens, I am trying to be serious," the deputy said frustrated.

"Gentlemen," Jack beamed, holding up a camera. "This is a DSLR digital single lens reflex that has the capability to distinguish orbs and natural mists from anomalies or spirits."

"What!" the scientist's eyes opened as wide as they could. "Come on now."

Nolin held up a smaller piece of equipment. "This is a DCEMF that can detect fluctuations in magnetic fields. This instrument ignores man-made electronic fields and only picks up the naturally occurring ones to be exact." "Now this," he continued on picking up a thermometer, "is a Centeck infrared laser that detects 'cold spots'."

"What!" the deputy laughed. "What in hell are you talkin' 'bout!?"

"Wait, deputy," the scientist interrupted. "From what I've seen – he's right. Well, I mean about magnetic fields etc. But I don't know how accurate or believable his equipment will be…"

"Listen to me – Usually in areas of spirit activity, the temperature drops." Nolin stopped to look at both men's reactions.

"Go on, Doctor," the scientist coaxed. "I like this."

"I have this Sony recorder. I can take the disk back to my lab and equalize the recorded sounds through a mixing board aided by compressors, effect boxes, noise gates, filters and other electronic devices. The sounds can be heard and graphed."

Both men, especially the deputy, put their hands over their mouths to keep from laughing out loud. Whispering in the scientist's ear, he said, "We got us a real nut case."

"You both think I'm crazy! Alright,! But let me tell you both one thing. I'm not! I have a PhD in philosophy and also teach metaphysical science. I conduct seminars all over. I have six published books under my belt…I know what I'm talking about!"

"So, Dr. Nolin," Dr. Stevens asked, "I think the deputy wants to know how you are going to conduct this paranormal investigation. Personally, so do I. I don't think you're crazy. In a peculiar way, I find you to be a very smart and fascinating man."

"How long have you been here, Dr. Stevens?"

"Since yesterday afternoon."

"Have you seen or experienced anything strange?"

"Like what?"

"Like seeing strange colors and weird sounds coming out of that large hole?"

"No," he laughed.

"How about you, Deputy?"

"Hell no!" he said, not having a clue as to what the psycho was asking.

"Well, I have, and I know of another person who has also."

"It's funny that I haven't," Stevens remarked. "Or any others – except you."

"The supernatural doesn't reveal itself to everyone." Dr. Jack cocked his head, wearing a sly grin. "So, to answer your serious questions, I'm going to film and record a supernatural phenomenon that will prove that this disastrous land eruption and destruction did not result from natural causes. That graveyard over there is causing it! Somehow the spirits of the dead are disturbed and angry."

"You really believe that!" Stevens blasted out, becoming even more interested.

"Sure I do. And I'll prove it!"

"And you are going to photograph and record them?"

"You damn right I am!"

The young deputy was getting bored and restless and then sported, "I've heard enough of this crazy shit! How long do you plan to stay here if I allow it?"

"I don't know."

"I do. You have two hours, and then I want to see you safely leaving here."

"I was hoping until twilight."

"Damn it, man! I could just order you to leave right now, but I'll let you stay awhile."

"Well, that's real kind of you, no offense intended."

"Likewise."

Jack sat on the back of his tailgate with his equipment ready and noticed no one close to the hole or the graveyard. No geologists, no seismologists, and no county deputies. "That's strange," he mumbled. "I guess they're over at the news vans and cameras, wanting to be in the spotlight," he said, talking to himself. "They just don't understand."

He looked at his watch, noticing an hour had gone by, and without any warning, he heard something. Crying sounds were coming from the 'hole.' He grabbed his camera in his right hand and recorder in his left, knowing he was just on the verge of witnessing and 'proving' a supernatural breakthrough. With good eyesight, he focused on the hole and began seeing these red bubbles emitting upward and out of the mysterious mouth of the crater. The sky began to turn dark. The bubbles turned a crimson red with flickering yellow lights inside them. And it wasn't the result of the sun's reflection. There was no sun! What happened to the sun? He quickly looked over toward the crowd. Everyone appeared unaware or could care less about the dark sky. And no sun!

Jack began taking pictures and turned his recorder on. "I have to get closer," he softly whispered to himself.

Stepping over the yellow tape, he moved cautiously in the direction of the hole, feeling a faint rumble under his feet. More bubbles were now floating out, and his excitement was rapidly building. He kept creeping toward the hole. The closer he got, the larger it got. He was now only four to six yards from the brink of much more than a hole. A frightening feeling began replacing his curiosity as he looked at a pit of reddish water bubbling inside the pit, The ground began rumbling and shifting as he could only stare in fear at the black smoke rising from the red inferno. With a shaking hand, he snapped a few shots until the land under his feet cracked open and he fell, becoming trapped in a

SLIT – a SLIT in the broken ground – shocked by sounds coming from – in a PIT – a PIT in the broken ground. A loud BLAST – happened FAST, shooting up cinders and fire – And dropping hot embers and hot ash on his body and face. HE SCREAMED! No one heard him. More flaming, red cinders shot out in all directions from a second blast only to burn him to a BLACKENED CRISP!

The skeletons came out – the spirits of the dead quickly grabbed his barbecued body and slung it into the open pit.

And the merciless SKELETONS from the dead knew that reporters were interviewing the curious people standing along the roadside behind the yellow tape. Of course, the fools heard the loud blasts thinking it was loud thunder coming out of the dark sky over the hole. Most of the people walking around acted as if they were at a flea market or the county fair. They just wouldn't care or become aware of the impending danger looming nearby…The general public! The SKELETONS laughed and laughed and laughed…

"And you, sir," the young, pretty anchorwoman, Rhonda Shields, spoke, holding her microphone. "Are you a resident of Lady's Island?" she asked a man from the general public.

"Shore am!" he blurted in the mic. "Ya'll from New York…ain't cha?"

"What are your thoughts on this terrible disaster?" she asked the man, a little reluctantly.

"Am I really bein' seen on TV," smiling wide with just a few teeth to show. Rhonda moved to another person. "And you, ma'am, what is your name?"

"Sylvie Nolin."

"Ms. Nolin, are you from Lady's Island?"

"My husband and I live in Beaufort."

"And what do you think is happening here?"

"I'm afraid to guess." She trailed off, glancing around, hoping to spot her husband. "Some people might think this place is haunted!"

"And that was Sylvia Nolin, from Beaufort, South Carolina," Rhonda said quickly, then rushed to another spectator in the crowd.

"I overheard you say you were Mrs. Nolin," the young deputy said, walking up to her.

"I am," she replied, surprised. "Why?"

"Let me ask…are you Dr. Jack Nolin's wife?"

"Yes, in fact I'm looking for him. Do you know my husband?"

"I met him, and I know where he is. He's at the back end, taking photos."

"Oh my – I should have known."

"Yeah, he's not supposed to be that far down, but he went anyway. I'll take you to him," he said with a friendly smile. "Yeah, he's got a bunch of video and recording gadgets. Said he was a meta – Uh, what is it? He was here yesterday."

"Meta physician," she said as she got in his car. "Yeah, he was here yesterday."

They drove slowly to the back end of the site, and the deputy broached the subject. "Do meta physicians look for ghosts?"

"They explore the intangible with a belief that the entire universe is energy and so are we. Actually, everything is energy, and everything in this universe of ours is interrelated. Energy can't be created or destroyed, so I guess ghosts and spirits exist."

"Hey, you're going over my head."

"I know. Mine too, but being married to Jack, I can't help but pick up on his philosophies, whether I believe them or not. I don't know about ghosts – but I believe he does. He can be eccentric and self-absorbed. And stubborn! I'm not surprised he came down here without permission. I saw the 'No Admittance' sign. You should have put the crazy fool in jail!" she shook her head, disgusted. "Why didn't you at least make him leave?"

"After talking with him, I felt it would be harmless to let him do a little investigating. But, of course, I told him not to trespass beyond the tape."

"There's his SUV." She pointed.

"I believe it is."

The young deputy and Mrs. Nolin stepped out of the patrol car and noticed his vehicle was vacant. The anvil case was lying on top of the tailgate with only the camera and recorder missing.

"Wonder where he is," she said, looking around.

"Dr. Nolin!" he shouted.

"Jack!" she hollered. "Where are you?"

There was no answer.

***

It was almost noon when Rob Pinckney walked inside the 'Iron Mike.' Since this was the new hot spot in town, he figured the Riley twins might have stopped here. He hoped they were calling their parents or already home. But they could have stayed there awhile. Or they could have met some decent kids and went somewhere else.

"Hello, Mike," he spoke to the owner standing behind the bar.

"Hey," he said surprised, not knowing this man. "Can I get you something?"

He flashed his badge and seriously looked him in the eyes.

"What is it, Detective?" he asked curiously.

He looked around the room, smelling the stale stench of beer and liquor. "Big night, huh?" Pinckney inquired.

"Packed! Spring break. Anything wrong, sir?"

"Did you work the bar last night?"

"Yeah. Me and Bubba did."

"Uh-huh."

"Anything wrong?"

"I'm looking for the whereabouts of these girls," he stated adamantly, laying photos on top of the bar. "Were they here last night?"

"Yeah." Mike nodded his head affirmatively. "Attractive girls."

"By themselves?"

"They were, but a couple of guys hit on them, and they left together."

"What time did they leave?"

"Detective, it was crowded."

"What time?"

Feeling nervous, Mike replied, "Around ten."

"So they left with two men?"

"Yeah, why?" Mike shrugged. "Something wrong?"

"Mike." Pinckney leaned across the bar and said, "These girls are reported missing, and their folks are highly upset. Tell me what you saw."

"They drank a few beers, and two guys came over and bought them a few more – and then they left. That's all I saw. How 'bout you, Bubba. Did you see or hear anything?"

Bubba nodded, "No."

"Where were they going?" Pinckney asked.

"Have no idea."

"Mike!" Pinckney barked. "I'm goin' to give you my card, and if you see those boys or those girls anywhere, you call me ASAP."

"Alright."

"And you better not tip these boys off. I'll know, and you'll be in trouble!"

"If I see 'em, I'll notify you. We don't want trouble."

Pinckney glanced around the room a final time. "Were they drunk?"

"I don't think so."

"Damn it, Mike! Did they all walk out sober, or were the girls stumbling out with the help of their damn escorts?"

"They walked out normal."

"I'm going to have to ask you one more time. You swear you never saw those men before?"

"Never seen 'em before."

"Or these girls?"

"No, sir. Never seen them before either."

"Alright, but I'm going to find out what happened." He turned to leave. "Help me by doing what you can. Find out who they are. Make that effort?"

"I'll do what I can."

"Alright."

***

Sunday afternoon, the door of the shack opened. It was THE MASKED MAN!

"Hello, 'Masked Man,'" Jennie said it rudely. "Did you bring us some more food and clean crappers!?"

He walked slowly toward them and laid down a basket of fried chicken and a pitcher of water.

"Masked Man, why don't you speak?" Jennie asked.

He stood staring at her and said nothing. He walked out briefly, then brought in clean chamber pots.

"Masked Man!" Jennie shouted. "Why don't you just let us go?"

He stared at her and then her sister. He stared through the slits in his mask – then just walked out. He said nothing.

The winds began to howl and rattle the sides of the shack. "I'm scared, Jennie," Lisa whimpered, pulling her blanket over her chin.

"I'm not scared," she lied. "I'm mad!"

"Are we gonna be all right?"

"Sure," she replied with questionable reassurance. "We'll be alright."

"I am so scared."

"Well, Lisa, at least he's feeding us," Jennie said, chomping on a chicken breast.

"I'm afraid to eat mine."

"It's good. Eat!"

"Alright."

"You know what I've been thinking?"

"No." Lisa looked over at her sister.

"I wonder what happened to those two assholes who brought us here."

"Why did they do it?" Lisa asked.

"They had to have been paid money to kidnap us, but how did they know where to find us? If they were just on a hunt – How's that masked man involved?"

"I guess the masked man paid them." Lisa guessed.

Jennie looked at her sister. "You think, Sherlock!"

"Yeah," she laughed foolishly, "yeah I think."

"Well, something is going on, and we're not here by accident."

"But what?"

"I know Daddy's in trouble. I could see it in his eyes," Jennie said as she threw her chicken bone across the floor. "I know!"

Chapter 7

STEVE WOKE from a restless sleep. It was 6:00 AM Monday morning as he got out of bed without waking Kelly. He made his coffee, pouring a splash of Irish whiskey in the cup, and walked out on the deck. Firing up a cigarette, he looked out at the ocean, feeling a slight hangover mixed with worry.

After three cups, laden with alcohol, he was almost able to shoulder the sudden avalanche of misery and worry that had dropped on him. It has to be a nightmare or punishment for something. But what? Only two days ago, he had it all. A beautiful loving wife, two sweet beautiful daughters, a successful career, and most of all – peace of mind. And now it was just crumbling away.

Kelly walked up behind him, placing her hands on his shoulders. "How long have you been up?"

"Hours," he answered absently. "I thought I'd take some time for self-pity."

"What are we gonna do?"

"I don't know."

"A little early to be drinking," she scolded, smelling the odor of whiskey escape his mouth.

"Just coffee with a splash of whiskey," he said, defensively. "But, you're right."

"Fix me one?" He looked at her, surprised. "You don't like whiskey with coffee."

"How would you know. I've never had it. Maybe I don't but maybe I do."

The phone rang, and it was Detective Pinckney. Steve was quick to answer. "Hello."

"Mr. Riley, this is Rob Pinckney. Is it possible I can come over and discuss a few things with you and your wife?"

"I'm glad you called. Our daughters never did come home."

"Is this a good time?"

"Of course. Hope you have good news?"

"I'll be over within an hour."

"What have you found out?" Steve asked, anticipating a positive response.

"We'll talk when I get there."

Pinckney arrived, and they all sat in the living room.

"I have some news," he spoke, tapping his knees. "I know where your daughters were last night., at least until ten o'clock that night."

"Where?" Steve jumped from the sofa and began pacing.

"I'm going to share some solid information along with some speculation. I just want you to stay calm."

"What? Tell us, Detective," Kelly spoke up.

"Your daughters were in a bar called the Iron Mike and left around ten o'clock that night with two young men."

"No way!" Steve gasped as Kelly started crying. "They wouldn't do that while visiting us."

"Especially that late," she agreed with him.

"Please stay calm. As difficult as it may be, it's important that you understand what I have to say."

"Alright," Steve groaned, and resumed his seat next to his wife.

"I have a statement from the owner of the bar that witnessed it. The good news is that they were not intoxicated or subject to any acts of coercion or foul play. In other words, they all left of their own free will."

"Where are they now?" Steve jumped from his seat.

"Mr. Riley, I know you're anxious and upset, I would be too, but I don't know where they are. Now, let me tell you what I think: That land deal you had with Mr. Sherburtt made me curious, Mr. Sherburtt might be responsible for your daughters' absence. That's what you both think. Right?"

"Yes!" Kelly loudly broadcasted.

"Now, listen to me. No one knows what caused that land to erupt. Folks, it's serious. It's drawing national attention!" Pinckney's eyes narrowed as he looked at Steve. "What happened over there?"

"Huh? I don't know. I wasn't there!"

"Uh-huh."

"Hey! What are you tryin' to say?"

Kelly looked over and said, "Steve, he's an investigator doing his job. Don't get riled. Let him talk."

"Listen," Pinckney continued. "I've contacted Greenville County, and we're checking out Sherburtt. I'm also going to find out where these men are who left with your daughters. They were driving a red Lexus."

"Why were you asking me about that land?"

"Alright, Mr. Riley – I believe you might know something that you're not telling me. Don't get me wrong – I'm just trying to use deductive reasoning, I don't think he would or could blame you for what happened – unless you're not telling me something."

"I don't know what happened! I don't know why he's blaming me! I don't know why he lost his mind."

"Take it easy."

"Alright," Steve stood up, patted his shirt pocket. "No cigarettes! I guess he has to hold someone responsible besides his damn self."

"Within one day of this land problem, he didn't know your daughters were coming?"

"No," he said finding his Marlboro pack in the kitchen. Nervously, he lit one.

"Well, from your statements about his recent behavior, I've decided to consider him a suspect. But I do have some reservations."

"Like what?" Steve exhaled, puffing cigarette smoke out like a locomotive.

"If he didn't know they were coming, how could he arrange for two unknown men to meet them at that bar and be able to leave with them?"

"He's smart."

"Well, he's not Merlin the Magician! I really need more to go on to be able to solve this puzzle." He stopped and looked at Kelly. "Anyway Mrs. Riley, I don't think your daughters are hurt."

"What makes you think that? Oh God – I hope you're right. Tell me you're right. Please."

"A club owner like Mike can read people. They watch the crowd because they absolutely don't want trouble. After hearing about your girls and their past reputations, I don't believe they would leave with unsavory men without resisting in some way. Now if Johnny Sherburtt orchestrated this, he went to a whole lot of trouble. But he doesn't strike me as a man who would harm two innocent girls."

"What's he doing? Why?" Steve asked.

"I don't know if he's done anything. I don't believe he's harmed them, that is, if he has them. Let's say he hired those young men, I'm sure he instructed them not to hurt your girls. Now here's the question – Do you think he wants money – or revenge?"

"I don't know!" Steve blared. "Maybe both."

"Since Sherburtt is out of a lot of money; he could be leading up to blackmailing you. I don't know. If that's his motive, why hasn't he already? I advise you not to have any more phone conversations with him. Sometime this afternoon, I'm gonna contact him. I assure you, he'll talk to me." He smiled at Kelly as he rose to leave. "I believe your daughters are safe."

"I certainly pray they are. But how would you know that?"

"I'm a detective following a pattern. He doesn't have a past criminal record or any trail leading to violent acts. I know because I've checked. But I'll know after talkin' with him if he's involved."

"I think he believes I'll get his money soon. If I don't – then he'll blackmail."

"That's possible but not probable. He's lost money but he doesn't want to ruin his life over prison. I'm trying real hard – to get a grip – on why he turned on you. You're not responsible for this land disaster – that is – you haven't told me everything."

"I've told you everything," he replied as calmly as he could. "I haven't held anything back. Johnny went crazy! I don't know why! I wish I knew why!"

"Alright Mr. and Mrs. Riley, I'll be leaving now. Oh, did I tell you that the sheriff is coming over in a few hours to talk further?"

"No. The sheriff!" Kelly said, surprised.

"Uh huh, and he's probably going to ask you pretty much the same questions. Have you met him?" Pinckney asked.

"No, we haven't," Steve replied.

"In fact, he might have some good news. He's a good man. Also smart."

"Thank you, Detective." Kelly smiled appreciatively.

Pinckney entered Price's office as the sheriff looked up.

"How did your meeting go with the Rileys?"

"They're upset."

"Of course."

"You ever find that missing red Lexus?"

"Not yet, but it'll show up."

"Bill, I believe it's possible Sherburtt has those girls."

"Like how?" Price asked, curious.

"Well, Mr. Riley had a bad pissing contest with him. They're both mad, and Sherburtt was threatening him for his money back," Pinckney said. "Riley don't have that kind of money, and that land deal was all legal. All the way to its present state! If he has the Riley girls, he's gone insane! The Rileys believe he has. What do you think?"

"Don't know. Doesn't add up. The first thing I have to do is get Mr. Sherburtt to admit something. If he can explain how he got torn up out of the frame and why he's blaming Mr. Riley, I'll know. So far, there are no records on him. Legitimate businessman with no criminal record."

"What if he snapped?" Pinckney asked.

"Three variables," Price said, scratching his head. "Money – insanity – revenge!"

"This is one of those cases where one and one make three."

"You got that right."

"I told 'em you were coming over early."

"I am. I got some questions Mr. Riley needs to clear up. I believe he and this Mr. Sherburtt might have something to do with the land suddenly exploding. I think maybe the missing girls might be tied up in this."

"Bill, I'm going to drive over to the site and see if anyone saw them. Plus, I want to check it out."

"You won't like what you see."

"Probably won't."

"Be careful over there. It's awfully dangerous around that hole. Don't get close to it!"

"You think they might be responsible for destroying the property?"

"Don't know. Like I said – none of this makes sense. Not yet anyway."

"I hope we get to the bottom of it before the FBI comes in," Pinckney said with a little animosity.

"You don't like those FBI boys, do you, Pinckney?" Price smiled.

"Not really." On his way to his office, Pinckney noticed the new female deputy sitting at her desk. She was a head-turner! Long blonde hair! Long legs! Definitely his type. He had his eyes on her for days and he finally mustered the courage to ask her out. He walked up to her desk. "Susan," he said, "you want to take a break and go across the street for a coffee?"

"Sure, that sounds great." She beamed.

"Great! Let's go."

Sitting in the small café, Detective Rob Pinckney and Deputy Susan talked casually until he ventured, "Susan, can I ask you something?"

"Sure."

"Are you dating anyone?"

"No Rob, I'm not," she quickly answered.

"Would you go out with me to dinner tonight?" His heart began to thump.

"I'd love to."

"Great. Where do you live? I'll pick you up."

She pointed. "Three streets up and turn right. It's the second on the left."

"Seven o'clock okay?"

"I'm looking forward to it. Now I better get back to my desk."

Pinckney drove out to the site and parked his car next to the yellow tape. He walked past the reporters and officials, flashing his badge. Susan was on his mind. He felt strong, confident and happy.

"I'm Detective Pinckney. This is an official sheriff investigation," he announced.

"Sir." A young man approached him. "Can I ask where you're going?"

"I'm investigating this property…"

"You're heading toward a disaster area that's very dangerous."

"I have to check it out."

"I warned you. Earlier, a man ventured from his vehicle, which is still parked over on the side of the road to take pictures, and never came back."

"Has it been reported?"

"I don't know."

"Huh." He frowned.

"He went over to the volcano hole and never returned."

"Do me a favor, will you?"

"What?"

"Go find an officer and tell him what you know."

"Yes, sir."

"And what is your job here?"

"I'm a seismologist."

"Uh-huh. And let me ask you what you know about this so-called volcano."

"Hopefully, we're going to draw a conclusion this afternoon. I do know that the land around it is not stable, and people have lost their lives here."

"We haven't found any bodies. So far, there's no evidence of deaths."

The young scientist looked at him and said, "Be careful!"

Pinckney started walking carefully, knowing that it was now declared a national disaster area, but he was going to investigate it.

Finally, he arrived close to the edge of the ghastly pit. Unbelievable! It was oozing out a reddish goop – a nasty stench filled the air! "What in the hell is happening here!" Reaching for his handkerchief.

The ground shook without warning, and he fell quickly to his knees. The land began giving way as a LOUD, violent BLAST burst from the THREATENING abyss! He picked himself up but lost his footing. A second BLAST shot up from the pit, raining wet muck mixed and rotten debris on him.

"SHIT!" Pinckney yelled, staring at the pit's opening. "WHAT THE FUCK," he shouted madly – Startled! With four years of combat training and active in *Desert Storm,* he was prepared for the unexpected. He wasn't going to be taken down by a few blasts of mud! He was wrong! – The skeletons came out – grabbing his feet, ankles, and legs. He kicked hard! But it was useless to fight these HIDEOUS monsters! They pulled him into their quagmire of HELL! Attempting a strong foot hold – at the edge of the brink – BUT HE felt his strength wane…The skeletons began mocking him. One mean and nasty one glared him in the face and chortled – jabbing a finger in his eye. "Fuck you too! Come on!" Pinckney yelled. And THEY CAME ON – forcing him closer to the bubbling pit. At the brink of falling into the fiery abyss – charged with adrenaline – he pushed his way through two attacking creatures – And scampered into the woods behind the grave stones. In a drenching panic – he became face to face with five glowing skeletons! Experienced in martial arts, his talents were futile against the hideous creatures of the dead. The mad, vicious skeletons dragged him out of the patch of woods. He FOUGHT – CURSED – STRUGGLED – while his foes GROWLED – HISSED – LAUGHED – dragging him along the ground's splitting surface – to a large, wide, crack – near the edge of the abyss – and slung him violently into the deep slit! ROB PINCKNEY disappeared into an unknown world – a spirit world – a world he wanted no part of – DOOMED under the GULLAH GRAVESTONES!

Sheriff Price received a report about a missing man named Jack Nolin, a Doctor of Philosophy, claiming himself a practicing metaphysician who vanished on the site. He shook his head in frustration and muttered, "A meta physician, that's all we need!"

He walked out of office toward Betty's station and said, "Betty…"

"Yes, Bill?"

"Call the Rileys, and tell them I'll be over there around twelve thirty or so."

"Alright."

Steve picked up his car keys off the coffee table. "Kelly, I'll be back in a little while."

"Where are you going?" she asked.

"Beaufort."

"The sheriff's coming. You can't leave here."

"I'll be back before then. Now, you stay here until I get back. Don't answer the phone if it's Johnny."

"I won't."

Steve raced out of Palm Island and drove straight to the Iron Mike, walked in, and sat down at the bar.

"Need a menu?"

"Where's Mike?"

"I'm Mike."

He laid down his daughters' photos on top of the bar. "You saw these girls Saturday night!"

"They were here, why?"

"These are my girls, and I aim to find them."

"Excuse me?"

"I know they were in here."

"Sir, a detective was here, and I told him everything. They were here but I don't know where they went," Mike said, becoming leery.

"I heard they left here with some horny ass boys!" Steve broadcasted with fire building in his blue eyes.

"Sir, I don't know what you want from me, but I can't have you yelling across the bar. People are coming in for lunch," Mike answered with authority.

"Give me a scotch."

"Alright," he said reluctantly. "This is my place and I can't let you get out of hand. You understand? I can tell you're mad."

"Yeah, I understand. Did you know those boys?"

"No."

Steve rose from his seat. "I want you to tell me where I can find them?"

"I don't know! Your girls met two guys, had a few drinks, and left. That's it. Now, I don't want any trouble from you!"

Steve leaned over the bar and stared at Mike. "Tell me who those boys are and where I can find them!"

A tall, bearded burly man walked up and said, "Mike, you see a problem here?"

"I'm looking for my damn girls!" Steve shouted.

"It looks like you're looking for trouble. You best leave now!" Mike warned.

"So you don't know those assholes or where they might be. I need to know."

"I done told you. I don't know! Now, do you want me to call the police and have you dragged out? Or you can leave on your own?"

Steve stood up, puffed out his chest, and said, "I'm goin' to find those boys!"

"Well," Mike spoke, "We don't know those boys. If we did, we'd tell you – and the detective. They were complete strangers here. Understand?"

"Yeah." Steve slammed his glass down and walked out, pissed.

***

Ross went down the corridor to the drink machine and popped out two Pepsis. *Damn I feel rough,* he thought. *Um, better get some cheese crackers too.*

Back in his room, he began listening to his recording and taking notes. He liked to drink but not that much. Yesterday was incredible, and today is a hangover, so far. He thought about running down to the lobby hoping he could sneak a bloody Mary out of the bar, but he didn't. He kept looking over all the notes that he received from Suzie Smith. He wasn't happy with her help. She didn't offer him testimonials on real Voodoo events like she had promised on their Internet communications. And she wasn't all that friendly. She just wanted fifty dollars. He looked at his garlic heads still on the dresser. "I must be crazy," he laughed. "Preston probably thinks so too!"

He slapped his face and remembered that garlic was for vampires. He needed a live rooster! "What!" he exclaimed. "I'm going back to bed!"

As Ross closed his eyes, the visions of the pit floated right into his mind. "Shit!" He jumped from the bed and started making notes of all the uncanny bubbles and screeches he saw and heard – at the Gullah gravestones.

***

The masked man barged through the door of the shack, holding a basket of ham sandwiches. He stood frozen and looked at the girls intermittently.

"Hey. How you doin'?" Jennie grinned. "Are we havin' a picnic?"

He said nothing.

"Can we go now?" Lisa whimpered.

"No, Lisa. The Masked Man is giving us a picnic lunch. Won't this be fun!"

He laid the basket down with a bottled Pepsi and turned to leave.

"What is it, Masked Man? You too good to eat with us?"

He ignored the remark.

"Hey, can you bring us a TV too?"

He didn't ignore that one! He walked over to Jennie and stood at her feet staring directly into her eyes. Reaching down to her ankles, his hand grabbed them and pulled her as far as her chain would allow. He let go of her ankles and kept his stare directly into her condescending eyes and face. He loosened his belt and began to unbutton his black shirt.

Jennie lay staring back at him, not uttering a word.

Lisa was watching while crying and the crying got louder until it turned into screams of terror.

The Masked Man looked over at her and put his forefinger to his lip while nodding no. *Shhhh!*

Jennie spoke. She was scared to death but wittingly brave. "Masked Man, did I hurt your feelings?"

He glared back at Jennie, fastened his belt back, made sure his black shirt was still tucked in his pants, said nothing – Nothing! Walked out.

"Jennie, you just about got us raped. Why are you teasing him. I was so scared and still am."

"He ain't goin' to do anything. I know he's got some kind of plan. He doesn't want to hurt us. What it is, I'm not sure. I believe Daddy knows we're here. He's goin' to save us."

"What are you talking about, He was about to rape us. Maybe even kill us because you keep pissing him off."

"Well, he didn't, did he! Look, I'm not afraid of him. He's a dumb stooge and keeps us fed good. Anyway, if he had gone any further, I'd kicked him through that wall."

"Yeah, I bet."

"You can't let bullies know you're afraid of 'em," Jennie lied. She'd been afraid of him since the start.

"I am scared of him, and you can't kick him through a wall."

"Yeah, I can."

"Whatever!"

***

Steve walked into the condo to find Kelly on the couch, staring blankly at a wall. He felt redneck and stupid.

"Well, where did you go?" she asked, sounding exasperated.

"I did something dumb."

"What?"

"I went to that bar and got the bartender mad!"

"No!" she shouted.

"I did. I feel stupid."

"What did you do?"

"I demanded him to tell me where those boys are. Yeah – in a redneck sort of way."

"Steve, you shouldn't have done that!"

"I know it! But I did."

"What happened?"

"Nothing. Hey," he said, throwing his hands up, "I figured he knew something! And was covering up something."

"Let the sheriff handle this. You're goin' to get in trouble. As a matter of fact, it's a good thing you came home when you did. He's on his way."

"Look, I did what any father would do in a situation like this."

"Now, don't get all huffed up at the sheriff if he says something you don't like. I know when you get anxious, your temper comes out!"

"I'll be alright."

"Just calm down and relax. Can you do that for me?"

"Yeah."

"Steve, I'm real upset and mad, but I'm doing everything I can to hold it in. We got to keep our wits. It's just not going to do any of us any good to fly off the handle."

"Yeah, but I didn't get mean in that place! I was just assertive."

"Assertive! Sounds like you showed your ass!"

"Well, I know one thing."

"What is that?"

"The lid is fixing to blow!"

Chapter 8

STEVE AND KELLY rushed to answer the front door after hearing the knock.

"SHERIFF PRICE?" they both anxiously greeted. "Good afternoon. I'm Sheriff Price and this is Chief Deputy Wilson. You must be Mr. and Mrs. Riley? May we come in?"

"Of course," Kelly said. "I see you have some folders. Please tell me you've found our girls."

"I'm sorry, Mrs. Riley. We haven't yet, but we're doing everything we can," he replied sincerely.

"Detective Pinckney was here earlier," Kelly said.

"I know."

"Sheriff, would you like to sit at the dining table?" Steve suggested.

"Thanks," he replied as he reached inside a folder and pulled out a copy of the *Beaufort Gazette*. "Have you seen this?"

"Yeah," Steve grumbled. "I saw it."

"Before we talk about your daughters, I have some questions I want to ask you about this land tragedy. Why don't you tell me what you know."

"I told Detective Pinckney that I know nothing about what happened over there," Steve stated. "Do you think that has something to do with our daughters?"

"I don't know. That's why I'm here. It might."

"How?"

"Okay, Mr. Riley, tell me everything about this land and your connection with Mr. Sherburtt."

"Like what?"

"Start at the beginning." Price rocked back in his chair while folding his hands. "The more I know about your land deal—"

"Whoa," Steve interrupted. "I really don't want to talk about that land! I was just the broker. And that's all."

"I understand, but go ahead and tell me what happened from the time you found it, sold it, and now," Price said calmly.

"Well, alright if you think it'll help."

"It'll help give me a clearer picture of what we're dealing with and possibly why your daughters are missing."

"Alright. Johnny wanted to purchase land for a condominium development at a good price. Checking block-map records in this area, I found that tract and notified the owner. She said she would sell it, and he closed on it in February. My wife and I decided to move here, and we bought this condo."

"Keep going, but please let me compliment you and Mrs. Kelly on your new home. It's extremely nice." Price interjected to keep the conversation at ease.

"Thanks. As far as this land problem, I really don't know anything about it."

"Well, this tract of land turned into a disaster. A large crater formed, and people lost their lives." Price hesitated. "This crater is now being investigated by scientists from all over, and nobody has a clue as to what caused it."

"I know, and the property is ruined. That's why Johnny is mad."

"I'm just surprised he got so mad at you but not surprised that he got upset over a deal gone bad. As I understand, you were only the broker. Now please don't take this wrong; why is he so mad at you?"

"I have no clue. Johnny liked the property. As I said, he wanted to get into coastal properties. I'm a broker, and I worked hard to find him this tract that showed enormous possibilities for a resort development that should yield high profits! Charleston and Myrtle Beach are too expensive now. This area is growing faster than the market values. I worked with him many years, and he certainly wouldn't have bought it if he hadn't thought it was an excellent investment."

"You had a long-term working relationship, and obviously you trusted him?"

"I trusted him. I've worked with him for years. We've never had any real problems." He lit a cigarette and confidently looked at Price. "He just snapped, and he's not the man I knew! I think he's gone mad! It happened as soon as he saw it. He's been calling me, harassing me and even threatening me!"

"He's threatening you? What is the threat?"

"He didn't say."

"Did he mean, no more business deals, a law suit or possibly violence?"

"He wants his money back!"

"Well, we all understand that. What I want to know is what he plans to do to you if he doesn't get his money back?"

"I don't know."

Price sighed and looked at Kelly. "What do you think, Mrs. Riley?"

"I'm shocked! I never cared too much for him."

"Why?"

"He's a very conceited and selfish man. My husband worked his butt off for him and now he's turned on Steve!" she said. "He's blaming him for something that's not his fault! He's a spoiled kid!"

"Folks," Price spoke, leaning forward and looking at them both. "Like I've already said, I can see why he's mad, seeing his expensive land ruined, but why would he be mad at you, Mr. Riley? You only brokered the deal."

"I don't know, Sheriff. He demanded that I get all of his money back – or else! He threatened me!"

"Or else what? That is what I'm trying to get you to tell me."

"He didn't say. That's why I think he's got our girls."

"After you closed on the deal back in February, did you have anything else to do with it?"

"No."

"So, he has been handling all the necessary preparations such as permits and, of course, the grading?"

"Right."

"You bought this home just after closing on the deal?"

"Yeah." Steve stopped. "Wait a minute. You don't think—"

"I'm trying to get to the bottom of this and why Sherburtt turned on you. You say he threatened you?"

"Yes!"

"What do you think he meant by 'or else'?"

"I don't know."

"Or else what!? What was he going to do if you didn't get his money back?"

"Good question. I don't know."

"Mr. Riley, a kidnapping involves an exchange of ransom money for the return of a person or persons. You haven't gotten word from him or anyone what the deal is! It's strange you haven't been told: 'your girls are being held captive and you this, or else'! Why is he being mysterious? Is he playin' a game – toying with you – ?"

Steve looked at him, at a loss for words. "I think he's sitting back waiting for me to get his money – and just holding them out of meanness!"

"Maybe." Price rubbed his head and changed the subject a little. "Alright, I'm going to ask you a question, and please answer honestly. Could Sherburtt have planted explosives, or maybe had someone do it for him?"

"What?! Are you serious?"

"I'm dead serious. Not long after the explosion, I went there and witnessed a large smoking hole."

"Who would do that?"

"That's what I'm trying to find out," Price said, and then cracked a smile and a chuckle.

"What's funny?" Kelly asked.

"There are those implying that it's not man-made or something caused by the natural laws. But they're not credible opinions."

"What are you saying, Sheriff?" Steve asked curiously.

"That the land is haunted." Price looked at him and then at Kelly, waiting for their responses.

"Haunted!" they exclaimed in unison.

"Well, I know this sounds ridiculous, but there is an old graveyard there, and rumors are that spirits of the dead rose up to stop this development. You have to understand that people around here are superstitious. Many believe in Voodoo magic – especially the Gullah people – and that graveyard is an old Gullah burial site."

Steve looked at him, he turned white with fright! The graveyard...

"Whoa," Kelly said, looking at Price. "We have two missing daughters, and you're talking about a graveyard and black magic."

"Well, I just thought I'd bring that up. Of course, I don't believe in that nonsense, but I wanted to mention it because you'll be hearing these rumors a lot and probably soon."

"But what's that got to do with our daughters?" she asked.

"Alright. I'm trying to arrive at a reason why Mr. Sherburtt would take your daughters."

"Yeah! Me too!" Steve burst. Not saying anything about the graveyard.

"Alright, here's my question: Do you have two million dollars to give him?"

"No, of course not. He thinks I can get it from the seller."

"You didn't tell me that. Why?"

"The old black woman gave all that money away to charities."

"Did Mr. Sherburtt know that before your daughters went missing?"

"I don't know."

"Alright, folks. We have to have a motive and a reason to consider him a suspect. He wants you to think he's got them, but he's smart enough not to own up to it. That's what you think, Mr. Riley. I think those explosions on the property might have been his doing. Why? I don't know. Or maybe someone else had some problems with him and out of revenge blew his land up. Anyway, there's a reason why he's acting like he is and I bet he's desperate for money!"

"He's got money. I can assure you," Steve said.

"Those explosions were caused by someone. Not the supernatural! How and why nobody knows. But I believe he knows why his land blew up. I suspect he could have orchestrated a kidnap and used these men your daughters left with – but it's far-fetched."

Steve interrupted. "You're saying he's just trying to scare me and that he hired those boys to take them until I get him his money? Then I'll get them back safe and sound?"

"If he's responsible, he's figured a way so no one will know he is. Not even your daughters. I think he might believe that out of desperation, you'll find a way to get his money. And, you'll be getting instructions of some kind."

"What makes you think he wouldn't hurt them?" Kelly said.

"Mrs. Riley, people leave tracks. He has no past criminal record."

"This is bizarre." Steve's head began to spin. Lula, Johnny – the graveyard!

"That it is," Price agreed as he rose from his seat and motioned for his sergeant to do the same. "We're leaving now, and we're going to keep exploring all possibilities, but I am completely confused as to how this man could plan and do all this in a short time. It's just too unbelievable."

"Now you're saying you don't think he did it?" Steve was getting frustrated.

"I didn't say that. It makes sense that he did, but how he was able to – doesn't."

"I just want my girls back safe," Kelly spoke.

"I know you do, and we're going to do everything in our power to make that happen."

Price looked at his watch and said, "Sergeant, we need to be getting back."

"Sheriff," Kelly pleaded, "I'm scared. Please find them."

"I know, and I promise that if Mr. Sherburtt has anything to do with it, he'll soon realize that he made a real stupid mistake!"

As they walked out of the door, Price looked at Steve. "Mr. Riley, will you do us all a favor?"

"What, Sheriff?"

"Don't go back in the Iron Mike with an aggressive attitude. You came close to getting into trouble. In fact, I don't want you going back in there."

"News travels fast," Steve said, embarrassed.

"Yeah, it does."

"I'm sorry."

"You're a good man, and I understand why you went there, but it could have turned out real bad."

"Yeah, I just thought the bartender knew more, I wanted them to know that I can't be taken lightly."

"Don't go back there. Let us handle it. Okay?"

"Alright, Sheriff. I won't."

"Now this is being turned over to the FBI since kidnapping is a federal offense. But I'll do what I can."

Steve got up his nerve and volunteered. "Before you leave, I'd like to say that you hit a nerve when you mentioned voodoo. The old woman that owned it warned us not to disturb the graveyard. She didn't say what would happen if it was, but I got a strong feeling that she believes that the grader hit into the markers caused it."

"You didn't tell us this. Why?"

"I didn't think about until last night. I believe the old woman was giving a cautionary hint. I don't mean to sound like a fool. She was a little creepy – maybe that graveyard might hold the answers to all the land problems."

"Steve!" Kelly blurted. "Have you lost your mind – too!"

"We have to go on facts," Price said with a warm laugh.

"I know…just brainstorming," Steve said.

"Goodbye, Mr, and Mrs. Riley, we'll keep in touch."

Price and Wilson left and headed back to Beaufort.

"What do you think?" Wilson asked.

"I've got some ideas but really not sure. I know Mr. Riley and his wife are innocent victims."

"What do you really think about the land crisis?"

"Good question. Wish I knew. Pretty much what I said back there."

"Sure is ironic!"

Price called into the station. "Betty, can you get some officers out to the site. We need to keep people off it. Scientists, geologists, and certain other experts that are trained to investigate will need their VIP badges with their names and titles."

"Will do."

"That graveyard is scary!" Wilson blurted.

"Dangerous is what it is."

"Dangerous and scary. You know that survey does show a graveyard, and the site prep map shows where it is. Supposedly it wasn't disrupted. But that survey is old. It was done in 1920."

"What are you getting at, Wilson?"

"I'm just wondering something."

"Keep goin'."

"The graveyard could have gotten a lot bigger over the years. In other words, there could be more graves outside of what that survey shows."

"That's possible." Price rubbed his chin. "But so...?"

"I know that people died there, including several of our own. And it can't be explained. There could have been Gullah gravestones that weren't marked. The man on that bulldozer could have dug 'em up, and spooks, haunts came out and killed that man and dragged him and his machine down in that hole. And somehow, the others were dragged in too."

"WHAT! Come on," Price burst from his seams laughing, trying to shuck the possibility that Wilson might be right. that something ghostly caused that tragedy. "You really believe that?"

"Maybe I do."

"Well, keep that theory to yourself. Listen, we got to keep onlookers and reporters away from that area. Let's make sure they stay only on the public road."

"Good luck with that."

Price changed the subject to a lighter view. "You know all this publicity is going to be good for the city. More business and more tourists."

"You believe that?"

"Wilson, I have to believe that this is just an unusual occurrence. It will be explained by our so-called engineers, scientists, and geologists. It'll all be explained."

"Voodoo can't be explained."

"Wilson," Price said, "they're taking soil samples along with trace and control, so put that voodoo stuff out of your head."

"I believe it's haunted. I don't believe soil samples will prove anything. Don't ask me why."

Price was silent as he reflected back to the other day when he witnessed the crater. His skin still was crawling believing men might have vanished into that hole. But he knew that he had to be matter-of-fact with this situation, especially around his people, and of course the media. Price was deceiving himself.

Again Wilson said, "That place is haunted."

"You keep that bottled up!" Price said, sternly.

"Of course, I will. But what exactly do you believe?"

"Wilson, I'm just going to humbly say this to you."

"What's that?"

"Do you know what I'm really afraid of?"

"I don't know. What is it?"

"That you're RIGHT!"

Kelly sat on the sofa, staring at the walls. "Why do you think the sheriff brought up voodoo magic?"

"I don't know. It took me by surprise."

"If Johnny has our daughters, how would he know about voodoo?"

"That's a damn good question, but the sheriff did make a good point."

"What?"

"He doesn't want anyone to know that he's involved. The sheriff was brainstorming that he might have them hidden out there or somewhere tied into it, and they would be convinced that spirits are holding them."

"What? That's ridiculous. He didn't say there were ghosts and spirits over there."

"I think he planted a seed without knowing it."

"Now that makes no sense."

"I think he believes it's haunted but not willing to admit it. Hell, I don't know what to think. But I know one thing."

"What is that?"

"The sheriff knows a lot about that graveyard."

"Like what?"

"Not sure." He lit another cigarette and let the smoke from his mouth drift slowly upward just in front of his face. "I have talked to a few people around here about the Voodoo customs."

"And?"

"We are living in an area where some people believe it and practice it. There are also people afraid of it and paint their houses blue to keep the voodoo spirits away."

"Seriously?"

"Yeah. You've seen the little blue house along the roads."

"Steve" – she rose from her seat – "voodoo is not real!"

"I don't know, but it seems a lot of people believe it is. I believe it is real if you believe it. Kinda like taking a vitamin C pill to cure a cold."

"I don't get it."

"The power of belief."

"Get real, Steve."

"No, I'm trying to make a point. Churches are full of people who are afraid of not believing that Jesus walked on water. They say they believe Jesus turned forty gallons of water into wine. They are afraid of going to hell. That's religion, but it's not spirituality. A spiritual person thinks in abstracts and feels connected to a higher power through his mind. People who live here are very spiritual, and voodoo is real if their minds are connected to it."

"I've never heard you ever talk this deep. I'm can't make much sense out of what you just said. Religion is based on faith. I consider myself a Christian and I don't think I'm going to hell," she said resolutely.

"I'm just saying that voodoo is real to the people who feel connected to it."

"No," she argued. "Voodoo is not real and has nothing to do with Jennie and Lisa."

"Yeah, you're right."

"Look, Red; I'm not stupid."

"I know, Kelly."

"My grandmother believed similar stuff."

"Really."

"Yes, but she was an Indian with no formal education." She popped him on the arm. "I think in educated, practical terms – not supernatural hocus-pocus."

"I was trying to say that a lot of people around here believe in black magic."

"They're superstitious and that's all I got to say."

"Okay, just voicing other beliefs and opinions."

"They're intriguing, but I don't buy their beliefs and opinions. I'm tired of arguing!"

"Kelly, I guess I was just rambling. It got my mind off our damn problems for a few minutes."

"I know, but I do know one thing."

"What?" Steve asked, pacing the floor again.

"I liked the Sheriff. I think he'll see to getting Jennie and Lisa back to us safely."

"We hope," he commented absently, as he paced back and forth across the room.

"Red, what's on that mind of yours? You're not planning on doing something stupid, I hope!"

"I'm not planning anything," he lied.

Chapter 9

THE LANDLINE phone rang. It was Johnny.

"Don't answer it, Steve!" Kelly shouted. She stomped her foot.

"I'm gonna answer it, damn it!"

"Hit 'record'!"

"Red!" Johnny said loudly.

"What do you want, Johnny?" he asked, already irritated.

"Hey, you remember Joe Browning?"

"Why?"

"Do you remember him?"

"What is this all about? I remember him. He sold you some land," he said, getting more irritated.

"Yeah, it was a seventy-five-acre tract off Highway Eleven."

"So?"

"I got a problem with that too!"

Steve bit his lip out of angry frustration and took a deep breath. "Well, I'm sorry! Why don't you just leave me alone?"

"Red, you listen to me. I talked with him earlier, and he said that he sold me that land for three thousand dollars per acre. You told me that he wouldn't take less than forty-five hundred an acre."

"What in the hell are you trying to say?" he asked, wondering if he was dreaming all this shit? This can't be real!

"Look, you son of a bitch, I paid three hundred and thirty-seven thousand dollars. You cheated me out of one hundred and seventeen thousand dollars!"

"You don't know what you're talking about."

"You dual contracted. You got away with stolen money. My money!"

"That is bullshit!" Steve shouted, confused and pissed. "I'm fed up to my ass with your shit!!"

"Oh yeah?"

108

"Yeah," Steve hesitated, simmered, gathered rational thinking, and said, "he wanted six thousand dollars an acre, and I got him to drop it to forty-five hundred."

"He said he only got three thousand."

"He lied!"

"Oh, really."

"It's all on record. Check with your lawyer – Look, I don't want to talk about that. I want to ask you something: WHERE are my daughters?"

"WHAT – I didn't call to talk about your daughters. I called to see if you're getting my money back. And are you going to pay me what you stole on that other deal?"

"No, I'm not! And did you hear me! Where are my dau—"

"HEY! You enjoy prison in about six months. I'm bringing criminal charges against you!"

"WHAT!"

"Yeah – Real estate fraud. Breach of trust. You name it."

"Let me tell you something, mutha-fucker! If you were standing in this room, I'd beat the ever-loving shit out of you!"

"Physically threatening me?" Johnny gave an arrogant laugh. "That's another serious charge, and, by the way, I'm recording this conversation."

"Don't you ever call me again!"

"Honey," Kelly consoled Steve, "it's going to be alright. I haven't seen you that mad in a long time. You had a right! That Johnny is just a money-grabbing evil man. I never liked him much, and now I hate him!"

"Yeah." Steve looked at his watch. "I have to leave for a while. Just rest and take it easy."

"Where are you going?"

"The Marina Bar," he said. "I'm going to meet Bob."

"Okay."

Steve walked to his car, got in, and dialed Bob. "Hey, I thought I'd call you. Are you busy?"

"No, Steve. I'm at the Marina Bar, just having a drink."

"I was hoping you'd be there. Can I join you?"

"Sure."

"Um, is it crowded?"

"No, why?" he asked.

"I want to talk some more about voodoo. I'll explain when I get there. I don't want anyone to hear our conversation."

"There's no one here. Come on," Bob said, appearing confused and curious.

"I'll be right over."

Steve walked hastily into the restaurant and saw Bob sitting alone at the bar.

"Steve, you want to move to a quiet table?"

"Yeah, I do."

As they sat at a table, Steve said, "You remember the other day when we talked some about voodoo? I want to talk some more."

"What is it? Damn if you don't sound worried about something."

"I am. By the way, am I keeping you from anything?"

"No, not at all. I'm just in here having a drink." He cracked a laugh.

Steve smiled. "You're not at work?"

"Spring holidays!"

"Oh, forgot, Bob, I have a bad problem that I haven't told you about. My twin daughters were kidnapped Saturday night."

"What?"

"Yeah, and the Sheriff's department is on the case, but it's complicated. Listen, I have a bad conflict with a client that I sold some property to. He's mad, and he's threatening me over a land deal on Lady's Island that went bad. I mean bad!"

"The 'site' over there?"

"That's it. He wants me to get his money back. He's mad and mean."

"I had a feeling that was the property you told me about. I haven't been there, but it's the talk around those parts." Bob stopped and took a big gulp from his drink. "What happened?"

"Some of it blew up, and no one knows what caused it."

"So this client bought it, and now it's ruined and he's blaming you?"

"That's right. I want to talk to a root doctor who can put a curse on him."

"You're not serious?" Bob's eyebrows furrowed, and he took another gulp. "I better get you a drink."

"Better not."

"What do you need me to do?"

"Find me a root doctor," Steve said. Desperate.

"Didn't I tell you about a man who works at the school. He's into all that. They call him Peabo."

"You know him well?"

"Sure. He's our maintenance man. You want me to call him?"

"Will you?" Steve asked. Eager.

"I guess. Let me step outside and see if I can reach him."

Minutes later, Bob returned. "You got time to run up the road?"

"Yeah."

"Peabo's at a restaurant on St. Helena. You want to follow me up there?"

"You sure I'm not putting you out?" Steve asked.

"No. In fact, I want to go. A place called the Tide Water. They got great food."

"I've seen it. Know exactly where it is."

"Well, follow me out there. You might be staying longer than you expect, and I'll be needing to get back home."

"Alright."

As the two men walked to their cars, Kelly was in the kitchen, pouring a healthy glass of Merlot. It was what she wanted and what she needed.

Steve followed Bob on their way to St. Helena. Gazing out over the sound, he got a whiff of an unpleasant stench and reached for a handkerchief in his console.

They pulled into the parking lot of the Tide Water. It was a small place that boasted low-country cuisine specializing in ribs, chicken, and gumbo.

As they walked inside, a tall, thin black man rose from a table and greeted Bob with a handshake.

"Peabo," Bob said, smiling, "this is my friend, Steve Riley."

He shook Steve's hand.

"Hey, Peabo," Steve said.

"Real name be Peter, but eberbody call me Peabo." He grinned, exposing a gold front tooth.

Bob stood silently and ventured to join in. "I've got to go. You'll talk, and I'll see you both later."

"Peabo," Steve asked apprehensively, "you know someone here who might be able to help me find my daughters?"

"Yu hab a seat, Steve. I bet you're hungry. I'll get you a big bowl of gumbo. It's de best around."

"Sounds good. Haven't been hungry today, but what I smell coming from the kitchen, how can I resist?"

"Mistah." Peabo looked at him, brown eyes wide open. "Bob told me ob yur problem. I know someone dat might can fix it. I knows he can."

Steve started in a rush, telling of his dilemma.

"Would yu like to see him now?"

"Of course I would."

"At least he'll get this Mistah Sherburtt off your back. If dat man has yur girls, yu'll get 'em back."

"Who is this man?" Steve asked as he gulped down the gumbo.

"Do yu believe in voodoo?" Peabo asked flatly, staring straight into Steve's eyes.

Steve didn't choke on his food, but he coughed. "Voodoo?"

"Dat is what I said."

"Um, I don't know enough about it. I figured it was just an old superstition."

"Nosuh!" Peabo was sure of himself.

"I don't know." He wiped his lips as he pushed his empty bowl to the side. "Tell me more."

"Voodoo has been around a long, long time. If dar ain't something real 'bout it, den it wouldn't be 'round today. In dis area, anyways. I can show yu in books where a sheriff of Beaufort used it. But dat was a while back."

"Isn't voodoo also called black magic? I heard it's supposed to be evil?"

"It can be for good, and it can be for evil."

"Well, let's cut to the chase. I'm not sure where this is going, but if it gets my daughters back, then I'm game."

"We need to go see de root doctor!"

"Well, okay. What's his name?"

"Dr. Blue Jay."

"Huh!"

"Dem det know him just call him Dr. Blue."

"Let's go see him."

"Awright. We'll go now."

"Is he home?"

"He's at his house. He never goes nowhere."

"Well, I'm ready if you are."

"Now, fore we go, I have to tell yu dat he don't talk to jus anybody. Yu not tell anybody or say where he lives."

"That's fine. I won't."

"You also gonna have to pay him money."

"That's no problem."

"Den yu can follow after me. But first, you finish eatin'."

Kelly left the condo, headed for the beach. After three large glasses of wine, she was feeling numb and walking unsteadily, but the numbness wasn't enough to keep tears from forming in her eyes. The sound of the ocean and a pleasant breeze began to comfort her. Somewhat.

"Kelly!" a familiar voice cried to her.

She turned to her left and saw her new friend, Elizabeth Ashley, waving to her.

Kelly walked over to her and smiled. "Hey, Elizabeth!"

"How are you?"

"Fine, thanks," she replied, then burst into tears.

"What's wrong?"

"Everything."

"Honey, let me walk you home. I can tell you're upset," she offered sincerely.

"I'm okay."

"No, you're not. Is that your condo behind us?" She became more concerned.

"Yes."

Kelly tottered along the boardwalk to her condo – and with the help of Elizabeth, she made it to the door.

"Let me help you inside," Elizabeth said, relieved she got her home.

"Okay."

They walked inside with Elizabeth holding tight to her shoulder.

"I'll help you to your sofa," she insisted.

"Okay."

"Can you tell me what's the matter?"

Kelly squeezed Elizabeth's hand. "Our daughters are missing, and I'm worried sick. Will you stay for a while?" she asked, beginning to sober a little.

"Of course! What happened?"

"Can you please pour me a glass of wine? I can't do it. My hands are shaking too bad."

"Just a little."

"Pour yourself a glass too."

"Do you want to talk?"

Kelly nodded her head affirmatively, and the two ladies began talking.

"My little girls came down from college and went to Beaufort Saturday night and didn't come home."

Elizabeth handed her a glass of Merlot, sat down beside her, and hugged her affectionately. "I'm going to sit with you awhile."

"Elizabeth, I'm awfully upset and scared."

"I know you are. I wish there was something I could do."

"You are," Kelly whimpered. "I'm glad you're here."

"I wish I could do more." She looked at her new friend in pure, honest sympathy. "What can I do?"

"Nothing."

"Why don't you try to relax or maybe get some sleep if you can."

"Alright," Kelly agreed. "You're right. The Sheriff's department will find my girls, won't they?"

"Yes, Kelly, they sure will. Now, you lie down on the sofa, I'm goin' to leave for now. Call me if you need me. I mean it. Will you?"

"I will."

"Go to sleep and try not to think about it for now."

"I will." She shook her head pitifully.

"Call if you need me, okay?"

"OK." Her head was beginning to hurt.

"Don't drink any more, okay?"

"OK."

Chapter 10

STEVE WAS EXCITED about meeting a voodoo witch doctor as he followed Peabo down a long sandy road to a purplish-blue block house. Climbing out of his car, he noticed the surrounding woods were full of large oaks dripping strings of Spanish moss, and the singing of birds were coming from everywhere. He imagined a mystical cottage within an enchanted forest – a place out of a book of fairy tales.

At the front door, Peabo knocked twice. An old Gullah man with a white beard and braided gray hair answered cautiously.

"Peabo, my mahn!" Dr. Blue said with a grin, exposing a row of gold teeth with sunlight reflecting off one. "Come in de house. And dis mus be a man dat needs my power?"

"I'm Steve Riley," he said hurriedly.

"Ahhh, Mr. Riley," Dr. Blue spoke, studying him from head to toe.

"Call me Steve." His knees trembled as he looked at the old black man wearing overalls, gold bracelets, gold watch, gold rings, glistening gold necklace – and a blue felt hat. "This is all new to me. Maybe this isn't such a good idea?"

Dr. Blue looked down at Steve's extended right hand but did not shake it. "Hold out yo left hand," he insisted.

Steve obeyed as Dr. Blue put his left hand on his and rubbed Steve's fingers while his thumb pushed into his palm. Not letting go, Dr. Blue motioned for him to sit down on the worn, dusty couch. Peabo sat in a wooden chair across the room, watching.

Steve broke into a cold sweat as he glanced around the room, dimly lit by an old recessive lamp. He noticed books stacked against the wall, and that was the moment he felt an extreme force of something he had never felt before – surge out of his hand – and run all through his body.

"What was that!?" he cried out.

Dr. Blue cracked a sly grin. "Yu felt dat?"

"Yeah! Why are you rubbing my hand?" Steve asked, frightened as chills ran down the length of his spine.

"Haa'kee, I be getting' de read."

"What kind of read?"

"Mistah Steve, you be in bad fix."

Peobo interrupted. "I'm going to leabe yu alone with Dr. Blue. I hab to go. Now yu do as de mahn tells you." Steve smiled thinly at Peabo.

"Peabo, I'm a little nervous. Maybe I ought to…"

"Yu be scart ob me?" Dr. Blue stared and stated. "I be here to help you. Don't be scart."

"What was that jolt I just felt run through me?"

"Haa'kee. Dat be Dr. Blue's power!"

"What does Haa'kee mean?"

"It mean dat oonuh LISTEN!"

"Oh."

"Aw right, den. Now yu tell me eberryting me hab to know. You be in trubble. I felt it in your sperrit. Me 'bout knows ebberting, but tell me yo' own self."

As Dr. Blue let go of Steve's hand, a cold shiver ran through him like lightning. He felt a power he had never felt before. It was real! It was only momentarily frightening, but now he was feeling a warm, relaxing peace he had never known.

He told Dr. Blue what happened since he visited the site planned to be a pricy condominium development and now turned into a land in ruins. He emphasized that Johnny Sherburtt blamed him and probably kidnapped is daughters.

"Oonuh beleeb dis Johnny hab yo chillins?" Dr. Blue asked.

"I think so. It's a long story. A wild and crazy one; but I think he does."

"Me git dem back."

"Can you?"

"Sho,' I do dat, But fus I gotta put a hex on dis Johnny. Me gwine make a root to gib him so it make him sick and scart – den e gib dem back to you."

Steve looked around the room and saw shadows dance across the walls and ceiling from the dim light of the lamp. "Really? How?"

"Some things you can ax, and some you can't."

"Like what?"

"De stuff I put in de root be me secret."

"Don't worry. I don't wanna know," Steve said.

"Me gwine need a clippin' ob his hair or fingernail." Steve shook his head, confused.

"You got any ob his clothes?"

"No." Steve shook his head.

"I could make powuhful potion if 'n we hab sometin offa him."

"Wait!" Steve almost rocketed from the couch. "I think I do!"

"Wuh dat?"

"He spit some tobacco juice out of the car window! I think it hit the outside of his door. I bet it's still there!"

"Oonuh hab dat?" Dr. Blue rose from his seat. "Me gwine look."

"Yeah. See that!" Steve pointed at the brown stain on his white Lexus.

"Yassuh, dat be bacca on dat door."

"That's what he spit!" Steve blurted.

"Me scratch it off. Me gwine get buttuh knife and plate. I be steady not to scratch yo' car."

Steve watched as he scraped the dried tobacco into a small plate. "You think it'll work?"

"Dis 'bacca' will be de poison dat gwine dribe him to sick. Now, I needs you to go back to dat grabeya'dd and get some du't dere. It called 'goofer dust.'"

"What?"

"Haa'kee! You git dat dirt! De grabeya'dd sperrits are de ones dat made Mista Johnny mean! Dey want dere grabes back."

"I don't understand. Am I really supposed to believe all this?"

"Dey want you to make him gib back dat land so dey can rest in peace. Dey want you to be de one. Yu hab to get some du't from dat place so I can finish de 'root.' When he gits de hex, e sho' gib you chillun back."

"So he's going to give back that land to the woman who sold it to him and also turn over my daughters free and unharmed – just because a hex made him sick!?"

"Dat's right. Now, here be de jar. You go get dat du't!"

"Alright, but I just don't understand all this. Is that all I do...go get dirt?"

"Dem spirits won't you to leabe dem sometin. You put a case quawtuh on de spot you get de du't frum."

Steve drove as fast as traffic would allow to Johnny's land and the Gullah graveyard. In an excited, confident way, he was feeling an exhilarated charge coursing through his body. He drove slowly up Lady's Island Road because it was crowded with people and cars everywhere.

He found one empty space to park along the road bordering the property. He got out and mixed in with the throng of curious onlookers. They weren't paying attention to him, and he was able to scoop some dirt, 'goofer dust,' into his jar. He looked at the black sandy soil in his jar and quickly reached for a quarter and placed it at the spot.

He couldn't help but notice and marvel over a strikingly good-looking lady reporter, watching her start an interview with someone important.

"Hello again. I'm Rhonda Shields with Fox News," she said confidently, smiling into the camera. "I now have with me Dr. Eric Stevens, head of the geology team here. Dr. Stevens, we all want to know if there is some explanation of this so-far unexplained occurrence. Do you think this was an earthquake?"

"The rumor of an earthquake is nothing more than mere speculation. Our team is finalizing our theory that no earthquake happened or caused this unusual destruction."

"Explain, Dr. Stevens."

"An earthquake would most likely have occurred on the coast and that would have been a devastating and tragic catastrophe. It would have thrown gigantic waves up and down the Atlantic coast, raging havoc and destroying most everything for miles inward!"

"So what do you think is happening here?"

"This area is composed of ocean, rivers, creeks, marshes, and solid ground. Marsh is wetland, but it abuts solid ground that's firm and intact. This area transformed into marsh due to pockets of water formed underneath by rivers and creeks. What happened is that a large sinkhole formed."

"A sinkhole?"

"Yes. Just imagine ice skaters on a frozen pond that appears solid. But, it breaks, and they fall through the ice; into the lake." He smiled proudly by his analogy.

"Dr. Stevens, are you trying to say that some of this land was weak and gave way to the water under it?"

"Exactly, but unfortunately it's giving way to a large lake. This has to be carefully studied. This land is very dangerous and until the problem is actually resolved, it needs to be guarded around the clock."

"Well, we certainly want to keep this area safe."

"The land that gives up to the forces of water is the result of what is known as alluvium. We are checking weak spots, and I hate to say, but the sinkhole is growing bigger."

"Thank you, Dr. Stevens. I'm Rhonda Shields, and our coverage of this devastating occurrence will continue."

Steve got into his car. "They don't have a clue!" he muttered, then sped back to Dr. Blue.

"Come in de house," the root doctor spoke loudly from inside.

Steve walked in and saw Dr. Blue sitting on the couch, playing an old acoustic guitar and singing an old blues song, 'Mojo Man.' "I got my mojo workin'. It gonna work on you." He then broke into 'Voodoo Chile,' and Steve was impressed. The only thing missing was the intense ripping electric guitar riffs from Jimi Hendrix. But not really.

"Alright den." Dr. Blue rose with a grin, laying his guitar down.

"I liked it!" Steve complimented him. "keep playin'…"

"Aw, jus' habin a lit'l fun, dat's all. I seez yu got me some 'goofer dust' in dat jar."

"Where do you want me to put it?"

"On dat table." He pointed.

Steve set the jar very gently on the wooden table next to the couch as if it contained nitro glycerine.

"Yu wait outside while I finish up root – den I bring it to yu."

Steve waited outside by his car for fifteen minutes until Dr. Blue came out.

"Dat good. I done got yu root." He handed Steve a small leather pouch, the size of a chestnut tied tight with a brown string. "Are yu flat foot?"

"What?"

"If'n yu aint' flat foot, me want yu to put it in yu shoe under the arch ob your foot. It will protect yu frum Mistah Johnny's evil."

"Whatever you say." Steve complied.

"Now, put dis round yur neck. It be an amulet to keep de evil away and make yu feel good."

Steve took it and put on a gold chain tied to a blue stone. The amulet rested nicely on his breastbone.

The old root doctor then handed him a sealed envelope. "Yu mail dis to Mistah Johnny. It be 'Goofer Dust Root.' Put Johnny's house numba on it and mail it to him. It be powerful!"

"Alright." Steve said, no longer nervous but feeling relaxed and confident.

"Yu take it ober to de post office and mail it to him on a one-day livery!"

"You mean one-day certified delivery?"

"Dat's right. Now, yu pay me five hundred dollars for dis. And yu got to keep dis all secret. Yo be hearin' soon from Mistah Johnny. He ain't goin' be happy. He'll be scart and sic. He be real happy te gib back yo chilluns. De spirits be mad he ruined de graves. Dey wants dat land back, and yu want yo chilluns back, dat right?"

"That's why I'm here."

"Den yu do what I done tol yu!"

"Alright, I will."

"It be his fault de grabe ya'd get ruined. He gotta pay de price. He had no bidness messin' wid dem graves. Nosuh. No bidness at all!"

Steve handed him the money, and Dr. Blue smiled and said, "Keep dat root in ya shoe. When yu bed down, put yu shoe in de closet."

"Alright."

"Wear dat chain all de time. Eben when yu bathes."

***

Sheriff Bill Price knocked on Lula Watson's front door, and she opened it.

"Ms. Watson?" he asked.

"Yessuh," she answered apprehensively. "Ooman de sheruf?"

"I'm Sheriff Price." He smiled at her assuringly.

She stared, motionless.

"Can I come in?" Price asked humbly.

"Come een de house, but don't let dem flies een."

He quickly stepped inside. She offered him a seat on her cloth couch, then sat down in her rocker and looked at him curiously.

"Ms. Watson, I need to ask you a few questions about some land you recently sold."

"Me hab nothin' to do wid dat mess dats goin' on obuh dere."

"Ms. Watson, I know you don't," he assured. "I just need to get some information that you might have."

"Wuffuh?"

"Well. I wish I knew what's happening over there?"

She eyed him suspiciously. Her filmy brown eyes grew large and bulged. "It be bad ober dere! De ground breakin' up and ebbuh thing. I warned dem men. It don't surprise me none, Mistah Sheriff."

"Warned them of what?" Price asked.

"I tol dem not to mess wid de grabeya'dd. Dey spose to leave dat part alone. Dat's de grabeya'dd of de Gullah Geechie. Now look wuh dey done. Dey got all de whole grabeya'dd stirred up!" she blurted in anger with her eyes wide opened.

"Who bought that property?" he asked, already knowing.

"A man from de upstate named Sherburtt. I sat wid him at de lawya table. He swunguh man dressed up like a demmy crack. Yessuh, he be a fancy Jim Dandy. Me don' like him."

"Why did you sell it?" he asked her.

"Git money to help de po' round here."

"No other reason?"

"Nossuh. But dat Mistuh. Johnny e bad omen. He jabbuh too much bout hiself."

"Do you know Steve Riley also?"

"Yessuh. He be a nice man. He came here and ax if'n I'd buy dat land back."

"I guess you probably told him no?"

"Call me Lula. Ebuhbody in dese parts calls me Lula."

"Oh," he laughed. "Lula, what did you tell him?"

"I tol him no like you sed. I don't hab money to buy it back."

"You made millions!"

"I did hab de money, but it be gone now. I kept a little, but I gabe it away to de chuches fuh de po. I tol dem men not to mess wid dem grabes!"

"According to the survey, the graveyard was not touched."

"It be touched."

Price rose from his seat, shaking his head in frustration, and said, "Lula, I have to leave. I appreciate you talking with me. If I need anything, I'll let you know."

As Price walked out the door toward his car, he heard Lula Watson holler at him.

"Sheriff, wuh goin' on ober dere is bekase ob dem spirits ob de dead. Awright? You hear me?!"

Price drove out Lady's Island Road in his gray Crown Victoria. Approaching the chaotic site, he grimaced on seeing spectators, news vans, and so-called scientists. He stopped, got out of his car, and was approached by a reporter from Fox News.

"Sheriff Price is here," the lady reporter spoke into a microphone as her cameraman began taking footage. "And what do you make of this catastrophe, Sheriff?"

"We've been told that this area is suffering severely from an unknown land disturbance. Maybe an earthquake. I don't know."

"You don't know what could have caused it?"

"No. I'm not qualified or have the expertise to answer that question."

"But do you know anything that we haven't been told?"

"The Beaufort County Sheriff's Department cannot speculate or discuss this tragic occurrence until it has further concrete information. Now, if you will excuse me, I must leave."

"That was Sheriff Price, and I'm Rhonda Shields, and this is Fox News."

***

A gust of wind hit the back side of the small shack, and Jennie Riley saw a beam of light shoot across the room. Rising from her blanket, she noticed a small hole in the back wall allowing light to enter the dark dwelling.

"The wind knocked a little hole in the wall," she said to Lisa.

"Really?"

"Yeah, and I can see out of it," she said, putting her right eye to the small opening.

"A round piece of wood is lying next to your blanket, Jennie. You're peeping out a knothole. Can you see anything?"

"I see a pasture and an old tractor. I see woods farther back. Wait a minute – I see a circle of rocks with a stone slab in the center."

"What is it?"

"I don't know."

"Is there anyone out there?"

"I don't see anybody. I'm looking at the woods, and there's a lot of large trees."

"I hear someone coming!" Lisa softly hissed.

Seeing the wooden knot, Jenny quickly placed it in the hole and jumped to her blanket.

The door opened. It was the masked man holding a basket in one hand and a large Pepsi in the other.

"Little late, aren't you?" Jennie smirked, feeling more gutsy.

Lisa looked over at her sister, surprised at her sassy remark.

Laying down a basket of fresh-baked biscuits, slices of ham, and the Pepsi, he picked up the metal pots and left.

"Hell, he left us a feast this time," Jennie said with a smile.

"All we need now is a bath!"

"That would be nice."

A few minutes later, he returned with their chamber pots. He set them down and walked back out, saying nothing.

"Well, Lisa," Jennie laughed, "we're fed and not dead."

"Yeah."

Jennie walked over to the wall and removed the knot. She gazed out over the pasture and studied the woods. She was determined to find a way out of the masked man's shack.

* * *

Steve walked into the condo and saw Kelly curled up on the sofa. The TV was on, but she wasn't watching it. At first, he thought she was just tired and had fallen asleep, but then he saw the empty wine bottle on the coffee table.

"Honey," he said softly. "Are you all right?"

"You're home," she slurred drowsily. "What time is it?"

"After five."

"I dozed off."

"Looks like you drank a bottle of wine!"

"Ohh," she moaned, pressing her hands to throbbing temples. "I think my friend Elizabeth helped," she said, rubbing her half opened blurred eyes.

"I hope so."

"Where have you been?"

"Oh, went to Beaufort," he lied. "Had to meet someone."

"You hired a private detective, didn't you?"

"Let's just say, I talked with someone who's going to get our twins back."

"I don't understand. How?"

"Can't tell you how. You have to trust me."

"Well, alright. I'm just glad you're home," she said. "I did drink too much!"

"You'll be alright," he said, "I'll rub your neck."

"What's that around your neck?" she asked as her eyes appeared to be focusing again.

"Oh, it's something I picked up in some souvenir shop."

"What is it?"

"It's an amulet. You like it?"

"You look like a hippie," she laughed. "Why in the hell would you buy that?"

"I don't know. I guess I wanted it."

"Why?" She laughed again, looking at the blue stone tied to a fake gold chain.

"It's supposed to bring good luck."

"Says who?"

"The Gullah woman at the store," he said, rubbing the stone with his thumb and forefinger.

"Steve, help me to bed. I need to lie down. I drank way too much."

"Alright."

She smiled at him with sparkles coming in her blurred, brown eyes. "I think I need a shower. Want to join me?"

His jaw dropped. "Really?"

"Yes really," she said seductively as she grabbed his arm and led him to the bathroom. She turned on the shower and adjusted the knobs until the shower head sprayed soft warm water just the way she liked it. "Why don't you take your new necklace off?" she whispered in his ear.

"I want to wear it." He came close to taking it off. No! He knew he better wear it!

"Don't be silly."

"No." He smiled as he tenderly held her soft, lean body close to him. "I want to keep it on."

"Well, I guess your lucky charm chain is working." She smiled, pulling him into the shower.

He massaged every inch of her body as she passionately pushed her long fingernails into his shoulder blades. The warm shower rained on them as if the water were falling from heaven.

When the water turned too cold for comfort, he turned it off.

Kelly looked at her husband. "I can't believe I'm feeling this good. Our daughters are missing, and we're behaving like this! I don't get it…I should be feeling guilty, but I feel good."

He smiled, not knowing what to say. He couldn't tell her about Dr. Blue.

"Can you put me to bed?" she coaxed. "And rub my back."

"Sure," he said, picking his shoes up from the floor and placing them neatly in the closet. "And don't worry. It's going to be alright."

***

Bill Price left his office and drove home. He was tired and didn't know what to think. Too much was happening. He wanted to believe Sherburtt was responsible for taking the Riley twins, but he had no evidence. He was trying – not – to believe that the hideous site was caused by something other than natural, explainable causes.

He sat on the front porch of his small antebellum home, gazing at the Beaufort River with a cracked-open beer in his hand. "I wonder what tomorrow will be like??"

***

Lisa looked at her sister. "Jennie, I wish we had a bath. I'm stinky, and my skin itches."

"Yeah."

"I need a bath!" Lisa spouted loudly.

"What in the hell do you expect me to do! You want me to holler for the masked man to come in here and wash us? Or maybe he'll just drive us up to the Ramada Inn and check us into a spacious room with a nice bath!"

"Stop it, Jennie. I'm sorry. I'm sad and scared."

"Lisa, it's going to be alright. There's a reason we're here. He hasn't hurt us. He's feeding us but I'm goin' to get us out of here soon – safe and sound."

"You think so?"

"Hey." Jennie bit her lip, seeing the fear in her sister's eyes. "Yeah, Lisa. I believe we're going to leave this dump soon."

"You don't think the masked man is going to torture and kill us?"

"No! We're going to be alright. Please try to get some sleep."

"OK."

"Close your eyes and don't think. Just let sleep come to you."

Chapter 11

TWENTY-NINE-year-old Ross London walked inside the Iron Mike. It was still early in the evening, and only a small group of people were there with just a few at the bar. He noticed an attractive young blonde sitting by herself at the end of the bar. Walking over, he asked if anyone was sitting next to her.

"No." She smiled, taking a sip from her beer.

"What you goin' to have ?" the bartender asked.

"Miller Lite."

He looked into the pretty young woman's bright blue eyes. "My name is Ross London."

"I'm Rhonda Shields." She forced another smile.

"I can tell you're not from here."

"No, I'm not. I'm from New York City," she said.

"Oh." He smiled. "I love goin' there. Wouldn't want to live there."

"You don't recognize me?" she asked, looking disappointed and surprised.

He brushed his hair back and said, "Uh I don't know. Oh, you're that actress—"

She quickly cut him off. "No!"

"I know a lot of movies are made in Beaufort."

"Why don't you guess?"

"Can I buy you a drink while I'm narrowing down the possibilities?" he asked.

"Sure. I'll take what you're drinking." She began smiling more warmly.

"Alright. I give up. Who are you?"

"I'm the anchorwoman with Fox News."

"Really!" He acted surprised. He seldom watched TV.

"I'm covering the land disturbance on Lady's Island. It's a big deal."

"I'm sorry I didn't recognize you. I'm embarrassed."

"You must not watch the news much."

"I do, but not lately. I've been on the road the last few days. I do know about the land disturbance. I went there. I know about the crater forming."

"What do you know about it?" she asked curiously.

"It's mysteriously volatile. I've decided to investigate it."

"Oh really. Let me see your badge."

"I don't have one." His face reddened. "I haven't applied for one." He lied. "Do you need one?"

"Yes – and just how are you going to investigate this crater when you can't get on the land?" She laughed. "No one gets onto that property without an official badge from the Sheriff's Department."

"I was on the property, and I saw things coming out of the crater. I wasn't the only one."

"Things like what?" she asked. "You serious, or are you just being funny?"

"Wait. Let me back up. I'm an anthropologist working on my PhD at Ohio State and researching the Gullah Geechees in this area for my dissertation. I just happened to find that site, and I went there…"

"Whoa there hoss! Slow down." She laughed then turned serious. "You know people have died at that crater. It's no joking matter!"

"I know that."

"Now you were saying something about being an anthropologist."

"Yeah, I've been coming here for over a year, studying the people and the customs of the Gullah-Geechee people who have been living here for centuries."

"What's that got to do with your insensitivity to people who have lost their lives on the very place I'm reporting on?"

"I didn't mean to be insensitive. Can we move to a table where we can talk more in private? I believe I can explain some things. You might want to hear about supernatural happenings going on there."

"Hey! You're crazy. I'm not going to a table with you!"

"I swear I experienced something incredible coming out of the crater over there."

"Yeah, I bet."

"I did, but I don't want others to hear me talk about it. You being a reporter should know…"

"Like what? What should I know, Ross?"

"I'll tell you – I don't feel comfortable talking about it up at the bar. Can we get a table in the back where we can talk privately? Please?"

"Hey Mike?" she called across the bar.

"Miss Shields. Is everything alright?"

"This guy sitting next to me wants me to go with him to a table. It's not what you think. It's business."

"He's okay. How about another round?" Mike said with a smile. "Yeah, Ross is alright."

"Well, okay. And yes, I'll have another," she said feeling hesitant but curious.

"Yeah," Ross said as he stood up. "We're going to move to a table."

"I'll bring the beers right over," Mike said.

Ross escorted Rhonda to a secluded table near the bandstand. There were amplifiers, chords, and PA equipment on the stage, but no band.

"Rhonda, there's a sacred graveyard on that land where the Gullahs have been buried for a long time."

"I know there's a graveyard. So what's your point?" she asked, becoming restless.

"I'm trying to tell you," he said, frustrated.

"Do you know why the land is cracking and forming a large crater that is scaring the crap out of everyone? I told you, people have died there."

"What do you think is causing it?" he asked. "Then I'll tell you what I think."

"Scientists believe it might be an earthquake." Ross looked at her, shaking his head no.

"A sinkhole formed?"

"Rhonda, I know what's causing it. I do. When I came in here, I didn't know who you were. I swear. But I believe you need to know what I know."

"How would you know? And why don't you just tell me what's causing it?" she asked him flatly.

"My doctoral thesis is on the Gullah Geechies, but I'm including something that some still believe and also practice – voodoo!"

"Voodoo!" she laughed.

"The Gullahs here take their beliefs seriously. They are all descendants of slaves, and they still believe and live by customs that go back to Africa."

"What is your point?" Her eyes danced around the room as she spoke impatiently. "Get to it."

He, too, glanced around the room, gathering his thoughts. "Voodoo is powerful magic! I believe in it."

"Ross, this has been interesting, but I think I want to leave now."

"Wait. Please wait. I'm trying to tell you that the graveyard disturbance on that property was no natural occurrence. It's the result of vengeful, angry spirits that are now causing havoc and disaster. They are spirits of the dead and have been awakened."

"Bullshit! I'm out of here." Reaching for her purse – rising from her chair.

"No, listen. I know what I'm talking about. I'm originally from Richmond and have heard many stories about the ghosts seen around the battlefields during the Civil War. Soldiers were brutally killed in battle. Even today, people see their ghosts. I've seen them!"

"Oh, I bet you have." She rolled her eyes. "I have to go."

"Respectable, lucid people have witnessed them. You've heard about the dead soldiers at Gettysburg that are seen still marching across the battlefields?"

"I guess I have but maybe I don't believe those stories."

"They died violently and can't rest!"

"Look, Mr. Parapsychologist," she mocked, "I don't know of any battle fought where we're talking about, so why would the dead be restless?"

"Rhonda, please sit back down. I believe in the supernatural. I believe that the spirits of the dead have risen! I don't know why they are restless, except maybe because of how they were treated in slavery, poverty, and whatever. I don't know. I do know that their resting place was dug out by a bulldozer, and they are mad."

"Well, I can't go on national TV tomorrow and tell everyone that the reason the land is exploding is because the angry spirits of the dead are mad!" She looked at him and laughed. "You know, you are fun to talk to. I didn't mean to be rude. It's just you're talking crazy."

"What if YOU had proof?" Ross's eyes twinkled in the dimly lit room. He looked into her eyes and could tell she was interested in him; and was becoming intrigued with the conversation.

"Well, yes!"

"I can get proof."

"Hey, I'm a reporter, and I think you knew that! You've got something up your sleeve. Just what is it you want from me? I don't know you. You better tell me what you're up to," she demanded, reaching for her purse again. "Maybe I should leave. Nice talking with you."

"Please hear me out! You don't want to leave yet. I'm serious, and I can help you, and you can help me. And no, I didn't know who you were. I just came in for a few drinks."

"What do you want, Ross?" she asked, laying her purse back down.

"I want to prove that the graveyard is haunted."

"Look, I'm not into the supernatural or ghosts. I don't believe it's haunted."

"I know it is, and we can prove it. You have access to a good camera and a professional recorder?"

"So what if I do."

"You'll be the first reporter on national TV to show actual ghosts to everyone!"

"So you're saying we can just go 'ghostbusting' and have factual evidence?"

"Ghost busting!" Ross laughed. "I am not a ghost buster. I believe we can prove with solid evidence that this place is haunted."

"With my camera and a recorder?"

"Yeah."

"Ross, you are the most ridiculous but interesting man I've met in a long time. But why do you need me? Don't you have a camera and recorder? Like you said, you've been researching here awhile – you must have your own equipment to work with?"

"Not high-definition enough. Can you get a professional Tascam and recorder?"

"Well, as a matter of fact, I have some pretty good stuff in my car," she boasted. "Now, you don't expect me to go out there tonight on a ghost hunt?"

"Why not?"

"You really are sure of yourself."

"I am."

"You really think we're going to document the 'supernatural' and show it to the world?"

"I do!"

"Why do I believe you? I don't believe in this voodoo or whatever you call it."

"You have a curious and impulsive nature. I can tell that you believe I know something."

"I must be insane."

"Trust me. We're going over there and see something that will shock the world!"

"Hey, we can't get in. It's taped off, and patrol cars are swarming the area."

"I can get in."

"OK, I'm crazy! I'm going to be the first reporter to have a chance to film ghosts in a destroyed graveyard. So, come out to my car, and we'll get the camera and recorder. Boy, I sure hope you know what you're doing – but for some reason, I trust you. This is going to be exciting!"

"You bet it will!"

"Wait!" She came to her senses. "I don't know you. I can't just leave with a stranger! Especially to go to a dark graveyard!"

"I'm trustworthy. Ask the owner, Mike. He'll vouch for me. I know him."

"Hey, Mike!" she yelled toward the bar. "Can you come here for a second?"

Mike hurried over. "Yes, Ms. Shields?"

"You told me that this guy's okay. Do you know him?"

"Yeah, he's an anthropologist doing research here," Mike told her.

"Is he trustworthy?" Rhonda asked.

"Oh yeah. Ross is a good guy."

"He wants to take me out on a ghost hunt!"

"Well, have fun," he laughed. "Don't let those Haunts get you."

"The what?" she asked.

"Haunts. He means ghosts, Rhonda. He's just kidding."

"Oh, alright. Well, let's go. And Mike, if my manager calls or comes in here – think of something to tell him."

They left the Iron Mike in Ross's white 4Runner and headed to the site. He couldn't get his mind off the beautiful reporter sitting next to him. And she's really going with him to the haunted land. *Damn.* He thought about how great this was going to be. He had a good-looking woman and expensive equipment to match. This was his lucky night, but he was falling for her. She had the looks, brains, and personality that got his endorphins running wild. He knew this was leading to trouble, because his attraction to her was getting the best of him. This was a dream come true, but deep down, he realized that this couldn't be a lasting romance. She was too attractive and in the national spotlight. She was definitely out of his league. He would put it in perspective and enjoy the moment.

They crossed onto Lady's Island and pulled into the small restaurant near the site, overlooking the Coosaw River.

"Why did we come here?" she asked.

"I know these people. I eat here a lot. We can leave my car and walk to the graveyard," he said, pointing across a grassy area leading to a wooded area.

"Are you out of your mind? I'm not going to walk through that marsh!"

"Of course not. Those woods over there lead to the graveyard. We'll walk along the road and cut through the trees."

"Are you sure?"

"Yeah."

"Why don't we just drive up there?"

"Like you said, 'It's being patrolled.'"

"Oh."

"The car will be safe here. Let's just kind of sneak up to the woods."

"Ross." Rhonda clutched his wrist. "I'm scared. I believe you. That place might be haunted!"

"Get your camera and recorder, and let's go."

They hurried up the narrow road and moved quickly through the underbrush and trees to the edge of the site. Kneeling so as not to be seen, Ross moved his eyes from side to side as his stomach began to churn. "Eerie place," he whispered nervously.

Rhonda nodded and held tight to his arm. "Glad I don't have high heels on."

He abruptly froze and grabbed her hand securely.

"It's a freaking gigantic pit!" Rhonda gasped as Ross placed a hand on her shoulder.

They stood in shock, gazing at the uncanny, frightening crater. "Jesus!"

"God, I never got close, but it couldn't have been like this earlier. It's a huge crater, and I can hear it bubbling! And what is all that rot I smell!?" she asked, overwhelmed with fear.

"This grave site is now a gigantic hole filled with hot nasty water with steam coming out," he stated, pointing his flashlight.

"Is it a volcano?"

"I don't know. Let's get a closer look. You got your camera?"

"Yes."

They cautiously walked to the edge of the pit, and Ross had a change of heart. "I think we need to leave!" he stammered and choked. Sweat running down his temples. "The ground is higher than the opening of the pit. It's like we're standing on a knoll looking down into it. DAMN it's huge. I DON'T LIKE IT! We need to get the hell out of here NOW! Somethin's BAD, wrong!"

"No shit!"

"Let's just leave."

"It's a volcano, right?"

"I don't know! I do know we'd better get the fuckin, hell out of here!"

As they turned to run, a SKELETON came out of the NASTY water – shot up the side of the pit's opening, and with its long BONY HAND, grabbed Rhonda's ankle. She screamed as its other bony hand grabbed her other ankle. "ROSS!"

Instinctively, he grabbed her hand and began pulling.

"Don't let those monsters get me! I'm goin' to fall in that hole! Pull!"

HE pulled HER. HE saw five GLOWING SKELETONS fly from the pit and land in a semicircle around him. He wasn't drunk and he wasn't dreaming. THIS was REAL!

"What the shit!" He began swinging his left hand at them while still holding tight to Rhonda with his right. The skeletons jumped back like small dogs. They began to GLOW yellow – and hissed – keeping the two at bay. But not long! They lunged at Ross, pushing him over the brink. Hands still joined, Ross and Rhonda tumbled into the watery hole. Thrashing in the hot slimy water – they couldn't swim out – SHE screamed in terror! The creatures of the dead – DROOLED and GRUNTED with wicked pleasure – as they bit at her face with wide rows of long teeth – swallowing the little bites of flesh! Staring into Ross's eyes, a skeleton grinned and screeched – then tore into his chest with long, sharp, bony fingers – moving through cracking ribs – piercing into his BEATING HEART! Still, barely alive, HE came up one final time before he drowned in the sucking mire. HE saw a man wearing a black mask, standing at the pit's edge. "HELP!" he gurgled and pleaded. "HELP US!"

The masked man walked up and just looked at him and calmly spoke, *"Curiosity killed the cats!"*

Chapter 12

JENNIE LOOKED through the peephole and focused only on the tractor. IT was old and rusty. Didn't appear to have been used in a while. She then gazed across the field of grass meshing into the nearby woods.

"I want to get out of here," Lisa whined.

"Don't you think I do too!" she snapped at her sister. "If we had a way to get out of these chains, then I believe we could."

"I know."

A beam of light shot in through the small hole in the wall, and Jennie saw something lying on the ground next to her blanket. She was able to walk over to it and noticed it was a thin piece of steel. It was a hacksaw blade.

"Well, Lisa, we just might have a way to get out of here."

"Really!"

"I see a saw blade on the ground. Daddy has some like these in his workshop. They can cut steel!"

"Can it cut off our chains?"

"Maybe," she said picking up the thin blade. "Not bad. It might work. Lisa, give me a piece of that ham with some fat on it."

"Why?"

"This blade is a little rusty. I can grease it and wipe it down with the end of my blanket."

Lisa handed her a fatty piece, and Jenny slid it back and forth along the blade, removing most of the rust. Feverishly she began sawing at one of the links in her chain but only a few flakes of steel fell.

"I can't put enough pressure on it. It needs a handle."

Jennie lay down on her blanket frustrated until she saw the wooden knot that popped out of the wall. "Just maybe."

"Maybe what?" Lisa asked in suspense.

"I think I can make a handle for the blade."

"How?"

"I can cut a groove in that knot and put the blade in it. I can hold the knot with one hand and push down on the blade with my other."

Lisa became silent, knowing it was best to keep quiet when her sister was preoccupied.

"I sliced it and the blade fits right in. I'm going to seal it with water so it will tighten around the blade."

"Really?"

"Well, it might. Anyway, I can wrap it with some string that should hold it. At least keep the blade from falling out."

Lisa just watched and listened appearing to have high hopes over the project.

"I can unravel some thread from the blanket and tie it. Lisa, you remember those arrow heads daddy's got? The Indians had to tie them! I used to look at the pictures in his books. They were just fashioned rocks tied to a stick."

"If you say so."

"I know so."

"How you going to keep the string from falling off the knot?" Lisa asked.

"Okay, the blade will be at the top secured in a groove. I'll cut notches on the other end of the knot to keep the thread tight then wrap and tie it."

Jennie grooved the knot and began fashioning the saw. She wrapped course string from her blanket over and around the blade and through the notches working meticulously and patiently.

Lisa watched her dominating twin sister wrapping and wrapping and wrapping the blade to the small handle. "You're something, Jennie!"

"Yeah."

***

Johnny Sherburtt sat at the bar in the lobby of the Hyatt Regency Hotel in Greenville. He was drinking a vodka tonic and talking with some bar buddies, "Wow!" Johnny's eyes widened as he spotted a sexy woman sitting across the bar, alone. "Look at that! I've never seen her in here. Have any of you guys?"

"No," one said. "She's hot! She could draw a blister on a sidewalk!"

"Looks strong," Johnny foamed. "Wonder where she came from?"

He kept eyeing the foxy blonde. Her hair was flowing from her head to her shoulders, sending shivers down his back. Her sexy blue eyes would melt any man in her sight. She glanced at Johnny and gave him a quick seductive smile.

He was quick to respond and smoothly walked over. "Mind if I sit down and offer you a drink?"

"Not at all."

"I'm Johnny Sherburtt."

"Lori Hampton," she shook his hand softly.

"Do you live here or just visiting?"

"I live here. Heard they have a good happy hour in this bar."

"Yeah, they do."

"I'm an advertising rep from the magazine 'You see it all.' I'm really from Atlanta."

"Wow, that sounds exciting."

"I love it."

"And what kind of magazine is it?"

"Fashion, of course, but a little riskqué." She laughed. "We just opened an office here."

"Interesting." He grinned. "I bet you do a lot of modeling too."

"Why would you think that, Johnny?"

"Why wouldn't I. You look like a model, tall, slim with long blonde hair."

"Well, I'm not and you don't have to blow smoke. I'm just a southern girl who grew up on a small farm. And what do you do for a living?"

"I sell and buy farms."

"Sure you do," she mocked.

"I do and then I develop them," he said.

"Oh, I see, you're a land developer."

"That's right," he gloated.

"Are you a Greenville boy or do you live somewhere else?"

"I live here but I'm originally from Charlotte – born and raised there."

"Well, I'm originally from Atlanta."

"I didn't know there were any farms in Atlanta." He gave a little, arrogant laugh.

"Smart ass. As a matter of fact, we lived just outside the city. But now it's been taken over commercially. Hey, let's talk about something else. What do you do for fun?"

"I live in a golf course community called Glassy Estates, so I play a lot of golf."

"I bet your wife likes living there," she quipped, sensing he was a player.

He looked at her, taken aback by that remark. "I'm not married."

"Sure you are."

"Lori, I'm not. I don't even have a girlfriend right now. We broke up three weeks ago."

"I'm sorry and regret what I said. It's just in my business, I frequently run across men that are."

"Well, I promise I'm not. Now let's forget all this and drink and have fun."

"I'll drink to that!" Holding her glass up expecting a clanging toast.

They talked and laughed for hours as the drinks kept going down. Johnny certainly wasn't dwelling or even thinking about his two-million-dollar land disaster at this moment. He was thinking about getting laid!

"I've got an idea," he said with a devilish grin. "We don't need to drive. Let's stay here tonight."

She giggled and nodded, yes.

He escorted Lori to the room as she stumbled a little in her high heels. "Great! A service bar," she happily slurred. "Can I open it and see what's in there?"

"Be my guest. Get what you want," Johnny said. This was too easy. Must be a catch somewhere.

She pulled out a mini bottle of vodka, cracked it open and turned it straight up. She then moved to the edge of the bed and coaxed Johnny with a curling forefinger. "Come here."

Johnny obliged and laid her across the bed. Looking down into her gorgeous eyes, he gave her a passionate kiss. She responded, panting heavily as their clothes were being yanked off. She wrapped her long legs around him with wild lustful pleasure, and the night was on.

Early next morning, Johnny woke and saw Lori standing in front of the mirror brushing her hair. She had dressed and showed no signs of guilt or regret as she looked at him and winked.

"I have to go," she said. "Got to get to work."

"Can I call you?"

"Sure!"

"Will you go out with me tonight?" Johnny asked. But he didn't want to know what he really knew – Lori was a slut!

"Are you asking me on a real date, Johnny?"

"Yeah," he said, wishing in a way that she didn't look so good. This is trouble! She knows she's trouble. "Yeah, I'm asking you out on a real date."

"Are you going to wine and dine me?"

"Of course." He smiled with head in clouds. He had never met a more desirable, sexy, gorgeous woman in his life. Swept off his feet, he could feel his stomach knotting and knew what that meant – he had fallen in love!

"What time?" She smiled at him.

"How about six?"

"Seven is better. That'll give me time to get ready. I don't get back home till 5:30."

"Where's home?" he asked curiously.

"Well right now they put me at the Hilton on 385. Room 318."

"I'll be there at seven," he said thinking that was an awfully nice and expensive hotel for a company to put out of town employees in. She must do pretty well, he hoped.

"Where are you taking me if I must ask?"

"The Chop House! Best steaks in town."

"I love that place, Johnny," she reached over and hugged his neck.

Johnny thought he had died and gone to heaven!

He walked the sexy attractive Lori to her blue Camry and kissed her goodbye.

Getting in his car, he luxuriated in his love for himself – and Lori – no way she could resist him!

It was still early morning when Johnny parked his black Mercedes in the garage of his custom-built home. Located in Glassy Estates, just outside of Greenville, it bordered a beautiful championship golf course and also gave a magnificent view of the Blue Ridge Mountains. He was feeling on top of the universe! *I have finally found the right one,* was his fantasy thought. Feeling too happy to go to work, he decided to play a round of golf. He called his office to let them know he wouldn't be in – not even aware of his hangover or thinking about that land disaster Steve caused him. He was going to enjoy this day and night. At least he thought he was.

As he settled in his den, flipping through channels on the TV remote, he began feeling nauseated. He didn't like it. He became worried and knew he was getting sick. Feeling his stomach twist and turn, he muttered, "Had too much to drink. Better lie down."

He lay on his couch and felt a nagging headache from too much alcohol but it wasn't bad enough to spoil his day. After a Pepsi and a Tylenol or two – he'd be alright.

Johnny heard the postman drive up – with a certified letter – and he signed for it. Curiously, he carried it inside, opened it, and a fine dust rose from the envelope and floated to his face. He started sneezing and coughing from the powder as he looked at the letter with a no return address; *Who sent this?*

"What is this shit?" he muttered. Then it struck him like a bolt of lightning – an excruciating pain shot through his head as he froze in an icy chill! Johnny started gagging, and his eyes burned with fire. His head now began spinning as he threw the letter on the floor while throwing up all over his nice Persian rug! His legs turned to rubber, and he fell to the floor. Barely able to breathe, he felt like his heart rattling and banging against his ribs. He fumbled for his phone and luckily dialed 911.

Steve and Kelly sat on their sofa as he ventured to ask, "How do you feel?"

"Great, but I shouldn't."

"Why not?"

"Steve, we should be scared and worried!"

He couldn't talk to her about Dr. Blue and the power he gave him that also rubbed off on Kelly.

She looked at him, "You still have that magic necklace on. Tell me the girls are fine."

"Honey, our girls are fine."

"Well, just who did you see yesterday that made you so happy and confident?"

"You're happy."

"Tell me."

"I talked with a lawyer in Beaufort," he lied. "He's getting the twins back from Johnny."

"What!?" She jumped from the couch – fist balled up – ready to knock his lights out! "Why didn't you tell me that yesterday! Are you serious? Don't mess with me!"

"I'm not. Take it easy."

"You didn't tell me!"

"I went out on the deck and made a phone call earlier," he lied.

She jumped from the sofa and poked a finger in his chest. "You better start talking, Red."

"They're at his house," he lied again. "My lawyer got him scared bad. He's goin' to bring them here today. And he's goin' to leave us alone."

"You're crazy! If what you're saying is true, I'll put him in jail!"

"No need for that."

Kelly looked at him with complete confusion in her eyes. "You're not making sense!"

"I wouldn't say it if it wasn't true." He looked at her with innocent eyes.

"It's not believable. Doesn't make any sense. He's just going to drive up with two happy girls and say, 'How's it goin?'"

"Don't worry about it."

Kelly laughed as the wonderful feeling she had begun to radiate again from her face.

"You feel happy again?" he asked.

"It must be your gold chain working. I feel good magic now," she giggled. "But are you going to tell me the truth or more BS. Hell, just keep on with your bullshit. It seems to be working."

He knew he couldn't tell her about Dr. Blue or his magic so he just hugged her and kissed her on the cheek.

"I don't buy all this crap," she said smiling and staring at his chain.

He looked down at the blue stone in his amulet and simply said, "Everything is fine. I just know."

"Well, I certainly hope you do!"

Sitting behind his desk, Price heard Betty knock on his door. "Bill, I hope you have a minute."

"What is it, Betty?"

"You know that anchorwoman, Rhonda Shields, with Fox News has been reported missing."

"Missing from what?"

"Didn't show up to the site this morning."

"So."

"Her manager is upset. He said she was at the Iron Mike last night and walked out with a young man."

"So."

"She didn't show up for work. Their entire production crew is very worried. They don't know where she is."

"Well, I guess she's somewhere with the young man," he said.

"Bill," she scolded. "She has time slots she has to fill. She would have called in. The production manager wants us to check up on her."

"Call him back and tell him that I will personally go over to the Iron Mike and see if I can't find out something. This is starting to get out of hand. Damn it!"

"Oh, I meant to tell you, an FBI Agent is on his way to talk with you about the Riley twins."

"Well, send him back to my office when he arrives."

"Okay."

"It's still morning! What's the rest of the day gonna be like?"

"I hope it gets better."

"Call the Iron Mike and tell them I'll be there at one o'clock. And tell them to be closed for business."

"Really?"

"Yeah, it might be best they're not open, I don't want to upset the customers."

"Doesn't the owner have an office?" she asked.

"I want to walk around and check out that room. Too many people are going there lately and wind up missing. I don't like it."

"Bill, now I have something new to say that you're not going to like."

"Well, go ahead and tell me." He sighed.

"Pinckney went to that bar yesterday and then drove out to the 'site.' His car is there abandoned and we don't know where he is?"

"Why wasn't this reported!?" he fumed. "He didn't call in."

"Just found out. And it is reported. We're worried."

"So am I. Wonder where he is?"

"You didn't hear me? He went to the site."

Price dropped his head into his hands and moaned. "This is all getting out of hand. Is there an APB out?"

"Yes," Betty answered him.

"Damn." He sadly shook his head. "I hope he's not where I think he might be."

"Where, Bill?"

"Down in the crater!"

"God! I hope not!" Wilson gasped.

"I guess you better call the Fox News people and tell them I'm going to check out that bar she was in while someone here finds Pinckney."

"I'll do that now."

Susan, the new officer on board, was at her desk when she heard the news about Rob. She had waited in her home, last evening, sipping wine, waiting – and waiting for him to show up – but he never did. She had a feeling he ran into trouble and tried calling him. She even called the department.

"Any news on Detective Pinckney?" she asked Betty while pretending to be reading a report.

"Only news is that his car has been at the 'site' since yesterday. We don't know where he is, but we pray he's alright. His car is being brought back now."

"Wouldn't someone have reported it yesterday and wouldn't we know he was missing," she asked in a saddened voice.

"You would think so, Deputy. But there's so much commotion and disorganization over there. It's getting out of hand. People are pouring in from everywhere to see that 'site.'"

"I know." A tear ran from her left eye; down her cheek.

"The Sheriff is highly upset and hopes he can get more help to keep that area under control."

"Why didn't he call?" she pleaded for an answer.

"You like him, don't you?" Betty asked sympathetically. Obviously, she had to feel her emotions.

"I do."

"We're all worried," she said and then smiled. "He might just walk in any minute now."

"I hope and pray so."

Betty started to head for Price's office.

"Betty," Susan spoke.

"Yes, Susan?"

"That site is bad news!"

"Yeah, I'm afraid it is. But Rob is a strong young man. He'll be alright." Deep down did Betty really think he was? If he was, why did he leave his vehicle there?

Johnny Sherburtt lay in ICU at the Greenville Memorial Hospital when a doctor walked in.

"Mr. Sherburtt, how do you feel?"

"I feel awful! What's wrong with me?"

"After looking at some tests, we have noticed you're low on potassium and magnesium, but your heart is okay. You might have had a mild stroke, but your symptoms indicate you probably had an acute panic attack. Do you take tranquilizers for nerves?" The doctor looked at him concerned and worried.

"Not really."

"What does that mean?"

"Okay, I have a prescription for valium but don't take them often."

"For anxiety?"

"I guess."

"You're very sick, Mr. Sherburtt, but we haven't been able to diagnose the actual cause."

"What kind of sick?!" Johnny shouted, "I've never felt this bad in my life!"

"I want to ask you some questions."

"What?"

"Alright. How old are you?"

"Forty."

"Do you know where you live?"

"Greenville," he answered weakly. "What is this? Don't my records have this information?"

"I am trying to find out how lucid you are."

"I'm lucid by God!"

"You appear awfully angry. We're going to keep you here over night. I'm going to give you a sedative after we run some more tests that should make you feel more comfortable."

"Whatever you say. I feel like crap," he said. "Did I have a stroke?"

"Now you rest, and I'll bring you something to help you relax."

144

"Wait, I have an appointment this evening," he said remembering his date with Lori.

"Not this evening."

"Well," he hesitated. "I'm too sick anyway."

"Yes, you are, but hopefully we'll get you feeling better soon." He looked into Johnny's eyes noticing they were dilated.

"Can you do something for me?"

"What?"

"I'm going to give you a note pad and I want you to write your name, the alphabet and the last three presidents of the United States."

"That's crazy."

"Can you do that?"

"Give me that notepad."

He took a few moments and handed the pad back to the doctor.

"That was quick!" he said and looked at the note pad. "This is bullshit!" is what Johnny wrote.

"You want to get well, Mr. Sherburtt?" the doctor asked realizing he had a reluctant, arrogant patient.

"Yeah! Of course, I do."

"Try being a little more positive and congenial."

Lisa watched Jennie saw into a link of her chain and said, "The masked man will be coming."

"It'll be awhile. I got him down like clockwork."

"You sure?"

"Two more hours and he'll show up. He's predictable. I tore out a piece of my blanket to plug up the knot hole. He won't notice."

"You got that handle tied pretty good."

"Yeah I do. I'm proud of myself. I can hold it with one hand and push down on the blade with my other. It's called torque. I'll get these chains sawed!"

"I'm impressed."

"Me too," she said giving a confident smile to her sister.

"We're going to get out of here, aren't we?"

"Trust me…we are getting out of here," Jennie said.

"I'll help saw."

Chapter 13

"BILL," Betty said, poking her head inside his cracked-open door, "the FBI agent is here. YOU want him to come to your office?"

"Yeah, send him on back."

"I'm David Stewart, FBI," a young thin man wearing a dark suit announced, walking into Price's office.

"Sheriff Bill Price," introducing himself, offering a handshake. "Please, have a seat."

"I'm here to take over a kidnapping investigation. Two young girls have been reported missing. Jennie and Lisa Riley. Is that right, Sheriff?"

"That's right. I submitted a status report," Price said. "It's an unusual situation. Complicated to be exact. One suspect without a reasonable motive. This whole case is a complete mystery."

"Yes, it is. Most are. And your report indicates that Mr. Sherburtt is the prime suspect. Is that correct?"

"For now."

"Sheriff, I'm aware of Sherburtt's and Riley's relationship and what's been going on but I don't think he's the culprit."

"He might not be," Price agreed, interested to hear the agent's assessment of the situation. He could tell he was new and eager. His thin face was a little awkward and funny-looking with a tiny mouth that probably hurt when stretching a smile.

"His only motive would be to make Riley get his money back. He's not holding these girls and demanding ransom. By law, Riley owes him no money. Sherburtt is a professional and successful land developer and would know this," he said, looking directly into the Sheriff's eyes. He continued saying, "There was not enough time for him to plan and execute such an undertaking. He would have to be an insane genus!"

"It appears that way but he is raging madly at Riley and harassing him with unreasonable threats to get his two million dollars back. Mr. Riley and his wife swear he's holding them."

"I don't believe it. He hasn't claimed he has them or demanding any ransom!"

Price looked squarely but honestly into the agent's eyes and said, "I want to believe it."

"You want to believe it! That makes no sense."

"After seeing pictures of those pretty, innocent-looking girls and the worry in their parents' faces – I wanted to believe it. Yeah, I confess I was letting my emotions get the best of me. I believed Sherburtt just wanted the money and was scaring Riley to find a way to get it. I strongly believed he wouldn't hurt those girls. I think his plan was to release them without anyone knowing he was responsible. He would have his money and they would have their girls."

"Sheriff, you can't build a case on personal feelings. Those boys would slip up, get caught, spill the beans and then he would be held responsible."

"I still believe he could be involved."

"Why?"

"Because of his financial loss and unreasonable behavior. It's just possible he used those boys and had a smart plan Of course it makes more sense to believe those bastards acted alone and just happened to have an opportunity to take those girls off somewhere – only to rape and kill them – but I'm not sure it's quite that simple."

"I'm going to talk soon with Sherburtt and the Rileys. Also, these boys will soon be caught and they'll provide us with the true answers."

"Well, I wish I could have given you more, but I've had my hands tied with this recent land disaster."

"I know you have and you can now leave this case to me. It's now an official FBI investigation."

Price looked at his watch. "I have an appointment at one o'clock."

"Okay, Sheriff. I promise I'll talk with Mr. Sherburtt. Whether he's involved or not, he'll be instructed to leave Riley alone."

"Good."

"I'm afraid your hotels will soon be overcrowded. You don't need a stampede with a bunch of rioting and looting." Stewart mentioned, rising from his seat.

"No, I don't."

"Alright, Sheriff, I'll be in touch," Stewart said, as he was walking out "Oh, by the way, is your chief of police involved?"

"Well." Price grinned. "If what you say is true about a stampede coming to Beaufort, he will be!"

"I can't believe I'm going to check on why a grown, successful woman didn't show up for her job!" Price grumbled to Betty before he left for the 'Iron Mike.'

"She's a celebrity!"

"Betty, we have six abandoned vehicles and no whereabouts of the drivers, along with two kidnapped young ladies, and I'm supposed to spend my time worrying about a celebrity who's probably drunk and coked up!"

"It's your job."

"Jesus!"

"I know," she agreed.

"Hell! One of the vehicles was turned upside down. I swear they are all in that crater. These damned expert scientists can't figure it out. I'm beginning to believe it's the devil's front door!"

"Calm down, and just talk with the owner at that bar. That's all you can do!"

"Yeah, I ain't happy with that place. I'm kinda looking forward to going over there." He sighed with relief as he looked at his watch.

"Guess I better go."

"Alright."

Price arrived at the Iron Mike and saw a solid built man sitting on a bar stool, "Is Mike here?"

"I'm Mike." The owner stood, seeing the sheriff of Beaufort County standing next to him.

"I'm Sheriff Bill Price."

"Yes, sir. I got the call, and we closed as you ordered."

"Well, Mike, I didn't want to disrupt your business, but at the same time, I didn't want customers in here during my investigation."

"What's this all about, Sheriff?"

"Two people were here last evening." Price pulled a photo from his shirt pocket. "Do you recognize this young lady?"

"Oh yeah. She's the Fox News lady! She was in here." He looked up from the photo. "Anything wrong?"

"Maybe."

"Like what?" Mike asked apprehensively.

"Was she here alone?"

"She came in alone," he answered, and pointed to a stool. "She sat right there."

Bill walked over to the stool, then gazed around the room. "Have a good crowd last night?"

"No, we actually didn't. Sheriff, can I ask what this is about?"

"Yeah, but let me ask you a few questions first. Did she leave with a man?"

"She met a man who I know. They sat up here a few minutes, then moved to a table."

"Did she leave here with him?"

"Yeah. She did."

"What time?"

"Um, probably around nine o'clock. Is there a problem?"

"I can't say."

"Sheriff" – Mike threw his hands up to his shoulders – "I didn't see anything unusual. They had a few beers and left."

"Relax. Tell me who this man is," Price said.

"His name is Ross London. He's an anthropologist doing studies here."

"What kinda studies?" Price asked with piercing eyes.

"He's working on his doctorate degree from Ohio State and researching the Gullah people. Been coming down here for about six months. Nice guy. And he always gets a room at the Quality Inn."

"So he comes in here for a short while and leaves with the almost-famous Rhonda Shields. Don't you find that a little strange?"

"No, not really."

"I know I do. At which table were they sitting?"

"That one." Mike pointed.

"Mike, what did they talk about? I'm sure you heard some of the conversation."

"I heard him say something about voodoo, but that's all."

"Really!"

149

"Yeah, and she seemed interested. I didn't think nothing about it. This is a bar. People are liable to talk about anything, and usually it's about themselves!"

Price laughed. "You're right about that!"

"Sheriff, all I know is that they had a beer at the bar and sat at that table and maybe had two more. I wasn't interested in what they were talking about. I just remember him uttering 'voodoo.'"

"Do me a favor. Try to remember anything else you might have heard."

"Wait!" Mike blurted, rubbing his forehead. "They were talking about that land disaster. And I did hear him ask her if she had a camera and recording equipment."

"Oh really." His eyebrows rose. "And?"

"That's all I remember."

"Alright, Mike, I'm going to leave, and you can open back up."

"Thanks. Hope I've been some help."

"You have. And I hate to say this, but too many strange things have happened recently to people leaving your place. You let my department know if you see or hear anything suspicious," Price said firmly.

"Of course."

"Your restaurant is now getting my attention!"

"Sheriff! The last thing I want is trouble," Mike said.

"You keep an eye out for suspicious-looking people. If those boys that took the twins come in, you call the department immediately."

"Of course, I will."

"I guess that's all, and sorry about the inconvenience."

"I understand. Oh, did I tell you Ross London stays at the Quality Inn?"

"You did. By the way, is the Iron Mike your nickname?" He smiled.

"No. An iron mike is a nautical instrument."

"Oh, didn't know that."

Price was back in his office when Wilson walked in. "You called Ohio State University, right?"

"I did," Wilson said. "Here's the lowdown on London. He's an assistant to an associate professor of anthropology and is working on his PhD."

"What else?"

"He's twenty-nine years old and lives in a small apartment on Arcadia Avenue in Columbus, Ohio, making six hundred dollars per week. He's originally from Richmond, Virginia, and has a good scholastic record – and he's well-respected and liked by his colleagues. He drives a 1999 Toyota 4Runner SUV, and his VIN is on file."

"Yeah, I was told he's doing his doctorate on Gullah customs and spends time here doing research."

"Yep."

"Okay, let's get a warrant and go over to the Quality Inn and see if he's there."

"What if he isn't?"

"You know, Wilson – I doubt he is!"

"I think I know what you're thinking."

"Just brainstorming. Mike over at the bar heard him talking about voodoo and needing state-of-the-art video and recording equipment. I have a feeling they went to the 'site' last night."

"That wouldn't have been very smart."

"No shit! Maybe that's why he's probably not going to be in his room. But I hope he is."

"How would they get inside the site area? That place is guarded!"

"Let's get over to the hotel. If he's there or spent the night, I doubt they went there. But if they did – Mr. London and Ms. Shields probably won't be coming back!"

"You know what I've been saying about that graveyard."

"Yeah, Wilson, I know."

Price and Wilson walked into the lobby of the Quality Inn on Bay Street. "Young lady, I'm Sheriff Price, and this is Sergeant Wilson. We have a warrant to search the room of one your guests."

"Oh," she said nervously, seeing their uniforms. "I'll call the manager."

"Yeah, and have him bring the head of housekeeping."

"Yes, sir."

A short bald-headed man along with a woman in her hotel uniform walked into the lobby. "I'm the manager. Are you Sheriff Price?"

"I am," he said, shaking his hand. "Is Ross London in his room?"

The manager looked at the receptionist and said, "Buzz Mr. London's room."

"No answer," she said.

"Alright," Price said. "Let's check his room. I need to know if he slept here last night."

The housekeeping manager opened the door, and they walked in. She looked around, patted the bed, and walked into the bathroom. The sanitary strip was still on the commode. "We cleaned this room after he left yesterday morning. It doesn't look like anyone spent last night in here," she said. "Unless he slept on the floor!"

"Alright, folks." Price smiled. "I appreciate your cooperation. If or when Mr. London comes back, contact the Sheriff's Department immediately."

"What's this about?" the bald-headed manager asked.

"Well, sir, just doing an investigation."

"What's going on?"

"We're not at the liberty to discuss it," Wilson spoke up. "Just let us know if he shows up."

"That's right. Call the department if you see him," Price said.

"Well, Bill," Wilson said as they got into the car, "where do you think Mr. London is?"

"You know where he is," Price answered.

"Are you saying they ran into trouble over at the 'site'?"

"What do you think, Wilson?" he asked, begging for a good answer;

"I'm sure they did – that is if they went there."

"You know they did!" Price stated wryly.

"They went there; didn't they?"

Price nodded his head yes.

"They're not still there, are they?"

Price shook his head no.

"What now?"

The light changed to green, and instead of turning left toward the office, he turned right, heading to the Beaufort River bridge. "Guess where we're goin'."

"I guess to the 'site,'" Wilson grimaced.

"You guessed right! Maybe we'll find some clues, but I doubt it. If we find any, we'll take back some control and trace samples to be analyzed. Hey, look how many people have vanished at this crater. I have a job to do."

"I guess. But just what are we looking for?" he asked curiously "The scientists are collecting samples."

"I want my own samples."

"I guess you know what you're doing."

"I want to get a little closer to that crater!"

"I don't know about that!"

"Yeah, just enough to be safe, but close enough to see what it is."

"This might be time to say a long prayer!"

***

"Jennie, you sure are working hard on that saw. Looks good!"

"Yeah, I believe it'll do. I just gotta keep the string tight."

"Shhhh, I hear footsteps," Lisa whispered. "I thinks he's about to come in."

Jennie nodded yes as she slid the saw under her pillow and quickly plugged the hole in the wall with some torn blanket.

He entered, carrying peanut butter sandwiches, a bag of potato chips and a large plastic bottle of Pepsi.

"Thanks," Jennie said and then mocked. "What would we do without our knight in shining black!"

He ignored her sassy, snide remark; and stared at her for several moments before putting their food and drink down.

"Have you got something you want to say, Masked Man?" Jenny asked him in a cocky manner. She appeared to be on thin ice.

He said nothing.

Chapter 14

"DAMN!" The sheriff shouted. "THE swing bridge is open. AND look, Wilson, it's just a little dinghy coming out of the sound!"

"It's going to take forever!"

"Maybe the wait will let me calm down before visiting our beloved 'site.' Yeah, everyone asks me what I'm doing about that place. Hell! That place is doing me!"

"I'm not sure what anybody can do," Wilson said.

"Look! That boat ain't doing a knot, and cars are backed up behind us all the way up Cartteret."

"I know. It only happens when you're in a hurry!"

"You want to know why I'm in a hurry to get there?"

"I think I know."

"Oh yeah, why?"

"You want to find out why no one can explain all this shit! I don't blame you – all these scientists are just walking around speculating and not coming up with answers."

"Um, No. I want to get there before I chicken out!"

"Yep."

"Let's see." Price wiped sweat from his face. "Two tipper trucks, two county-owned patrol cars, an SUV, and a turned-over pickup with no one in them!"

"And nobody there has a clue?"

"No! Experts spending taxpayers' money for days can't tell whether that damn hole is caused by an earthquake or not."

"I know."

"Wilson, we've talked about this. Do you really believe that graveyard is haunted?"

"Yep!"

"Why? Tell me again. I'm trying to make factual sense out of all this. I just can't tell all the people in Beaufort County that spooks out of a graveyard are killing people and tearing up a big tract of land without proof! They'd remove me from office!"

"The grading company got too close and scraped up some headstones that the survey didn't show. Spirits of the dead want revenge," he said.

"On who?"

"The owner – and maybe – anybody else who's curious."

"What about all these experts there? Why wouldn't they have a problem with all these so-called spirits?" He stopped. "I'm talking crazy! The bridge is closing, and we're going there and find out everything our stupid-ass minds can. Fuck those scientists! I'll find out what's caused all this. I believe Sherburtt blew it up – somehow!"

"I don't know about that."

Price and Wilson arrived at the 'site' at midafternoon. Onlookers lined the road, taking pictures. The news media were there jabbering in microphones. Scientists walked around talking in their small recorders or waving clipboards at others.

"Here we are," Price said as he parked his car at the edge of the taped-off area next to a news van. "Good to see such a fine turnout!"

"Well," Wilson commented, "at least everyone is behind the yellow tape."

"Yeah, and there's no hot dog stand that I can see. Now that would piss me off. And look at all these fine scientists with their fingers up their ass. God, this is great. Just great."

Wilson forced a chuckle masking his fear. "I don't have a real good feeling about all this. What are we goin' to do?"

"Walk over to that crater!"

"Come on, Bill. We better study on that!"

"Oh yeah, I don't think we have a choice. I think it's a death trap."

"I know it is," Wilson quickly agreed. "You really want to get close to it?"

"I'm going. If you don't want to, then stay here."

"You know I can't let you go alone."

"What's that?" Price looked up at the sky.

"What's what?"

"The sky is clear all over the county except for here. I see only black and gray clouds overhead."

155

"Haven't had rain in a week. 'bout time for a storm. You reckon?"

"But why just here?"

"Don't know. But look, Bill." He pointed to the dark mass overhead. "It doesn't move."

"No wind."

"I don't like it."

"Well, come on," Price said as they headed to the crater – or a sinkhole or an earthquake or?

A man wearing a VIP badge rushed up to them panting. "Sheriff, I'm a seismologist, and I need to warn you not to get any closer. You are really headed toward harm's way!"

"Sir, we have to get as close as we can. We need to check out that sink hole. It's our job."

"Sinkhole!" he blurted loudly. "It isn't a sinkhole!"

Price looked at him and asked impatiently, "Well what is it? An opening to Hell!?"

"Look Sheriff. I'm a scientist trained on these matters. You're making a bad mistake if you get too close to the crater. I promise. I'm a realist."

"A realist!" Price laughed. "Well then, you tell us what's real here. No one else can. I have too many people that I personally believe died here, and it's my job to find out why."

"We're all afraid of it now!"

"Oh really. Will you start telling me in layman's terms just what you know? Can you do that?"

"I'll take you to the safest place, and you'll see what we're dealing with. Yes, it was reported as a large and growing sinkhole that has now turned into approximately a one-acre lake. A lake of hot, dirty water with steam emerging. Step around these trees and you'll see it."

"Alright," Price said. "I'm sorry but I didn't catch your name."

"Dr. Nelson. John Nelson."

"And I guess you're a seismologist. Where are you from, by the way?"

"Oregon."

"You're a long way from home, Doctor."

"That I am, Sheriff. Now this as far as we can go without sinking. It's bad. Right?"

Price and Wilson stood petrified and speechless, their jaws hanging as they stared at a huge body of water making steam and bubbles. The hot lake began emitting loud and violent screeches. They stood in frozen awe until the scientist, John Nelson, spoke.

"Sheriff, can I say what some others are saying?"

Price nodded his head yes, his face becoming ashen.

"This is a scientifically explainable occurrence that has yet to be explained but somehow will be explained. Like I said, I'm a realist." He stopped and then continued, "I don't know!"

"Jesus Christ!" Price spouted to Wilson. "Is he talkin' shit or do they call that double talk?"

Wilson looked at Price, ignoring the question, and spoke flatly. "This place is haunted. We're standing at the edge of Hell. Let's get out of here, Sheriff!"

The scientist looked at the sheriff with eyes full of terror. "Sheriff, he might be right! Ten minutes ago, it wasn't this bad! We better leave now!" He was almost petrified. "This is too unbelievable! This can't be explained. I'm in total shock!"

"Back away. Everybody, let's back away!" Price demanded.

"I don't understand!" the scientist cried out. "I don't know what it is or what's causing it!"

"It's the work of the devil!" Wilson blurted out.

Price caught his breath and said, "I think the rest of your crew coming down from Oregon, Washington, and wherever else – is in for a serious, rude awakening."

"I'm not sure any of this property will still be here when they arrive," the scientist added.

"I'm not sure Lady's Island will be here much longer!" Price shouted. "We have to all get out of here now before we fall through the ground. 'Come on, let's go!'"

"Look!" Wilson screamed, pointing at the ghastly lake. "I saw a skeleton jump from the water and swim back under."

"The hell you say!" Price shouted disbelievingly. "You saw what???"

Two skeletons came to the surface, looking at the three men, and started climbing out. They were glowing a bright scary yellow and hissing like mad cats.

"Back up!" Wilson shouted. "BACK far away! HELL – RUN!"

The scientist RAN away like a rabbit. Price FROZE in his tracks. Wilson SCREAMED out in terror, "I've seen enough horror movies in my life, but I ain't ever seen nothing like this! Bill – Did I see skeletons come alive? I swear I did – I TOLD YOU!"

"They're swimming around in that hellhole," Price said, pulling out his Glock and firing nine-millimeter rounds at them. "Those goddamn graders dug up their graves."

"Hey!" Wilson shouted, "Bill, get back! PLEASE! Have you lost your mind? Come on!"

The high sheriff put his pistol back in the holster and began running, hoping to catch up with his sergeant.

As Price and Wilson began approaching the crowds, they walked slowly so as not to draw attention.

"God, what are we goin' to do? Did we really see that?"

"Yeah, Wilson, we did. I hope it's some insane fool's joke! It ain't funny!"

"What now?"

"I'm goin' to pretend I didn't see what I saw."

"Hell, I saw it! You believe me now?"

"Alright, Wilson." He looked at his chief deputy with a disturbed face and calmly said, "Here's what we're goin' to do. We're goin' to get everyone off this land. Can you call the office and have a mayday alert put out – and get some of our boys down here."

"I can but is that a good idea?" Wilson asked, still panting heavily.

"What do you mean?"

"I don't think anyone needs to come here."

"This place has to be cleared out, so what do you suggest?"

"I don't know!"

"I want eighty percent of our force down here now, and hopefully run everyone off. Call our chief of police and get his ass in gear. Hell – what else can we possibly do?"

"We've been blindsided!"

"An understatement!"

"You think I should get the office to call Parris Island and have troops sent here?"

"No!"

"What about the air base?"

"Noooo!"

"You want me to call Betty?"

"Yeah, but don't tell her what we saw. Just tell her that this place is a hell of a lot worse than we thought."

"Alright, people!" Price shouted at the crowd. "We got to ask you all to leave."

A reporter ran up to them. "What is it, Sheriff?"

"I'm goin' to order you and all news people and vans to move to the main road. As of this moment, this place is off limits to everyone!"

"Can you tell us why?"

"That disturbance down at the other end is extremely dangerous, and no one is safe here. I have nothing else I can say. So please inform your people to leave – and do it in an orderly way!"

Price and Wilson sped away from the 'site,' seeing a flood of police cars approaching.

"Well, you saw it!" Wilson exclaimed.

"Yeah! Mayhem has come!"

"Are these creatures going to climb out of that lake?" Wilson wondered out loud.

"Hell! I don't know what them crazy fuckers are gonna do! I think they can do whatever they want; that is they're real." Bill stopped, looked at Wilson. "They're real."

"You know if people knew – this whole country would be in a panic!"

"Just a matter of time! They'll know real soon." Price banged his hands on the steering wheel. "We can't tell anyone about Gullah spirits coming out of a graveyard that is now a large lake of horror! My stomach is in knots, and my hands are shaking. If I hadn't seen it for myself, and someone told me this, I would think they needed to be committed. But I saw it! It's starting to hit me bad! I can't close my eyes without seeing those skeletons. You know what, Wilson?"

"What?"

"I hope and pray that the Riley twins aren't down in that hell! I hope Sherburtt has them and they'll turn up soon."

"Bill, I'm surprised that you're able to think about those girls after what we just saw. I'm in a state of panic!"

"Right now, I don't know what I'm thinking!"

159

"I know! It's called SHOCK!"

"I'm thinking movie people will be down here, and there's going to be a lot of publicity happening – a lot more than we've seen so far."

"Hadn't thought of that. You're probably right. But I ain't sure this place will be here for them to come to! Damn!" Wilson spouted in fright. "I'll never sleep at night again!"

Price's phone rang, not the radio, and he answered. It was Betty.

"Bill," she said.

"Yeah, Betty."

"Bill, a trawler coming up the Coosaw spotted a red car bogged down in the marsh not far from the 'site.' The captain said you can get to it by Marsh View Road. I'm sending two cars over there."

"I guess we'll go by there. Call a wrecker."

"Okay. And it's a red car. It might be the one those young men had who took the Riley girls, you think?"

"I don't know. Might be."

They turned on the sand road and saw two of their cars parked near the wet bog.

"Damn it, Wilson. I don't think we need too much more excitement!"

They stopped at the edge of the wet marsh and saw the top of the car with black muck caked on it. If it hadn't been for the reflection of the sun, it probably would have gone unnoticed.

The wrecker arrived, and the red car was pulled from the bog to the sand road. No one was in it. Price slowly walked around the car, shining his flashlight on the muddy windows.

"Someone get the keys out of the ignition and open the trunk," he ordered.

They approached the trunk as a deputy was opening it. A strong, sickening stench filled the air. Two dead men lay across each other, covered in blood and black muck.

"Jesus!" Price shouted.

"Sheriff," Wilson said, "these might be the men who picked up those twins."

"I believe they are! Someone slit their throats!"

"I'll radio the coroner."

"Yeah."

Price looked at the deputies. "You boys see if you can get their driver's licenses and any other identification."

"And tape this area off," Wilson shouted. "And take photos."

"Should I tow it in?" the driver of the wrecker asked Price.

"Not yet."

"What do you make of this?" Wilson asked, astonished.

"Two dead men in a trunk," Price answered flatly.

Later that afternoon, Price looked up from his desk at Betty as she handed him some reports. "From the coroner's office," she said.

He opened them, called the coroner, and left to meet with him and the M.E.

"They look mighty young," the coroner said, observing the photos. "They definitely match their pictures on their driver's licenses. I'm still studying them, and I have observed the bodies."

"Throats were slit," Bill commented.

"Yeah, they were," he said, scratching his head. "Clean wide cuts."

"With a knife?" Price asked. "Died quick, didn't they?"

"They were killed with a machete," The medical examiner said factly.

"Machete! Who in the hell from around here would use a machete?" Price was dumbfounded.

"Maybe whoever did this wasn't from here."

"Yeah, maybe – whatever – shit."

"It's obvious it was done quick and sudden. Not much sadness on their faces. Surprised shock is more like it. Who would do this? Do you know who these men are?"

"I think they're the boys that kidnapped the Riley twins, but I can't understand why they were murdered with a machete and placed in a trunk." Price stopped to think. "I don't think those girls are hurt, and I don't think they visited the 'site.' If I had to guess, just going by past experience, someone hired those guys to do a dirty deed, and didn't plan on paying them."

"How come you think the girls weren't hurt?" Wilson spoke up.

"It just looks to me that someone wants something bad and those girls are their key. I thought earlier it was highly possible that they were at the wrong place at the wrong time, The men saw an opportunity to have some fun and took them off only to rape and kill them. Now seeing those boys with their necks slit, someone had a complicated plan to kidnap these girls."

"It could be a drug deal gone bad?" Wilson posed.

"I don't think so. I'm going to do a hell of a background check on these men."

"You really think they had those twin girls?"

"I think they took them to someone and he or she is holding them for money or information. I believe it's information. Maybe leading to the site. I've got two problems. One is why would someone used these guys and then kill 'em with a machete. A damn gun seems more logical. And the second problem is where are the girls?"

"Well, Sheriff, here are their licenses and ID," the coroner interrupted. "I'll send over the photos of their bodies in a half hour."

Price put their driver's licenses carefully in a baggie for trace evidence and left.

Back in his office, he was studying the reports and the identifications when Wilson walked in. "Got some information on those boys, Bill."

"Let's hear it."

"They're from Savannah and had been in jail for eight months in Reidville for larceny. They're low-life hustlers."

"What else?"

"Went to work at the Toyota distributorship here but got fired two days later."

"Guess what?"

"What?" Wilson asked.

"I'm going right back to the Iron Mike with enlarged photos of these scoundrels and put them on his notice board. Someone has to know them."

"You want me to go with you?"

"No, you make sure the damn site is secured."

"You don't want the scientists on the hallowed ground!"

"Hell no! Make sure our boys keep them off. Clear that place out – and see if you can arrange a helicopter to hover over that hellhole. But make sure they don't hover too close!"

"Got it."

"Bill," Wilson said, "how did those boys get two supposedly nice girls to leave with them?"

"Fed them a bunch of bullshit."

"Now you think someone paid them to steal the Riley twins?"

"I think so. I always had a feeling they didn't act alone."

"Mr. Sherburtt?"

"Wilson, according to Riley, Sherburtt paid cash for that property."

"That's right. He mentioned that."

"Where did he get two million dollars?"

"I guess he's rich. I don't know."

"There's no mortgage on that land. He just happened to have that much money laying around? Let's say he does – real estate investors don't use their own cash. They either borrow or use other people's money."

"I reckon he could have used his own," Wilson shrugged his shoulders.

"I doubt it! Now I can see him seeing a huge profit on that land but couldn't get the financing. But he got someone to put up the money. And that someone wants it back!"

"Two million dollars is a lot of money – especially if you got it from the wrong group of people. Ain't that right?"

"Hell yeah, if that's the case. I don't know if he's involved, but let's just say he is. Alright. So why would he kidnap them and not demand a ransom. He would need the money, wouldn't he?" Wilson asked.

"Yeah. He would need the money. Especially since the land is now worthless. And I guarantee that whoever loaned him the money wants it back."

"Wait a minute, Bill. If what you say is true – the FBI could find out how he paid for it. They'd check all his records and assets and whatever. He'd be up to his ass in gators!"

"Exactly, but that's our FBI boy's job," Price said.

"Question. What do the girls have to do with it? If Sherburtt lost his money, how will he pay that so called debt back? He never actually asked Riley for money?"

"No, he didn't. I hate to say this, but he could have arranged to sell the Riley twins to cover his debt."

"What!"

"If Sherburtt owes that much money to the wrong people – he's liable to do anything to save his own neck."

"Are you implying that he might be offering those girls as sex slaves!"

"Possibly. And if so, they're still alive and unharmed. But damn – how did he do it with so little time to arrange and execute such a plan. Unless he's a miracle worker, it would be virtually impossible."

"What if those girls have already been sold and shipped off?"

"I don't want to think that! But I'm going to tell Mr. Stewart with the FBI about this; and that time is of the essence. I know one thing, Wilson, money makes tracks and so do dead bodies! Yeah, I have to leave this kidnapping mystery to them and hope they act fast. I mean fast!"

"What about the site?"

"I'm putting that out of my mind for now."

"How?"

"Well," Price looked at him, "I don't know, but I'm going to the Iron Mike with photos, and I want you to go to the Toyota place and do the same. And, Wilson, find out why they were fired and if they were associating with any suspicious people. Also run a check on those plates. I want to know who owns that car. That car might be the key to a lot more than we know. Now I have to call the FBI agent."

"Alright, I'll do that." He brushed one side of his hair. "Bill, changing the subject, you've heard of that Sheriff that claimed to be a witch doctor, years back?"

"Yeah, Wilson. Hadn't thought about him in a long time. What are you trying to get at?"

"He was Sheriff of Beaufort that believed in voodoo and black magic; claiming he could solve cases with it. I think we should find someone like him to talk to; and maybe get answers to this problem. Someone who really knows about this voodoo magic. Have you given any thought to that?"

"No, but what I saw today, I might."

"You saw it at work!"

"I saw the goddamn underworld of hell!"

"It might take magic, not scientists, to solve this problem."

"Yeah!"

"Yep!"

"You go talk to Toyota, and I'll talk with Mike. After that, we'll explore this voodoo – but this is between you and me," Price stated resolutely. "There's no way we can let anyone experience what can come out of that crater. I mean it."

"I understand."

"And when you visit that Toyota lot, find out if Mr. Sherburtt had any dealings, conversations, and whatever with those boys." Price stopped, then stated with frustration, "You know more about voodoo than me. You find someone we can talk to. But let's get these matters out of the way first," he said, overwhelmed, balling up a sheet of paper and throwing it in the trash can. "Let's go and try to be back around four o'clock. This day is not done."

"Betty," he yelled.

"Yes, Sheriff?"

"Get Agent Stewart on the phone for me."

"Aright."

"And, Wilson, let's go into the conference room and talk before we make our investigative visits," he said and then hollowed to Betty. "Hold that call to Stewart. I'll call him later."

They sat down across from each other, and Price hesitated, then furrowed his brow. "I try to be a reasonable and understanding man and I can see both sides of a coin. I've lived here most of my life and heard all the legends and beliefs of the Gulla Geechies and never believed in their magic or ghosts. All this voodoo stuff is too overwhelming – but I witnessed horrifying events that are just plain too much for me. My bones are turning to ice! You asked me earlier to investigate and understand voodoo magic."

"I don't think you have a choice."

"No, but what do I do?"

"You know that land is cursed!" Wilson stated. "I have read about voodoo magic and talked with a lot of Gullahs who believe in it. Voodoo magic might be considered folklore and superstition, but it's been going on for centuries – and before then."

"But what do I do?"

"II think we need to talk to someone who knows about this kind of stuff a lot more than me. Someone credible!"

"Then find someone who is credible, and we'll meet with him as soon as possible. Can you do that?"

"I'll work on it when I get back."

"Good. Now I'm headed back over to see Mike."

***

"Hey," Price said, walking into Mike's place.

Mike looked at him. "Back again, Sheriff?"

"Take a look at these photos," he rushed, handing them to Mike. "Recognize those men?"

"That's the guys who left with those girls."

"Thought so. Their vehicle was bogged down in the marsh, and they were found dead and stuffed in the trunk – with their throats slit."

"God Almighty!"

"Put these posters up and make sure that if anybody – and I mean anybody – knows them, to contact my office."

"I sure will!"

"I'm leaving – and Mike, you stay in touch with me."

"I will."

There was about an hour of sunlight left when Wilson came back to the office.

"What did you find out?" Price asked.

"Nothing. Just two deadbeat lazy boys who couldn't sell cars."

"No one suspicious?"

"The sales manager said he didn't notice anything except that they just didn't do anything. Didn't sell one car between the both of them."

"Worthless – and now they're dead. I'm starting to believe something, Wilson."

"What?"

"I'm not sure I suspect Mr. Sherburtt anymore."

"Um, who then?"

"Someone who knows a lot about that hellhole. I don't know. but we never got to find out." Price's curiosity was lighting a fire. "By the way, who's the owner of that car?"

"Ross Hawthorn. One of the men."

"Just my luck. I hoped it would be someone else."

"Bill, I called Dr. Chris McLeod at USCB. He's a history professor but also teaches cultural anthropology. He knows about Gullah voodoo."

"Really?"

"Yep. I think he can enlighten us."

"You didn't tell him what we saw?"

"No, but he might just fly off his saddle if we do!" Wilson gave an excited grin.

"When can we talk to this man?"

"Seven o'clock – in his office."

"I'm game."

A waiter at the Coosaw restaurant looked out a window. "Preston," he said. "Yeah?"

"That white Toyota SUV has been here since last night. You want me to have it towed?"

"Naw, he's a friend of mine. That's Ross London's 4Runner. He'll come back for it."

***

Jennie's saw was hidden under her blanket when the masked man walked in with another bottle of Pepsi and a bag of potato chips.

"Hey, Masked Man, did you bring us anything else? We were expecting something nice and special," Jenny laughed.

He ignored her and picked up their metal pots as he laid down clean ones.

"Wow! Thanks a bunch. Lisa and I just love those beautiful crappers!" She got brave again.

With no sound or expression, he walked out.

"Jennie, quit messin' with him!"

***

Price and Wilson sat in Dr. Chris McLeod's office at the University of South Carolina Beaufort.

"Sheriff, you got you a good man working for you. I've known him a long time. In fact, he got his criminal justice degree here," he said.

"Oh, yeah?" Price quipped.

Wilson looked at him, surprised.

"Yeah, Professor…he's a good man…couldn't do without him."

"Well, gentlemen, what do we need to talk about?" McLeod was curious.

"Voodoo," Price said.

"Alright. That's an interesting subject. Voodoo is a broad religious belief. What came from Haiti might not be the same as some other versions of this belief such as those from Madagascar."

"Excuse me, Dr. McLeod. I guess I want to know what you believe and what you know from the people here in Beaufort County." Price hastily interrupted him.

"Well, I must say, not bragging; I'm a scholar when it comes to old beliefs. I believe in voodoo because it's been around for a long, long time. Even though the Gullahs are adapting to the modern ways – some haven't let go."

"No?"

"Well, it's fading, but black magic is believed by many – you know that!"

"Normal sane people don't believe in it," Price paused. "Seriously, is it truly real?"

"Of course, it is." McLeod shook his head affirmatively.

"So you accept the fact that it's possible to place spells, curses, or whatever through magic?"

"Magic?" Dr. McLeod raised his eyebrows. "Was Jesus's turning water into wine magic? Did a god make the world in six days? Did Noah place two of every animal on the earth on the ark and float for one hundred and fifty days?"

"But what's the point?" Price asked, slightly confused.

Wilson interrupted. "Bill, I think the point he's making is that Christians are expected to believe that those events really happened. And we aren't considered superstitious believing them. Maybe without knowing it, we're believing in a sort of magic too."

"Okay," Price nodded. "I see the point. Now, tell me, how powerful can this voodoo be?"

McLeod rose from his chair and stood in front of his desk. "That's a good question. Not everyone is vulnerable or subject to its power. I believe the more vulnerable you are to the supernatural, the more powerful the force is. And I believe only a small percentage of us are. It's never been proven there are ghosts or anything supernatural. It's a pseudo-scientific belief from hypothetical and some theoretical conclusions. It's not fact. It's abstract."

"But you believe in it and consider it factual?"

"Yes, I do," Dr. McLeod replied resolutely and honestly.

"Have you experienced the supernatural?"

"I have."

Price looked at Wilson suggestively and nodded. "Wilson, tell Dr. McLeod what we saw."

It was almost eight PM when Price and Wilson finished relaying their experience along with all else that had happened at the 'site' to the professor. Though all ears, he was shocked but sincerely believed what they were saying. He was more concerned in solving the problem instead of reacting in surprised amazement! He appeared to be a self-assured, confident man around sixty years old. Casually dressed, he showed a sincere demeanor with a well-rounded, friendly attitude that Price liked.

"This is unbelievable!" He rose from his chair. With his arms folded at his chest, he walked to the window and gazed out over the campus grounds. "But I believe it."

"Professor," Price said, "when we saw it, there was a scientist with us who knew about it. Why is it that no one else knew?"

"They weren't vulnerable to the force."

Bill scratched his head. "Then what should we do?"

"You get a root doctor from St. Helena to put a stop to it!"

Price looked at Wilson and said sarcastically, "Well, Wilson, go get us a root doctor and hurry back."

"I'm serious, Sheriff," the professor stated, obviously affronted.

"I know. I meant no offense," apologizing for his callous remark. "I'm trying to convince myself that it's not real – hoping it's a cruel joke. But I have to come to grips that I witnessed frightening, supernatural forces at work. So how do I fix it?"

"I guess it won't be that easy. I'm trying to come to a solution. Maybe have the graveyard resurveyed and get the owner to sell it to the Gullah Society here in Beaufort. Then the restless souls of the dead can lie in peace."

Price rubbed his face, thinking hard, then commented. "As crazy as it sounds, that might not be a bad idea."

"He's got a good point," Wilson jumped in and said, "That oughta work."

"Well, unfortunately that graveyard is part of Sherburtt's property. He would have to agree to sell or give it away. I don't think he'll give it away, and after talking with this man, among other things I know, I find him to be awfully shrewd, cunningly smart, extremely greedy and would ask a fortune for it. Especially when he thinks he's holding the key for everyone's future safety."

"I think if he no longer owns that graveyard then you won't see any more spirit activity!" the professor stated firmly, not offering a solution to the foreseeable problem.

"Um, Bill, what surveyor is going to be willing to mark off Hell?" Wilson volunteered a probable snag.

"You haven't seen hell yet!" the professor spouted. "But you just might if you don't get it deeded back!"

"Professor," Wilson spoke, "That might not work. They don't think like us 'cause they're spirits! I believe they've seen a higher plane somewhere outside our universe. In other words, the graveyard might not be what they want…?"

"How do you know they have seen a higher plane?" The professor smiled at Wilson. "Their souls could be trapped, and they can't progress into the knowledge of the universe, or should I say 'salvation'?"

"Well then, what were they doing all that time under their graves when it was normal?" Wilson asked.

"Good question. I don't know for sure; but obviously some haven't left."

"Maybe souls don't automatically float up to heaven when they die," Price joined in. "I think getting that graveyard away from Sherburtt is a good idea. We're going to force him to deed it back to the original owner, Ms. Watson."

"And have a root doctor put a blessing, not a curse, on it. Then the land should change back and be as it was," the professor added.

"Bill," Wilson asked, "who is goin' over to that lake of fire to survey it off?"

"Gentlemen," the professor suggested, "get that land back to the ORIGINAL owner, and it should calm down! It's your only option. But if he won't give it up?"

"Eminent domain!" Price jumped up and yelled. "Yeah! The county will have to get it back and give it to the old woman through the process of Eminent domain! Damn that's the answer!"

The three men looked at each other in agreement.

"Wilson, come by my house a little later, OK? We'll sit on my porch and drink a beer or two," Price insisted. "And Professor, thanks for everything you've shared with us – but keep all this under your hat!"

"Of course. And good luck – you're going to need it!"

They sat on the back porch of Bill's small house looking out over the Beaufort River.

"I like sitting out here in the evening gazing at the river. It always calms me," Bill said, drinking a beer. "But I'm not calm."

"Yep, I know," Wilson was quick to agree.

"Are you calm, Wilson?"

"Right now…I'm tryin' to be."

"I'm looking at the river and damn it! All I see are skeletons coming out!"

"You need some sleep, tonight."

"Hell, you saw them! How am I gonna sleep?"

"Yep, I saw them. I'm just as shaken as you. I just wonder if that scientist saw them. You know, Dr. Nelson."

"I don't know, but if he did, he's not talking to his little group about it."

"You're right. He probably ain't."

"I know one thing, we're not the only ones that experienced that shit…we're just the only ones alive who 'can' talk about it. But I don't want to talk about it – I want to forget it. But how?"

"I know what you mean."

"I think I'll get another beer. Want one?"

"Thanks – I'll drink one more. You know as I stare out at the river, I remember, as a young boy, an old black man that walked up and down Bay Street," Wilson paused, appearing deep in thought.

"What about him?"

He would sing a little song that went: *I wakes to de mornin' dew, glad me not in Chuck Town and me house be painted blue.*

Chapter 15

Steve came out of the kitchen early the next morning holding two cups of coffee, one for himself and the other for Kelly, and he was still wearing the necklace. "Here Kelly – I brought you a cup of coffee."

"Thank you," she said, yawning.

"How do you feel?"

"I feel good." Kelly smiled, crawling out of bed. "I see you're still wearing that chain."

"It keeps me happy."

"Well, good," she sounded flippant.

"I feel like calling Johnny!"

"Are you crazy?"

"No."

"Why in God's name would you call Johnny?" she asked as her eyes became clear and piercing.

"I want to know how he's feeling."

She just looked at him. Reality was wanting to bite.

He dialed Johnny's office, and his assistant told him that he was in the hospital. She said Johnny had dialed 911 and was rushed to the emergency room. Steve hung up the phone and stared at Kelly.

"What?" Kelly asked. "Was he not there?"

"He's in the hospital."

"Why?" she asked despondently.

"His assistant gave me his room number. I guess I'll call him."

"What's wrong with him?"

"Don't know. It must be serious since he called 911."

"Call back, and find out before you call him."

"I'll just call him."

"No!" she insisted. "Call his office and find out what that hussy assistant of his knows!"

"Sherburtt Developers," the young voice answered.

"Yeah, it's me again. Is Johnny all right?"

"Don't know. They think he might have had a stroke."

"I'm sorry to hear that," he lied, as his mind screamed victory. "What else did they say?"

"He's under close watch," she said. "He was in ICU. They told me he has lesions on his body like small burns. Go ahead…give him a call."

"Alright, bye," he said, then hung up.

"What did she say?" Kelly asked.

"Maybe a stroke."

"Oh really," she simply replied.

"I guess I'll call him," he said flippantly.

She shook her head, confused and frustrated.

"Hello," a weak voice answered.

"Johnny, this is Steve…"

"Uh, hey."

"What happened?" Steve asked, anxious to find out if the hex was working.

"I'm in the fucking hospital! They think I had a stroke," Johnny snorted.

"Hate to hear that," he lied.

"Yeah, I'm in bad shape. I feel like shit!"

"Yeah, your assistant said you called 911 yesterday morning."

"I fell in my den. I don't remember too much except being in the emergency room. I was real sick! They got a bunch of damn wires hooked up to me."

"Oh yeah?" Steve grinned wide.

"Look, Steve, I don't feel like talking."

"I do!"

"What do you want?" he grumbled. "I don't feel good."

"Do you remember threatening me?" Steve asked.

"I don't need this." Johnny moaned. "I'm not well."

"Too bad! I've got a real problem with you! You had a problem with me, so now we need to talk," Steve said rushing to the main problem – HIS GIRLS!

"I don't feel like talking."

"Well, before you hang up, I need to discuss a few things."

"What?" he asked him.

"I had nothing to do with your property after you bought it. You threatened me, and I think you kidnapped my daughters."

"Huh? Do what!?" he sounded surprised.

"My daughters have been missing since Saturday night, and I think you either have them or know where they are. You're a real son of a bitch, but I didn't think you could stoop that low!"

"What the hell are you saying? You're not making sense."

"Where are my girls, Johnny?" Steve demanded.

"I know nothing about your girls. Have you been drinking?"

"You better tell me where they are, and they better be all right!" Steve shouted.

"You hold on!" He rattled off. "I have no idea what you're talkin' about. Why would I know where your girls are? I doubt I've even seen them in a year."

Steve looked at his wife, his Irish face was turning red.

"I said, I don't know," Johnny reiterated. "What happened to your daughters?"

"Hey, you got mad as hell at me when you saw your property caving in. You told me to get your money back, or else!"

"I was mad."

"Look, asshole, you better tell me where our girls are."

"How many times do I have to tell you? I don't know."

"I don't get it!"

"Alright," Johnny spoke calmly. "I was upset and reacted pretty bad. I was beside myself, and I knew it wasn't your fault, but I just exploded. I couldn't help it. I turned into a madman. I'm sorry for that but I don't know anything about Jennie and Lisa. I hate hearing that! Have you called the police?"

"What?" Steve asked, trying not to believe that he might be telling the truth!

"I wouldn't do anything to hurt your girls. You know that," he pleaded. "I'm sorry for everything I said, but I swear, this is news to me."

"You want me to know that you have them, but without me being able to prove it! You've figured I would raise two million dollars – give it to you – then miraculously, Jennie and Lisa would show up!"

"What!? That's ridiculous! That don't make any sense! I don't know what happened to your daughters. I told you that something came over me when I saw my property in ruins. I don't know, but I became a different person! And

174

I don't know why. There ain't no way I could do what you just said – even if I wanted to."

Steve was silent. Was it possible Johnny was under a spell? Maybe – but maybe not.

"I care about you and your family, Steve."

"Don't spoon-feed me shit out of a Dixie cup!" He said, still pissed but confused.

"I'm not."

"You don't care about me, or my family. You just care about yourself!"

"Yeah, I'm selfish. But come on now – I couldn't hurt you, or your family. I'm sorry about the way I've acted; but I couldn't control myself. I really am sorry, Steve."

"You're sick! You feel helpless," Steve said, waiting to see if he's getting sicker.

"I was under some spell!"

"I'll call you back," Steve said.

"Why don't you tell me what's goin' on. I have no clue. Tell me more about what happened. You say they've been kidnapped? I can't believe you would think I took them! But – I can't believe I turned into a raging lunatic. Someone else is behind this mess. Why?"

Steve ended the call and put his hand on Kelly's shoulder. "I'm confused. I don't think he has them."

"You don't believe him, do you?" she asked.

"I think I do."

"He's lying, Steve!" she sparked.

"No, I don't think so," he muttered sadly, plopping down on the sofa.

"I'm telling you, he's lying. He's going to prison damn it!"

"Ow!" he screamed, jumping from the sofa.

"What's wrong?" Kelly asked him, startled.

"Shit!" he yelled, feeling the amulet burning his chest. "Look!"

"Steve! Your chain's turning red! Take it off!"

He ran to the kitchen, ripped his chain off, and flung it in the sink.

Kelly came running in and saw it lying in the drain, sizzling.

"It's on fire! That blue stone is a red-hot ember!" she screamed. "Oh my God! It burned a hole in your shirt, and it's all the way into your chest! Let me get some ice cubes. Go lie down on the sofa!"

Steve felt his chest burning while his stomach began to knot. The hex put on Johnny had backfired. But why?

"Steve! Are you all right? What in the hell is going on?"

"I don't know!"

"How did that stone turn red-hot? Did it have a battery in it?"

"No."

"Well, what caused it? Damn, look at your chest. You're burned to your ribs. I better call EMS."

"No, don't. I'll be alright. Get me some salve."

"Alright," She hurried to the bathroom and brought him some cream. "It doesn't look good."

"It'll be alright. I just need to rest. Kelly, I haven't told you everything." He looked at her, pitifully.

"This may be a good time to start," she said, rubbing ointment on his chest.

"Kelly, I visited a root doctor, and he put a curse on Johnny."

She looked at him and puffed a short laugh. "You did what?"

"I said that I saw root doctor and had him put a curse on Johnny. That's why he's in the hospital."

"I'm not in the mood for jokes! Now tell me what's really goin' on."

"He gave me that amulet to wear so that I would feel safe and happy while Johnny was getting a hex put on him."

"You have lost your freaking mind!" Kelly spouted as she quit rubbing his chest and stared into his eyes. "Excuse my French! Your fucking mind!"

"No, the root doctor told me that Johnny would get real ill and that would make him return Jennie and Lisa back to us."

Looking disgusted, she began pacing. "Are you asleep and talking to someone in a dream, or are you trying to talk to me?"

"I'm talking to you."

"A root doctor?"

"Yeah," Steve said. "I really did."

"How in the hell could you possibly do that? Are you stupid?"

"I don't know."

"Steve," was all she could say at the moment.

"I was told there was a man who lives on St. Helena who could work magic. He could get Johnny to release Jennie and Lisa. He assured me they were alright. So I g—"

"I guess you paid him money," she interrupted, disgusted. "How much?"

"Five hundred dollars."

"You said you went to a lawyer. You lied."

"I didn't think you would go for the idea."

"Sherlock! What would give you the idea that I wouldn't go for it? Hell, I'd give you another fifty so you could tip him good. What am I going to do with you?" she said mockingly. "This is ridiculous."

"He gave me a hex to put on Johnny and told me to wear that chain."

"Wait! You said you got that chain at a novelty shop."

"Do what? Did I tell you that?"

"Tell me the name of the store so I can call them."

"I got it from the root doctor."

"I'm completely confused, mad, scared and whatever – all at the same time."

"Look, I was skeptical at first, but when I met this man, I felt his powers, and I thought that getting Johnny sick would bring the twins back. I meant well."

"This is absolutely ridiculous." She rolled her eyes. "By the way, what is this witch doctor's name?"

"Dr. Blue."

"Dr. Blue!" She burst out laughing. "I don't know whether to laugh or cry."

Steve's face turned pale, and he ran to the bathroom. "I'm going to throw up!" A few minutes later, he came back and fell back down on the sofa. "I'm pretty sick."

"What's wrong besides a burned-up chest?"

"Not funny!"

"Well, what then?"

"Can you drive me to Dr. Blue's house?"

"I can call EMS."

"Please!" Steve begged.

"Steve, forget this Doctor Blue."

"I got to get him to take the curse off Johnny. And now it might be on me!"

"There is no curse on you or Johnny. You ate something bad that's making you sick. That's all."

"Please."

"Okay," Kelly said, throwing her hands up in the air. "Let's go see your witch doctor!"

"He's a root doctor."

"Whatever." She shook her head. "You need a Coke?"

"Yeah."

"Alright. I'll grab two out of the fridge, and we'll go."

"Thanks."

"We're not goin' to some spooky place, are we?" she asked, leaving the island.

"No, you'll like it."

"Oh, I bet I will!" she said sarcastically. "How far is it?"

"Not too far. Just over Johnson Creek."

"I'll stop at that little store and get gas. You need anything?"

"Cigarettes and a Budweiser."

"I thought you were sick," she stated.

"I am."

"'No cigarettes! No beer!'"

"One beer?" He coaxed. "Just one. I'm nervous."

"Nope." Kelly's tone was short.

"You mad?"

"Nope."

Suddenly, the front end of the Lexus dipped to the right with a flip-flop sound.

"Damn!" she blurted. "What happened?"

"Sounds like a flat tire. Stop. I'll get out and look." Steve said aggravated.

"Oh, that's all we need." She banged her hands against the steering wheel.

"It's a flat alright. I'll fix it, but don't feel like it," he remarked grumbling.

He fumbled the jack and wrench from the trunk and began loosening the lugs.

"Hey," Kelly shouted. "You know what you're doing?"

He ignored her.

"You need help?"

"No."

Ten minutes later, they were back on the road. She reached over and squeezed his hand. "I'm sorry I've been rough on you. Just tell me where to go."

"There's a road to the left once we pass the marina. It leads to his place."

"I want to see this Dr. Blue! This might be a thrill." She hesitated, "That is – if he's real."

"Hell, I hope he's home."

They drove right up to the little blue house and parked. A middle-aged black woman rushed out the front door and stood on the porch, looking at them suspiciously!

"Who's that?" Kelly asked. "She doesn't look too friendly."

"I don't know."

"What you folks doin' here?" the black woman hollered. "This is private property. What's yur bidness?"

Steve stepped from the car and said, "We came to see Dr. Blue."

"Yu what?" she shouted, offended, "Yu best be leavin'. There's no Dr. Blue here! Nawsuh!"

"I was here the other day and talked with him for hours."

"Nawsuh, yu didn't!"

"Ma'am, I'm sorry, but I was here. I met and talked with him."

"I'm sorry but you betta leave!"

"Please let us come up to the house. We mean no harm," Steve pleaded.

She looked at him and his pretty wife who was now getting out of the car reluctantly. "I say, what be your bidness?"

"Is he here?" Steve asked her. "The older man with a beard?"

"No I told yu!"

"Will Dr. Blue be back?"

"Dare ain't no Dr. Blue living here no mo. He passed away years ago. And buried in his grabe!"

"Come on, Steve. She doesn't want us here, so we better go," Kelly said nervously.

He ignored her and spoke to the black woman. "I'm sorry, but I was here and talked with him. I need to see him!"

"That's not possible."

"Why?"

"He don't live here anymo, and we don't call him Dr. Blue. His name was Joe Keaton, and he be dead ten years now. He was my pop!"

"I saw him!" Steve resolutely said.

"No yu didn't."

"I watched him play guitar."

She hesitated looking alarmed and astonished. "What did he play?"

"Mojo Man."

"Mojo Man! Yu heard him play dat ole blue's song?"

"I did!"

She ran from the porch and joined them, yelling, "Follow me! I be Lucinda Keaton. My pap never played dat song for nobody he didn't know or like! And you saw him play gitar and sing? Dat's impossible."

"I was here, and I heard him play."

"Follow me!"

"Where?"

"I shos yu."

Kelly and Steve followed her into the woods behind the house until the trees opened to a small clearing where two headstones lay.

"Dat be where Pap and Mama rest." She pointed. "That's their grabes. I keep up dis place 'cause I don't wanna sell. Forty acres it be. Price ob land here keeps goin' up."

Steve looked at Dr. Blue's headstone: "Joseph Keaton 1910–1990." The one next to it read "Lyda Keaton 1915–1985." He was speechless, and his face turned white as he began getting a weird but spiritual feeling.

"Steve?" Kelly asked. "Are you alright?"

He looked at Lucinda and asked, "Can I be alone here for just a while?"

"Uh, yeah, I guess dat be alright."

"Thank you."

Lucinda and Kelly walked away, headed for the house. Kelly didn't know what to say. He stared at the headstone, oblivious to the sounds of a thousand birds. He sensed a power coming to him and was no longer feeling sick. He felt Dr. Blue's thumb probing into his left palm, offering a peaceful warmth – but suddenly, the birds quit singing, and a strong shiver ran down his spine. He looked back behind his shoulder, and Kelly along with the black woman, Lucinda, was out of sight. He was alone, standing in front of Dr. Blue's grave.

The birds were quiet, and there was no breeze. A fine mist rose from the ground around the headstone and developed into a bluish white smoke with an apparition forming. An anomaly?

The smoke cleared, and he was face-to-face with the spirit of Dr. Blue. He wanted to run, but his feet were frozen to the ground. He wanted to scream, but his throat could not make a sound.

The spirit looked at Steve, holding out his hand, expressionless. Steve was awestruck as he offered his left hand to the ghost of Dr. Blue.

"Yo feel me spirit?" Dr. Blue communicated through his thumb pushing into Steve's palm.

"Yes." Steve nodded.

"I tawk – you listen!"

He nodded yes as he began receiving pure clarity from the ghost.

"Dere are things yu mus' know."

"What?"

"Haakee!"

"What does that mean?"

"It means, 'you to listen to me good'!"

"I will."

"I be the spirit of Dr. Blue and be livin' in the invisible world. What you saw was not me but was a 'plateye.' Dat be a conjured-up spirit by a root doctor to perform his magic or curses. The plateye can take on any form to look like anyone. Yo root doctor used *'me'* to make yu think he was 'me'."

"What!?"

"Haakee! It wasn't me dat did da spell. You were fooled into believing dat Mista Johnny hab yo girls but he don't. You was to make him sick and he would gib back yo girls. But dat not be de truth. When Mista Johnny die frum his sick, de land he bought and the grabe yadd would go bac to Lula Watson. Dat what de plateye be doin'. Lula's boy be de one dat conjured up de plateye."

"Wait!" Steve jumped. "I'm totally confused. I never wanted Johnny to die!"

"I know. Peabo want him dead."

"Peabo! What's he got to do with this."

"Peabo be Lula's boy. He was tol by a spirit frum de grabeyadd to put a hex on Johnny to either give back the land or die frum sickness. Peabo knew dat he wouldn't gib back de land so he had to die. Dats why he got Johnny crazy and made you believe dat he took yo girls. He didn't want to do dis bad deed on his own, so he made yu think it was me. Peabo thinks you gonna gib him money to git yur girls back."

"How do you know all this?"

"I lib in de invisible world. I know things!"

"Oh, so you say that Peabo tricked me into believing Johnny kidnapped my girls so I would get mad enough to have a curse put on him? And then blackmail me!?"

"Dat's right. Den he was gonna ask you fer a lot ob money to get dem back."

"And I was supposed to believe that I would get my girls back from Johnny?"

"Dat right, but now yu gotta get Mista Johnny to gib dat land back to Lula."

"Why was I given that amulet?"

"De Amulet were to make sure yu got Mista Johnny to gib de land back by makin yu feel good and not worry. It do ward off evil spirits."

"It burned me and made me sick."

"Dat was to git yu to come to me fer help. Now listen. Yo girls were taken by Peabo, and he hab dem now, and de be safe and unharmed."

"Why would Peabo want me to come back to you?"

"Not Peabo. De Plateye couldn't finish de hex when he knew dat you knew dat Mista Johnny didn't hab dem girls. De spirits didn't like de way Peabo tricked yu, and you was showed to me so yoose culd know eber thing."

"Tell me where they are – please!"

"Fust yu gotta make Mista Johnny deed dat land and grabeyard back. You gotta take care ob Peabo, and den you'll hab yur girls."

"I have to confront and kill Peabo?"

"Yu gotta let him know eberthing and he gib dem to you. Yu might hab to kill him but I gabe you powers dat work. Don't be feared ob him."

Steve nodded yes, mesmerized.

"Now Yu git dat deed and take it to Ms. Lula so de grabeyadd spirits can rest."

"Can you help me when I talk to him? He won't just give it back, freely."

"Yu tawk to him. You'll know what to say. Hol my hand and I'll gib yu some power."

The spirit of Dr. Blue started to vanish as Steve stood at his grave, overwhelmed – almost in shock. The GOOD feeling was coming back as he walked slowly back to the small house. He saw his wife and Dr. Blue's daughter, Lucinda standing on the front porch and smiled with joy at both of them.

"Mistuh Riley," Lucinda spoke, "You look better den when yu got here. Yu was lookin' peekid. Yu look real happy!"

"I am."

"Why did yu wanna be down by yoself at Pop's grave?"

"Yeah, Steve?" Kelly asked, obviously waiting for a good answer.

He shrugged his shoulders. "I just did."

"Are you ready to go?" Kelly asked impatiently. "Ms. Keaton has work to do."

"Yeah, I'm ready."

Waving goodbye, they left the house and headed back to Palm Island.

"Have fun at the tombstones?" Kelly smirked.

"I wasn't there for fun."

"Don't you tell me that you saw or talked to the witch doctor!"

"I saw and talked with Dr. Blue, but he was only a spirit."

She looked at him as she turned right onto the main road. "And just how were you able to do that?"

"He talked to me. He told me to get the deed to that land and give it back to Ms. Watson."

"I guess he just popped up out of the ground and said that!" she asked sarcastically.

"Something like that."

"I think when we get home, I'm going to give you a Valium and put you to bed."

"Don't need a Valium. I need to call Johnny."

"No, Steve! Give me a break, please!"

"I could use a beer," he said, without a worry in the world.

She whipped the Lexus into the parking lot of a small country store. "Alright – go get your beer, and why don't you get me one!" she said, giving to defeat.

"Alright."

He came back to the car, holding a six-pack of Budweiser. Getting in, he held out his left hand and asked Kelly to grab it.

"What are you doing?" she asked, curiously.

"Feel my hand. You'll get the power again."

"Steve! There is no Dr. Blue. I talked with his daughter, and his name is Joseph Keaton. He was a farmer! There is no Dr. Blue!" Kelly flat stated – adamantly.

He looked at her with a sly grin as he rubbed her hand. "You feel anything?"

"I'm starting to feel more relaxed, but I don't believe you saw any witch doctor. Wait! I do feel something!" Her round brown eyes opened wide. Real wide!

"You believe me now!"

"I feel good! But why? How?" Even her nose was smiling at him.

"I have the power back and I'm sharing it with you."

"I can't believe this! Let's get home." She hesitated and smiled at him. "Is everything going to be all right?"

"Oh yeah!"

"You sure?" she begged, as he popped open two beers.

"Yeah, here, drink this."

"I don't drink and drive."

"It's not far. You'll be fine," he told her.

"I don't want to get stopped for open containers."

They walked into their condo, and Steve said, unusually demanding, "Sit on the couch while I call Johnny."

"I'm trusting you, but I don't know why."

Steve picked up the phone and dialed Johnny's room.

"Hello," he answered.

"Johnny, just calling to check on you."

"Steve?"

"Yeah, are you feelin' better?"

"Don't feel so good. They're still running more tests."

"What do you feel like?"

"Weak and dizzy. I got bad stomach cramps, but the good news is; I didn't have a stroke or a heart attack. They don't really know what's wrong."

"Can you talk a few minutes?"

"I guess. What do you want? You're not going to cuss me out again, are you?"

"No," Steve said assuring.

"Good, I don't feel like hearing it."

"Do you trust me?" Steve asked seriously.

"Um, Yeah, I trust you."

"I want you to deed that land back to Lula Watson," Steve said.

"What are you saying?"

"You got to give it back."

184

"This isn't making sense," Johnny said.

"Now listen. You didn't get a loan against that property."

"You know the money came from equity in other properties."

"No mortgage on this one?"

"No."

"Well, then you can deed it back to her," Steve simply said.

"Why would I want to do that?"

"Brace yourself?"

"I'm listening."

"Johnny, that land is now haunted. You've been in Greenville and you don't know how frightening and tragic your property has become. You saw all the people there. Well, it's gotten worse. Now I'm in real estate and I foresee the county taking your property through condemnation proceedings."

"Really?"

"It's a death trap and they'll probably destroy it."

"What? Wait a minute. There's a sink hole I probably can get fixed."

"Just listen to me, okay?" Steve demanded.

"I'm trying."

"Johnny, that land has a centuries-old graveyard on it that was disturbed by the grading company. The reason your land's disrupting is because the spirits of the dead were disturbed and they're viciously angry. You saw it! I know it sounds crazy, but I know it's no joke. You will witness a powerful, supernatural force that is beyond your control and you will DIE unless you give them what they want. They want this land back, and it has to be given back to that old Gullah woman – NOW!"

"You're serious. Hell, you're starting to scare me."

"People are dying on that property. And it's those graveyard spirits doing it – because that damn grading company you hired, dug into their graves!"

"You expect me to believe this shit!"

"Hey you said you trust me."

"Steve, there are no ghosts or whatever coming from there! Are there?"

"Why do you think you're sick? They put a voodoo curse on you, and if you don't give that land back, you'll die."

"I was pretty fuckin sick! But how can I believe this bullshit!?"

"You better believe it!" Steve stated loudly and firmly. "This ain't a joke!"

"Well, they can buy it back from me!"

"You're not listening!" Steve rubbed his temples in frustration. "I'm not getting through to you. I'm telling you that you're going to die if you don't give that woman back that deed. She can't buy it back. She gave all the money she made off the deal to charities. That's why she sold it so she could have money to help all the poor people around here."

"What if I just keep it?"

"You'll die. Don't you remember at the closing, she said not to mess with the graves? – Damn it, Johnny, I can't go into everything right now BUT YOU WILL DIE!"

"Why me, Steve? Why am I cursed to die? Tell me."

"Did you not hear what I told you? Your grading company caused all THIS!"

"I heard, but I can't believe that land is being destroyed by ghosts any more than I'm dying from a voodoo curse!"

"You better believe it!" Steve began pacing and rubbing his face, trying to organize his thoughts. He had to convince him somehow. "You have to believe it."

"If what you say is true, Steve, then I will have lost over two million dollars," Johnny said, still feeling sick. "I don't want to do that."

"Hey." Steve brightened. "Put a clause in the deed that if government research wants to use the land, or a motion picture company makes a movie, then you get the proceeds they offer paid to you. I tell you. It's a big deal. That will happen! Maybe more, such as books and magazine royalties!"

"Hadn't thought of that." Johnny pondered.

"You might come out making more than two million." Steve put his right forefinger to his lips as a jester for Kelly to not laugh.

"Well, why don't I just keep it and still get the rewards?"

He thought hard. "Because the old woman, Lula, has to own it. I swear you gotta have faith in me and do that. If you sincerely give that land back only by your own free will; you won't be sick. But if you don't, you won't leave that hospital bed." He paused then calmly continued, "The spirits want their land back. I can't go into the details over the phone. Do this for yourself, not for me, but just say you'll give it back freely."

"Alright. I'll humor you."

Johnny agreed to deed the land back and a few moments later he shouted, "Steve! I'm starting to feel a little better. Is this real or just power of suggestion?"

"It's real, Johnny. Just relax and ask for the doctor. I bet you'll be like your old self before he sees you, and you'll be able to go home," Steve assured, amazed that getting him to give back the land – really worked.

"I really do feel better. Is it magic?"

"Yeah, it really is. Now can you get your lawyer down to your room with a drawn-up contract and deed, and overnight it to me?"

"I can but let me ask you. Are you goin' to fill me in on everything? I mean everything!"

"I will. Johnny, I believe this is the best real estate deal you've ever made, but do what I said and go ahead and put these possible future stipulations in it."

"Maybe tomorrow you can enlighten me over these money stipulations."

"This is not the time to be greedy, I need that deed! Just have a contract stating that any money made due to the result of this tragedy – goes to you."

"You'll have it in the morning!"

"I know you think I'm crazy but I also believe you know me well enough to be honest. Everything I've told you is an absolute fact. We happened across supernatural forces. When you feel like it, I'll explain it all. I know why you got angry. I know why I thought you had my girls and I know why the graveyard erupted."

"OK. I believe you. Hell, we'll talk about it later. I feel like sleeping. Bye."

Kelly looked at him, "I didn't hear what Johnny said, but there's no way he could buy all that crap?"

"It's not crap. You should know that by now. He's giving the property back."

"I just can't believe you told him to sign that land over. There's no way Johnny Sherburtt would just give it back for free because you told him it was haunted."

"He's getting his lawyer to draw up the deed. I should have it in the morning."

"Steve. I'm still in the dark. Why don't you start at the beginning and tell me exactly what's goin' on. And what's this Hollywood movie deal you were feeding him?"

He told Kelly the whole story and assured her that Jennie and Lisa were fine – but hid the fact that he had to confront Peabo.

"So your golfing friend, Bob, got you in touch with him?" she asked suspiciously.

"Pretty much, Kelly."

"How do you know he's not involved in all this?" she asked curiously concerned.

"He's not."

"Hey, all this happening just can't be real. Bob pulled something on you. Why?"

"No – Dr. Blue would have told me! I got to talking to Bob and asked him about voodoo out of curiosity. That's all. Bob has nothing to do with this. I know."

"But you let him find a witch doctor? That doesn't sound like you."

"I wanted our girls back! I was desperate to do anything. Look how Johnny was treating me."

"Promise me that everything is going to be alright. I don't understand all this, but I'm trying."

"And you believe it now?"

"I believe in you. Yeah, I believe it."

"I promise it will all be over tomorrow. All I have to do is to take the deed over to Ms. Watson's."

"And you're bringing my girls home safe?"

"I promise, but do one thing for me."

"What?" she asked.

"Don't touch or pick up that amulet," he warned strongly.

Chapter 16

PRICE drove his Crown Victoria along Bay Street, not noticing the morning sun's reflections along the Beaufort River. He could only fear what this day might hold. Reaching his office, he was unpleasantly surprised to see a large crowd standing in front of the County Administration Building along with the news media. "Wilson, what do I tell all these damn reporters?"

As he got out of his car, a reporter approached him. "Sheriff Price, tell us about what's developing on the 'site.'"

"All I can say is that it is now off-limits to everyone."

"Are you saying no one can enter the property?"

"That's right. If anyone is caught trespassing, they'll be arrested."

"Really! What about the scientists and other experts? Have they drawn any conclusions as to the actual cause of the catastrophe and what needs to be done?"

"I don't know." He bit his lip. "It's off limits to everyone. I mean everyone for now. I'm really not at liberty to discuss any more about this. Now if you'll excuse me; I have work to do."

Price was sitting at his desk when Wilson walked in, handing him two sets of reports. One folder pertained to the murdered young men, and the other to Shields and London. "This should make interesting reading for Agent Stewart," Wilson said.

"He just called. He's got all the info on the boys and their car. I was surprised one of them owned that Lexus and had the title and registration. I told him that."

"What did he say?"

"He wanted me to know that the 'site' is now an official disaster area," Price said.

"I won't comment on that."

"Guess the feds will be storming here soon!"

"Yep, and I can't wait to see how they're goin' to handle this shit. What are they goin' to do? Nuke it?"

"Who knows." Price threw up his hands. "You know it might come to something like that – that is unless the professor's ideas don't work. Anyway, how did you sleep last night, Wilson?"

"Doctor called me in some tranquilizers. They helped and don't feel least bit groggy."

"I drank too much."

Betty burst into the office. "There's someone here who has information on the Riley case."

Price jumped up from his chair. "What?"

"There's a man in the lobby who saw the two men before they were murdered that night not too far from the 'site.'"

"Show him to the briefing room. I'll be with him in a minute."

A small middle-aged man sat quietly in a chair at a wooden table when Price walked in.

"I'm Sheriff Price."

"Joe Rogers." He rose to shake the sheriff's hand.

"Please keep your seat, Mr. Rogers. You have some information you wish to share?"

"I do. I saw those two men – they were standing next to a red car along Marsh View Road talking with someone I know. I recognized them from the photos posted in the Iron Mike restaurant."

"When did you see them?"

"It must have been around eleven thirty Friday night. The night before those girls were reported missing."

"Who were they talking to?"

"Peter McKee. He works at Beaufort High in maintenance. I'm a teacher there and was drivin' home when I saw him and those men but I didn't stop – didn't think anything was wrong."

"You live close to McKee?"

"I live on his road, four houses up from his," he said.

"Did you see anything else? Did you see two girls?"

"No. I saw those boys leaning up against the driver's side while Peter was talking to them. It looked like he was giving them orders or something."

"What do you mean by 'something'?"

"I mean it looked like he was doing all the talking. I really didn't pay much attention to what was going on – but when I saw the posters of those boys; I thought back. He was giving them instructions to do something, I believe. I didn't have any idea he or those boys were up to anything criminal!" He paused and continued, "I wish I could tell you more."

"Does McKee live alone?" Price asked.

"He lives with his mother, Lula Watson. I don't really know McKee. I just see him walking on the road and see him at the school."

"You mean his mother is Ms. Watson who lives just off Lady's Island Road? An elderly black woman?" Price asked, very interested.

"That's right."

Price turned to face the door of the room to hide his sudden astonishment. "Will you sign a statement attesting to what you just told me?"

"Of course, Sheriff. I hope I've been of help."

"Sir! You've been of more help than you can imagine!"

They left the room, and Price motioned for Wilson to follow him back to his office.

"You're not going to believe this," Price said. "Those young guys were seen last with Lula Watson's son. Get a report on Peter McKee, and then I think we need to pay him a visit."

Wilson walked into Price's office, holding several sheets of printed reports.

"What you got?" Price asked anxiously.

"Peter McKee is a forty-year-old black man, six foot one and weighs one hundred eighty pounds. He's a maintenance worker at the high school and has a near-clean record. He has a nickname – 'Peabo.'"

"What do you mean, 'a near-clean record'?"

"It's stupid. He got some complaints from a family a couple of years ago for promising them they could win on a Georgia lottery ticket if he worked a little voodoo magic for them."

"What?"

"Yep," Wilson laughed. "He was going to get forty percent of their winnings."

"Did they win?"

"No, but he took a five-hundred-dollar deposit and wouldn't return it. He said that covered the effort."

"That's ridiculous!"

"He's a root doctor!" Wilson burst.

"I think I'm going to lose my mind. Let's go visit the school," Price assertively suggested.

"Can't. Closed for spring break."

"After I get something to eat, we're goin' to drive over to Ms. Watson's house. I hope he's there, and if he is – he'll have a lot of explaining to do!"

"That he will."

Jenny spent hours during the night sawing at their chains. The small wooden-knot handle wobbled, but it did the job.

"Okay, Lisa, it's time to leave this hellhole of a place, but let me peek outside first," she said quietly, tip toeing to the door. It creaked when it opened, and she winced, but fortunately, there was no one outside – the absence of the masked man being the most important observation. Silently stepping outside, she peeked around the corner of the shack and noticed the tractor sitting in the small field. "Come on." She motioned to Lisa who now had her head poking out the open door.

They moved quickly and silently out the door and Jennie turned around looking at the small, falling in shack laughing. "I hate leaving this place. I just wish our host had talked to us more."

Lisa just pretended not to hear her sister's snide sarcasm.

The girls dashed across the open clearing into the woods. "We made it!" Lisa exclaimed.

"What do you mean we made it, Lisa. We have no idea where we are, but I believe we're on Lady's Island. Remember they didn't drive us far after crossing the bridge," Jenny whispered. "We have to be quiet."

"What do we do now?"

"We're gonna move through these woods and find help – and hope we don't run into 'you-know-who.'"

"I know."

The girls crept through the thick, prickly underbrush. "I'm scared," Lisa whimpered. "This is creepy."

"Now's not the time for whining. We gotta keep moving and find somebody who will help us."

"What if we don't? Jennie, I can't help being scared. I don't want to be chained back up."

"Hey, quit it. I'm scared too, but at least we're not still chained in that god-forsaken room."

"You're right."

"Wonder where that crazy masked man is? We can't let him find us," Jennie muttered, her eyes dancing around hoping to spot someone – a house, a car or anything that would get them home.

"I bet he lives nearby. We better stay hidden. It'll be bad if he finds us," Lisa said quietly.

"Yeah. We have to keep our voices down and stay out of sight."

***

Steve was wearing out his living room carpet, anxiously pacing back and forth. He wanted that deed desperately. It was time to tell Kelly what was really going on.

"Kelly," he said loudly, "can you come in here?"

"What is it?"

"I'm waiting on a package that's extremely important. How do you feel?"

"I don't know how to explain how I feel. But it's good!"

"Can you trust me?"

"I trust you. What is it?"

"You still believe I talked with Dr. Blue?"

"I believe you talked to him or someone, or something! At first I thought you were going crazy, but I know you're not – Steve. I guess there is something to this voodoo!"

"When I get the deed from Johnny, I'm going to give it to Ms. Watson. Our troubles will be over."

"And our daughters? You swear they're alright!"

"You damn right!" he said. "I wouldn't be doing this if not for them. Johnny had nothin' to do with it. He doesn't have them. Ms. Watson's son does. When I explain this deed to her, she'll be happy. Hell, she ought to be jumping for joy since she got two million dollars and gets her land back for nothing."

"Where's the deed?"

"It's being FedEx to me. I'll get it anytime now."

"This is so unbelievable, but when you grabbed my hand, I felt something pure and powerful. I believe you know what you're doing – And I feel GOOD!"

193

"I was given a lot of help – and I'm goin' to need it. I'm bringing back our girls!"

"I'll go with you."

"No, Kelly. Trust me. I have to go alone."

"Alright, if you say so. You be careful."

"I will. I'll call you."

"Please. I'm scared!" she said, hugging him. Laying her head on his shoulder – she began crying.

The doorbell rang, and he ran for the door!

"Steve Riley?" the uniformed lady asked.

"Yeah, that's me."

"Sign here, please."

Steve took the package, kissed Kelly bye, ran to his car, and sped to Lula Watson's house.

***

Price stepped in Wilson's office. "You ready to visit Mr. McKee?"

"Yep. Is there anything you want me to bring other than my gun and cuffs?" he quipped.

"Come on, let's go."

They left the office. After crossing the Beaufort River bridge, Price said, "I'm hungry. There's a restaurant on the right where we can get something to eat."

"I thought you were eager to see Mr. McKee."

"I am, but I'm hungry. Let's stop at the Coosaw. They got the best grouper that I know of in these parts."

"Don't they though," Wilson agreed. "Damn if you ain't got me hungry!"

"Yeah. I really need to eat. Gotta feed my hangover!" Price smiled.

"Yep, I know."

"I'm really looking forward to meeting McKee – but I like postponing the suspense. Also, I do better on a full stomach."

"We ain't gonna have a day like we had yesterday, are we?" Wilson posed.

"God, I hope not! This is goin' to be a great day – I can feel it."

Price and Wilson pulled into the Coosaw and couldn't help noticing the parked white Toyota SUV.

"See that white Toyota?" Price said.

"Yep. Ross London's?"

"You got the license number for Mr. London's Toyota back at the office. I hope you gave it to Betty."

"Yep, I sure did. I'll call her right now."

After flipping his phone off, he looked at Bill and said, "That's Mr. London's."

"Well, let's go on in."

"Sheriff Price," Preston greeted him. "Having lunch with us today?"

"Yeah, how's the grouper?"

"Fresh as you can get it!" He laughed. "Just kiddin'. It's always fresh."

Price laughed. "Can you bring us both a sandwich, fries and iced tea."

"Coming right up."

"Oh, Preston. I have to ask you about that white SUV parked outside."

"Yeah, that's Ross London's car. He must have come by here and left it. I know him and didn't want to report it. I figured he'd be woulda gottin' it by now."

"He might not be coming back." Price looked over at Wilson. "Go ahead and have it impounded."

"Damn, I hope he didn't run into trouble; wonder where he's at?" Preston said curiously, looking at Price.

"Let's just say I have an idea where he is, and he might have run into trouble."

"I saw him a few days ago. He came in and was goin' to do some research. Hadn't seen him since. I hope he's alright. Where do you think he might be at?"

"I can't say right now. He's probably not somewhere he wants to be."

Preston was silent for a moment and said, "Your sandwiches will be up any minute."

"Wilson, have you not thought about McKee? I have."

"Like what?"

"I believe McKee took the Riley twins, and Sherburtt isn't involved. I think McKee knows more about this land and graveyard than we could imagine. Remember, his mother owned it! Also, you said he was a root doctor."

"Yep, and I think I know where you're goin' with this."

"Mr. Riley brokered that land to Mr. Sherburtt. The graveyard is haunted. McKee is a root doctor, and his mother owned the land!"

"But you don't think Sherburtt is involved?"

"No, I don't. I think McKee stole those girls."

"Why would he steal the Riley twins? Coincidence maybe?"

"Not sure. Somethin' keeps running through my mind that doesn't set well. McKee's mother gave away a fortune. I mean millions – to the needy – and I bet that didn't go well with McKee. At first, I thought Sherburtt could have possibly been pressured to come up with that money, fast! And by his attitude and demands toward Steve Riley, he hoped to get it from him. But since he's an experienced, successful land developer with no trails leading to shady dealings, he wouldn't take money from loan sharks or dangerous thugs – especially to buy land!"

Preston came out with the food and headed back to his kitchen. Price continued on with the conversation. He was confident that Peter McKee was behind it all, including the graveyard, and knew the reasons why. But figuring out how he was doing it was mind-boggling impossible!

"Peabo. What a name!" Price laughed.

"Bill, can I say something?"

"Sure."

"You're acting like a cat playing with a chipmunk before the kill."

"That's funny, Wilson."

"Well?"

"I'm trying to picture how he's going to explain his involvement with those young men. I'm taking my time. Gotta get my thoughts together, you know. I believe he's the key behind everything. Hell, I know he is! I also know he ain't goin' be real happy to see us and asking questions. I bet he's got those girls somewhere close, I hope. And I bet he knows about all those skeleton creatures living in that crater. Yeah – he definitely has some explaining to do!"

"He could get hostile, Bill."

"He might, but I doubt it. Hell, let him. I really don't care!"

"He could get violent?"

"Well, let him get violent. I don't believe he will. If he does – shoot the son of a bitch! No, I think he'll do a little dance around everything I ask him. I'm going to study his reactions to my questions. And you do the same."

"Of course!"

"You know what I'm going to ask him first?"

"No, what? Um, maybe his name?"

"I'm going to ask him if he owns a machete," Price said with a cocky smile – stroking his sandy-brown hair from his forehead.

Chapter 17

STEVE LEFT Palm Island in a rush to meet with Lula Watson. HE HAD THE DEED – the deed to give back the seventy-acre tract that she sold to Johnny. The entire ordeal will be over – that is, if Lula's home and takes the deed? *Please Lord – please let her be there!* Steve prayed.

The swing bridge crossing Johnson Creek was open to traffic. *Good,* he thought, *only eight more miles to go.* He was on pins and needles as his right hand trembled trying to light a cigarette.

Turning onto Lady's Island Road, he saw an unwanted roadblock and stopped behind a waiting car. A county patrolman approached his window.

"I'm sorry, sir, but this road is closed," the deputy said.

"Officer," he spoke respectfully, "I have business with a woman who lives near this road. It's less than a mile."

"Sir, things are mighty hectic along here. The Sheriff's Department has ordered that no visitors are allowed on this road, only residents."

"But, I need to see this woman."

"Sir, it's too dangerous. Hell! This area has been designated a national disaster!"

"I know, but I need to see her about something important!"

"I can't let people come down this road, unless it's a real emergency or they live on it. I have strict orders from the sheriff."

"I understand, but I have a deed that has to be delivered and explained concerning 'this' property. It's really important."

"What's her name?"

"Lula Watson."

"What's she got to do with this 'off-limits' property?"

"She owned it, but recently sold it, the business I have with her just might help explain all the havoc and destruction that's goin' on."

"Oh really?" he asked, curiously. "Well, let me look at my roster. You're right, she's a resident but not on this road. Go about a mile and turn right on the second sand road."

"Thanks, Officer," he said, knowing exactly where she lived.

"Oh, I need to see your identification and also let me glance at that paperwork."

"No problem," Steve said anxiously.

The officer looked at the papers and license, then handed them back. "Alright, but be careful on this road."

"I will and thanks again. You don't know how much I appreciate it."

Driving too fast, he bounced and slid along the narrow road before slamming on brakes at the side of Lula's house. Jumping from his car, he ran to her door with deed in hand.

She answered the door after the second knock.

"Whu goin' on Mistuh Riley, sho's good to see oonuh?" She smiled.

"Ms. Watson."

"Lula!"

"That's right. Lula, I have something I want to give you."

"Whu dat?" she asked.

"A nice surprise! It'll make you happy."

"Trabble on in de house and set yo-self on de couch. You hungry?"

"No, thanks, Lula. I'm not hungry. My stomach feels a little tight."

"Whu wrong. Hab mis'ry? Oonah need to eat somethin. Dat make you feel bettuh." She looked at him with her big round eyes.

"I have something I want to show you."

"Whut dat be?"

Steve began pulling the deed out of its folder when she said, "I got a chick' in de pot and greens."

"Yeah, I smell 'em?" Steve came to his senses and realized he'd better eat some of her food. He had no choice.

"Hab you awready eet?"

"Yes, ma'am, had some breakfast. But I think my stomach quit hurting after smelling your cooking. I can eat," he said, anxious to get down to the matter at hand. "I want you to look at this deed. It's a deed to the seventy acres that you sold to Mr. Sherburtt. He wants you to have it."

"Makes no nebbuh mind – Lula hab no money," she said walking to her kitchen.

"He's giving it to you, free. You don't have to pay a cent."

"Why e do dat?" She eyed him suspiciously, after turning around from the kitchen.

"He doesn't need it and just wants you to have it back. Lula, I'll eat in a few minutes. Please sit down so I can explain all this to you."

"He know dat land hab haants en' e be 'fraid ob dem haants!" she said, then plopped in her rocker.

"He knows that if he gives it back to you, the spirits will be happy and can rest peacefully, while the land turns back to normal."

"Nosuh! He don't gib no nebbuh mind 'bout souls restin in peace. E hab jaw tee' en debblement! I see dat at de lawya' table. I sol' dat land fuh me people, en now it don come back to haant ebbuhbody. Nosuh, Nosuh!" Lula reached for her handkerchief.

"No…He knows giving it back to you will make everything alright. Lula, you've done nothing wrong. Please don't be upset. Try to be happy and glad he's doing this."

"He jis' gib it back en dat all, Mista Steve?"

"Yes, Lula, I know why you sold your land. You wanted to help people, but you need to understand that Mr. Sherburtt didn't destroy the graveyard. It was done by a grading company that wasn't careful. He didn't know anything about it. Please don't blame him."

"E swonguh mahn – E gib me back de land – Wuffuh? 'Fraid e be too late fuh dat!"

"No. By giving it back to you, everything will be alright. He wants to do the right thing," he lied. "He really wants me to give you this deed. I want you to have it – I really do."

She looked at him with skepticism and confusion.

"I have the deed made out to you. I have a contract that says if any money is made from any and all the events that have happened, it will be given to him up to the purchase price. You can also get one half of the money that's received over the purchase price."

She looked at him. "Is dat right?"

"Yes. What I'm saying is that you get your land back and maybe you might get money later that you can use to keep helping people – that is if you want."

"Awright, let me look ober dem papuhs!"

"It's a free and clear 'Fee Simple' deed to your property."

"Lawya' tawk!"

"No. It's your deed. You own the land. And this is the only way the souls of the dead can rest again at the graveyard."

She wiped her tears away and smiled. "You be good man! No gubment or nobody goin' git dat land frum me if'n me hab it back!"

"Lula," Steve replied, "Like I said, you should get a lot more money. What if someone wanted to write a book or magazine articles about it?" he asked.

"Shishuh! Mo' money?"

"What if no one, and I mean no one, can touch that graveyard? It will be secured except for you and those who have family buried there."

"Awright Mistuh Steve. Go on mo' 'bout dis."

"Well, by owning it, you will have more control or say-so than if you don't."

"En wid mo' money!" She grinned and laughed.

"Yes, ma'am! Um – maybe."

"Gimme dat papuh work!"

Steve Riley breathed a sigh of relief.

"Oonuh ready to eat?" she asked.

"What kind of greens?"

"Collads!" she spouted. "Got chick' leg wid peppa and winiguh."

"That sounds good," he said as he was beginning to feel hungry.

"I gwine bring it."

She came back with the food and began talking, "Mistah Steve, I hab no eddycashun but I hab ecknowledge and be smaa't ooman; not eegnunt. Let me tell you, we Gullah folks be proud ob way we lib. Le'm'lone. W'se'f. We be libbin' on dese iluns fuh a long w'ile and hab no reasons to change or leabe. We happy. De grabeya'dd hab many ob good sperrits and it too hab e few bad uns. De gubment wanted de grabeya'dd w'ile back; and de sperrits come to me saying, NO! I felt dem sperrits at de lawyers table and I feel dem now. Dey happy, e be gib back to me. Bekase I be de ooman dat took berry good care ob dey grabes. De spirits dat came out de eart' – hab no mo' anger. Dey be at rest agin."

"Lula, you gave all that money to charity. They know that."

"Dat right…Mr., Steve, how you know dat! Dey tawk wid you?" She posed, cocking her head in astonishment.

"I just know," Steve said, truthfully.

"Yu bettuh eat dat food fuh it get too cold!"

"Yes, mam."

***

Jennie and Lisa climbed out of the woods and underbrush onto a lone sandy road and spotted the rear of a small house not too far away.

"Is that Daddy's car parked beside it?" Lisa asked.

"Jennie squinted her eyes and said, I believe it is. Damn, what's it doin' at that house, I wonder. Yeah, that's Daddy's Lexus."

"You think? For sure?"

"Who else around 'here' drives a brand new, white Lexus, with a South Carolina Game Cock sticker on the windshield?"

Lisa shrugged her shoulders, put her hand over her mouth to muffle a laugh and said, "No one."

They both scanned the area looking for the best way to get to that house without being seen.

"Look, Jennie, I see a man. He's walking out of a shop building headed for the house. Get down before he sees us. It could be the masked man."

"You might be right. Same size." Jennie studied him. "Yeah, that's got to be him."

"Yeah. What do we do?"

"I don't know. Let me think."

"Why is Daddy and the masked man there?"

"Hell, I don't know, but it's the first time I'm glad to see a Carolina Gamecock sticker."

"Me too. I hope Daddy's not in any trouble. He wouldn't be – would he?"

"Lisa, I don't know. I have no idea what's going on, but I'm gonna sneak up to that house and find out."

"I'll go with you."

"No, you won't," Jennie ordered.

"Yes, I am. I'm not staying here by myself."

"I might run into trouble, so stay here and run for help if I do."

"No."

"Alright, but we got to be careful," Jennie insisted. "If the masked man sees us, he'll chase us down and put us back in that shack!"

"I know."

"Well, are you ready?"

"Yeah. I'm ready."

"Come on, follow me to those bushes. Now Lisa, you gotta be quiet. And please stay out of sight."

"I know what to do."

The masked man wasn't wearing a mask but walked slowly with the same slow swagger. The girls knew it was him, black pants, black shirt. Who else could it be! They quietly approached Lula's house, ducking behind trees and shrubbery. He didn't see them as he walked in a back door to his bedroom.

Peabo plopped down on his bed and realized it was time for Johnny Sherburtt to die. His duty to the graveyard spirits was a success. At least he thought – but he was wrong. With no idea that Sherburtt had given the land back. He began to think about the Riley twins. *"Steve Riley will be sadly disappointed when he finds out Johnny Sherburtt is dead and doesn't have his girls. He's going to have to give me one million dollars to get them back and will never know it was me. I got it all figured out."*

Peabo snapped out of his thoughts when he faintly heard a conversation between his Ma and a man at the other end of the house. He went to his dresser and pulled out a Colt 45 revolver and softly walked toward the living room.

"Now, that was good," Steve said, laying his plate on the table beside the couch.

"I put sugah on it. I put vini-ga and peppa on it too. Yu liked it, Mistuh Riley?"

"I did. Now are you ready to sign?"

"Yea, rekin so."

"Sign the form and I'll make you some copies and bring them to you tomorrow. I have to file the deed at the courthouse."

She walked over to her old secretary, retrieved a pen, and signed the document. Handing it back to Steve, she said, "Yu bring me back my copy!"

"I will," he said happily. And now it was time to ask her where her boy might happen to be!

Peabo walked into the living room and froze, speechless, seeing Steve standing next to his Ma.

"Peter! Or should I call you Peabo?" He bolted, surprised to see Peabo so soon. He knew this initial confrontation would happen soon after Lula accepted the deed. Dr. Blue was right – *It's now showdown at high noon!*

"Ya'll know each udder?" Lula asked, looking surprised.

"Where are my daughters, Peabo? I know you got 'em. Bring them to me right now!"

"I don't know what you're talkin' 'bout, Mista Riley."

"Oh yeah you do! I know you have my girls, so you tell me where they are! Are you hearing me!?" he shouted.

Peabo turned and faced his mother. "Ma, go in the kitchen and fix me somethin' to eat?"

"What goin' on?" she asked her boy, she appeared awfully frightened and bewildered. "Ya'll be mad at one an udder. Wuffuh?"

"I need to tawk wid this man. Go in the kitchen, Ma."

"Yeah, Lula," Steve agreed. It's going to get nasty and he didn't want her to be around it.

Lula Watson went to her kitchen walking pitifully, muttering under her breath, "Lula hab to leab de room. Dat right…Lula hab to leab de room."

"Alright, Peabo, you son of a bitch – I'm going to ask you one more time – where are my daughters?"

"Look Mista Riley, I don't know nothin' bout your girls or where they are."

"You're lying – damn it! I know you have them. I know everything. You used me to put that curse on Sherburtt that was supposed to just make him give back the land and then he would free my girls. But since he didn't have them, he would just die, and then you were going to blackmail me! You greedy son of a bitch! Yeah, when you found out your mother gave away all that money, you took my girls knowing I would later pay you a large ransom. That was pretty clever, believing you would satisfy the graveyard spirits and then extort money from me! But your plan couldn't work until after Sherburtt died. Didn't it cross your mind that the spirit world knew about your evil scheme? I'm going to make sure your ass goes to prison! And if you've hurt my girls – I'll break you in pieces!"

"Oh, really?" Peabo replied as he reached behind his back for his gun, then pointed it at Steve's face…standing far enough away to where it couldn't easily be slapped out of his hand.

"Put the gun down!"

"I'll put it down after I put a hole in your head!"

"Put it down."

"No. I can't do that. And you ain't gonna see your girls. And I ain't gonna see prison. I'm gonna hab to kill you, Steve."

A loud noise suddenly exploded in the room as a brick came through a window, shattering glass everywhere. Peabo was startled, and Steve instinctively jumped him, wrestling him to the floor. As Steve struggled for the gun, the revolver fired. Peabo moaned, clutching his bleeding chest. while Lula came running to him in a panic. She fell to her knees and hovered over him, cradling his head. Steve slowly stood up, trembling! "I'm sorry Ma," Peabo cried, as he slowly closed his eyes and died.

"No…Peabo. Pleeze don' die on me." She hugged him, crying tears that ran like torrents down her face – all the way to her shoulders.

Price and Wilson had just pulled up to the house. Hearing the gunshot, they rushed inside and saw Peabo lying on the floor in his own blood, with Lula crying over him in hysterics.

"What in the hell!" Price yelled. "What happened!"

"He had a gun on me, and I wrestled him to the floor. He was going to kill me, but the gun went off when I tried to take it from him." Steve's voice was shaking, and his face was white as cotton. "I might be a fairly strong man, but I was in a tough struggle. I've never been that scared in my life. I knew he was about to fire his gun at me, but I somehow turned it. I was trying to just get it out of his hand – but – he was a strong man!"

"Obviously for your sake, you were stronger."

Wilson helped Lula to the couch as Price looked around the room, shaking his head.

"Sheriff," Steve gasped, "he kidnapped my daughters and now I don't know where to find them."

"That was awful brave of you, charging a man at gun point." Price said, "And we'll find your daughters. I promise."

"There was a sudden crashing noise and it startled Peabo, so I rushed him."

"A crashing noise?"

"Like something heavy came through a window." Steve paused and looked at a smashed window on the right gable end wall. "Hey, that window wasn't broken earlier!" Price looked around the room and saw a brick lying on the floor along with broken glass. "It looks like someone threw a brick through that window from outside. Who did that?"

"I did," Jennie cried out as her face poked through the window.

"Jennie!" Steve yelled, running out the door.

Jennie and Lisa ran into his arms, and tears streamed down all three faces.

"Wilson," Price said, "stay here with Ms. Watson, and get a report on all this. Call Betty, and make sure we have ample transportation for these victims. They might need to go to the hospital and get checked out."

"Yeah. Um, I believe Ms. Watson is in shock and should go to the Crisis Center."

"Yeah, and call the coroner's office. I'm going to talk with Mr. Riley and his daughters."

"Well, Mr. Riley, it seems everything turned out good for you and your twins." He smiled and looked over at Jennie and Lisa, "I've been worried about you two. Are you OK?"

"Yeah," they both said grinning. "You wouldn't believe it!"

"Oh, I bet I would," Price spoke warmly. "And we're goin' to talk all about it, soon."

"It's been only days but seems like an eternity – a long and unbelievable nightmare," Steve told the sheriff, wiping away tears with the back of his hand.

"I think I know the nightmare. I believe the nightmare is now over. But I must say, you and your daughters are very brave."

"Daddy," Lisa sobbed, "Call Mama."

He dialed Kelly's cell.

"Steve!" She was quick to answer. "Are you alright? I'm worried sick to my stomach. Didn't you…?"

He handed the phone to his girls, and without a moment of hesitation, they screamed as loud as they could into it, "MAMA!"

Epilogue

The land and graveyard had miraculously calmed to normal, looking solemn in the twilight, as the last of the scientists, reporters and authorities were leaving the seventy-acre site – except one perplexed seismologist lingered behind – as he nervously approached the graveyard.

"What could have possibly caused such a mayhem with no explainable scientific reason?" he asked himself. And now – no signs of a recent chaotic earthquake, a volcano, or…? He knew there has to be logical reasons, and he planned to find the answers. He was desperate and determined to solve a mystery that no one else could – or can – and he would!

Noticing darkness beginning to close in, he decided to wrap up his investigation for the evening and return early in the morning when there would be daylight.

Hearing a faint cracking noise, the scientist jerked his head back quickly, looking behind him. Apprehension and anxiety caused him to pick up his pace, changing his steady gate to a brisk jog heading to his car. He had no desire to be here after dark.

As the curious but leery scientist shakily got in his car, the moon slowly rose behind him, hauntingly illuminating the entire site. He didn't hear the next cracking warning sound as the land began to subtly tremor from the pulsing heartbeat of the Gullah Gravestones.

THE END

CPSIA information can be obtained
at www.ICGtesting.com
Printed in the USA
LVHW081530030323
740864LV00011B/464

9 781638 291824